The
Cuckoo
Tree

OTHER YEARLING BOOKS YOU WILL ENJOY:

YEARLING BOOKS/YOUNG YEARLINGS/YEARLING CLASSICS are designed especially to entertain and enlighten young people. Charles F. Reasoner, Professor Emeritus of Children's Literature and Reading, New York University, is consultant to this series.

For a complete listing of all Yearling titles, write to Dell Readers Service, P.O. Box 1045, South Holland, Illinois 60473.

The Cuckoo Tree

Joan Aiken

Illustrated by Susan Obrant

A Yearling Book

Published by
Dell Publishing Co.
a division of
The Bantam Doubleday Dell Publishing Group, Inc.
1 Dag Hammarskjold Plaza
New York, New York 10017

Yearling® TM 913705, Dell Publishing, a division of
the Bantam Doubleday Dell Publishing Group, Inc.

ISBN: 0-440-40046-5

Reprinted by arrangement with Doubleday & Company, Inc.

Printed in the United States of America

April 1988

10 9 8 7 6 5 4 3 2 1

CW

The
Cuckoo
Tree

1

A wild westerly gale was blowing over the south downs one November evening when a chaise-and-pair, having slowly ascended the long, gradual hill on the London road some five miles north of the Port of Chichester, came to a halt at the top.

A girl put her head out of the carriage window. "Why've we stopped here?" she inquired.

"Why d'you think?" growled the driver bad-temperedly, without turning his head. "So's to give the nags a layoff, o' course! I spose in the furrin parts overseas where you was raised, horses goes on for weeks together without a bait or dram?"

It seemed to be his own needs he was consulting rather than those of his horses, however, for he pulled a black bottle out of his pocket and took a swig from it.

"I was raised in London if you want to know," retorted his passenger, "and where I come from, nags don't need a rest half an hour after they start off! It'll be a month o' Mondays afore we gets to London at this rate! Where are we now?"

She looked with disfavor at the dark wooded hillsides that surrounded them. Volleys of leaves rattled against the carriage windows and swept the rutted road; fitful bursts of rain made the horses stamp and shiver. A faint green strip of light still showed in the west, but elsewhere the sky was piled with cloud, and in fifteen minutes it would be true night.

"Where? Top o' Benges, that's where—if that means owt to you." He took another long swallow, upending the bottle.

"Not a thing! All I knows is, we must still be a perishing long way from London. Hey! Steady on wi' that tipple, mister! Don't forget we've a sick passenger aboard."

"Shick—hup—passenger be blowed," grunted the driver. "It's the gray *I'm* worried about—if he don't go lame afore we gets to Petworth, I'm sucked in! Why was I ever such a maggot as to say I'd drive ee to Lunnon tonight? Gee woot, you!" Angrily he shook up the reins, almost shaking himself off the box in the process. The chaise started again, and gathered speed on the downhill slope.

"Oh croopus," muttered the girl, withdrawing her head from the window. "I jist hope we gets to London this side o' Turpentine Sunday, and all in one piece."

"What's amiss, my child?"

[10]

The other passenger appeared to have been dozing. It was dark inside the chaise and little could be seen of him, save that he was a tall man, muffled in numerous capes and rugs. Except for an eye slit, left so that he could see out, his head was entirely wrapped in bandages, over which he wore an enormous fur hat. He spoke weakly, but with an air of authority.

"It's our driver," returned the girl in a low voice. "I suspicioned he was a bit bosky at the start, and now I reckon he's just about half-seas over. Trouble was, none o' the drivers would leave for London at five o'clock in the evening."

"I cannot imagine why not! They might ask what fee they liked, since we are traveling on government business, with dispatches for the Admiralty. Did you not tell them they should be handsomely rewarded?"

"Didn't make a mite o' difference. None of them'd stir—said as how we might meet with Gentlemen on the road." The girl glanced doubtfully at the black trees on either side.

"Gentlemen!" her companion exclaimed weakly but testily. "Pish! What moonshine!"

The driver had evidently caught some part of their conversation, for he suddenly burst into raucous song:

"Captain Hughes and young Miss Twite
Went for a drive—hic!—one shiny night
If they don't end in the Cuckoo Tree
Pickle my brains in eau-de-vie!"

[12]

"Attend to your business, my man!" snapped the bandaged passenger, for the horses were now dashing faster and faster down a long, winding hill, and the carriage was beginning to sway alarmingly.

But the driver only replied, "Tooral-eye-ooral, fiddle-eye-ay!" and cracked his whip in a very carefree manner.

"Put your arm through the strap, Cap'n!" young Miss Twite exclaimed anxiously, and since, blinkered as he was by his bandages, her companion was unable to find the arm hold, she scrambled across the rocking vehicle and slid the heavy leather loop over his elbow.

"Ah! Thanks, my child!"

She had secured him only just in time. Next instant the coach gave a particularly violent lurch and overturned completely. Young Miss Twite still had hold of the strap; she clung to it tenaciously as she and her companion were flung backward against the padded seat, and then down on to the door of the carriage, which had come to rest lying on its side.

"Cap'n! Cap'n Hughes! Are you all right?"

No answer. Anxiously, Miss Twite felt his chest and discovered that he still breathed.

"Fry that coachman!" she exclaimed, attempting to disentangle herself from her companion.

"Who are you? What's happened?" he muttered confusedly.

"It's Dido, Cap'n—Dido Twite. We've had a turnup, but don't fret; I'll see to everything. *Mussy* knows how," she added to herself, "seeing I don't even know how I'm a-going to get *out* of here—and the driver's about as much use as a herring in a hockey match. Maybe he's dead. Anyways, thank goodness the Cap'n isn't."

By stretching up to her full height (which was not great) she was just able to reach the arm strap dangling from the upper door; she pulled herself up by this, digging her toes into the indentations in the upholstery. Luckily one of the windows had fallen open, and she was able to edge her way through and climb on to the hedge bank. Searching about, she found the coachman, dead or unconscious, in a patch of long grass and thistles; he had apparently been thrown off his box at the first jolt. One of the horses stood with hanging head, very lame; the other was plunging about nervously; it had kicked its way clear of the shafts but was still held by its traces.

"Easy now, mate," the girl said, approaching it warily. "You and me has got to get better acquainted. Here, have a slab o' Sussex pudden; it's a bit squashed, but the landlady at the Dolphin said it would do for supper and breakfast too; you're welcome to the soggy stuff if it'll settle your spirits. It's better inside you than in my pocket, anyways."

The large, damp, sweet lump of suet pudding did prove soothing to the horse, and Dido was presently able to unhitch it, and lead it around to the side of the overturned coach.

"Cap'n!" she called. "Can you hear me, Cap'n Hughes? I can't get you out by myself, and I can't right the coach, so I'm a-going for help. All rug? Shan't be long—I hope," she added to herself.

No reply came from inside; it seemed likely that the unfortunate captain had fainted again. Dido led the horse alongside the hedge bank, which was about three feet high, and from the top, managed to scramble on to the animal. Unused to being ridden, it started affrightedly, threw up its head, and set off at a canter; clinging like a monkey to its mane, Dido was jounced in a most uncomfortable manner from side to side of its broad back. By now her eyes were accustomed to the darkness and she was able to make out that they were in a narrow muddy lane with wooded hills sloping away on either side; no lights or houses were to be seen anywhere.

"Of all the God-forsaken spots to get tippled up in! *Don't* pull so, what's-your-name, Dobbin, my arms is weaker than seaweed already with all that scrabbling about in the coach."

Fairly soon the horse slowed to a steady trot better suited to its solid build; this was even more bone-shaking for Dido but she did not feel in such imminent danger of being tossed off and having to continue her quest on foot.

"How much o' this nook-shotten wilderness is there?" she wondered. "It seems to go on forever—not a house, nor an inn, nor a bakery shop anywheres! Downright wasteful it is, if you ask me."

After about ten minutes' riding she came to a cross-roads—or to be more accurate, a spot where four or five tracks met.

"Now where?" Dido wondered, dragging on the traces to bring her steed to a halt. "Choose the wrong path and I reckon I'll be wandering for hours—and never find my way back to the carriage, which is worse; and if I don't get back with help pretty nippily, poor Cap'n Hughes is liable to *die,* I shouldn't wonder, with all this hugger-mugger on top o' that head wound he's got."

She bit her lip in anxiety and indecision, but at this moment a dark shape emerged in complete silence from the trees over to her left, stepped up beside her, and whispered,

"Tarrydiddle?"

"*I'll* say it's tarrydiddle," Dido replied. "Likewise hocus-pocus and how-de-do! Who the blazes are you, hoppiting about in the woods like a poltergeist?"

At this reply, evidently not what the newcomer expected, he put his fingers to his mouth and let out a soft whistle; in an instant seven more figures darted out from the trees; somebody took hold of the horse's bridle. Dido felt cold metal pressing against her leg, and saw a gleam of light move up and down something that looked extremely like the barrel of a blunderbuss. She also smelt, rather surprisingly, a strong, sweet scent, roses and cloves, mixed with ambergris and orange blossom.

"Who are you?" somebody hissed in her ear.

"Who'm I? I'm Dido Twite," she replied with spirit. "Our coach tippled over along there, acos the coachman was drunk as a wheelbarrow, and there's a hurt man inside, and I'm a-going for help. So I'll take it kind if you gentlemen will step back along with me and turn the coach topsides, and tell me where there's a house or a barn or *summat* where I can take poor Cap'n Hughes for the night."

As she spoke, the word *gentlemen* reminded her of the landlady's warning: "You'll not find a driver at this time o' day, love, they're all too scared o' the Gentlemen. All except Bosky Dick that is, and I wouldn't call him reliable."

"'Tis a child," somebody whispered. "Do ee reckon that be a true tale?"

"The nag be Ben Noakes's gray from the Dolphin, sure enough. I did hear tell as how Bosky Dick was hired to drive a party to Lunnon town."

"Who else be in the coach, maidy?"

"Cap'n Hughes, I tell you, and he's hurt bad."

"What like of a cap'n is he?" someone asked suspiciously. "Be he one o' they Preventive Men, Bush officers?"

"What's they? No, he's a navy cap'n, and he was wounded at sea, in a battle—oh, *please* come and help me with him!"

"Us can't do that, my duck. Us has to goo t'other way to meet some friends, see? That's one reason, and another is, we dassn't, do we might meet some niffy chaps as we don't fancy."

"Well, then, can you tell me where I *can* get some help?" said Dido impatiently.

"Arr! Ee wants to goo upalong to the Manor House.

Owd Lady Tegleaze'll help ee surelye. She'll send some o' the chaps from the estate, sartin sure."

"Which way to the Manor House, then?"

One of the men holding the bridle turned Noakes's gray and led it into the track on Dido's left.

"Up yonder, my liddle maid. Through the big gates and on up the dene till ee see the lights. They'll help ee, up at the Manor. But don't ee goo speaking arter now, about who ee've seen here, eh? 'Twouldn't be wise, see?"

"How can I?" said Dido tartly. "I *haven't* seen you. Who are you anyways?"

She heard soft chuckles in the darkness. "Wouldn't ee like to know? Well, then, listen: we're Yan, Tan, Tethera, Methera, Pip—"

"Sethera, Wineberry," the other voices took it up, "Wagtail, Tarrydiddle, and Den! Now ee knows all that's good for ee."

"And a mighty big help you've been *I'm* sure," Dido muttered—rather ungratefully, since they had, at least, set her on the right way—as her horse cantered up the loamy ride, under an avenue of tall trees whose branches creaked mournfully in the wind overhead.

Just before she left them she heard one phrase not meant for her ears:

"Quick yourselves a bit, then, lads, or us'll be late at the Cuckoo Tree!"

This reminded her of the coachman's rhyme,

> "If they don't end in the Cuckoo Tree
> Pickle my brains in eau-de-vie!"

She wondered vaguely what it meant, but almost at once anxiety about Captain Hughes drove out all other considerations. Luckily she soon came to a pair of massive stone pillars, evidently the gates the man calling himself Yan had alluded to; when she passed between them the path took a sharp bend to the left around a hummock of ground, and beyond this she could distinguish a cluster of lights not far ahead. Five minutes more, and Noakes's gray drew up in front of what was plainly a very large mansion, set in a fold of the hillside, with a dark mass of trees behind it and a broad sweep of grass in front. Little else was visible in the dark rainy night. Considering that the time could not yet be much after eight o'clock, Dido was somewhat surprised not to see more windows lit—there seemed to be but half a dozen, and these with wide spaces between them, as if the inhabitants of this great place were so unsociably inclined that they preferred to keep as separate from one another as possible.

There was a portico with white marble pillars, and some iron staples, roughly driven into these, were evidently meant for tethering horses.

Dido slid off the gray's back with relief. "Though dear knows how I'll ever get back on," she thought, seeing no mounting block. Ignoring a slight palpitation of the heart at the grandeur of this place—the double doors, under the portico, were so huge that a medium-sized whale could easily have passed between them, given enough water to swim in—she tugged briskly at a brass bellpull.

The house had seemed so silent, as if all its inmates were elsewhere or asleep, that she was a little startled when the doors flew open at once; they had been pulled back, she discovered, by a pair of liveried footmen in powdered wigs, and directly in front of her a butler stood bowing.

"Can you help me—" Dido began. He interrupted her with raised hand.

"This way, my lady. Please to follow me."

"Poor old fellow," Dido thought, following. "I suppose in a place as grand as this he ain't allowed to give orders for help on his own, but has to ask the lord or duke or whoever lives here."

They crossed a wide hall, decorated with a great many pairs of deer's antlers, ascended several flights of marble stairs—very slowly; the butler was a very aged man—and proceeded along several wide passageways until, it seemed to Dido, they must have reached the very end of the house.

"Coo, it's a big place, ennit?" she remarked. "Must take a deal o' sweeping. I'm right sorry for the house-maid."

The aged butler, in the act of knocking at a door, turned and surveyed her with some surprise. The sight of her clothes, which he had not observed in the darkness of the portico, appeared to surprise him still more.

"I'd take it kind if you'd ask someone to keep an eye on my nag while I'm up here," Dido added. "If I'd a known we'd have to come sich a perishing way I'd a tied him up a mite tighter."

"But—did your ladyship not come in a carriage?"

"That's just what I'd a told you if you'd waited—" Dido was beginning impatiently, when an equally impatient voice inside the door shouted,

·"How the deuce many times do I have to say, come in?"

Flustered, the butler threw open the door, bowed, stood aside, and announced, as Dido entered,

"The Lady Rowena Palindrome!"

"There! I might a known there was some mux-up," Dido said. "Bless your socks, *I* ain't Lady Rowena Thingummy."

"Never mind, I daresay you'll do just as well," said the room's occupant. "Come in and sit down. Can you play tiddlywinks? Gusset, there's a draft; don't stand there, go out and shut the door behind you."

"I beg your pardon, Sir Tobit. But if the young lady *isn't* who she said she was—"

"I didn't say I is, I said I isn't!" Dido put in. "My stars! I was told I'd get *help* here, not a lot of argufication—"

"I had better inform her ladyship," the butler muttered worriedly. "She won't be best pleased, I'm afraid. What name *did* you say, missie?"

"I didn't say *any* name, but it's Dido Twite."

"Dido Twite. Dwido Tite. Twido Dite. Twito Died. Dwighto Tied," the butler repeated, and left the room, closing the door.

"Oh, bother! Now Grandmother will come along and there'll be a lot of fuss. Why did you have to say you weren't Rowena Palindrome? What does it matter who you are? Sit down, anyway, and amuse me till the old girl comes—it'll take her a while to get up."

"I haven't *got* a while," said Dido crossly. "There's a chap out there, dying, maybe, in an overset carriage, and the driver's knocked silly—not that he was much at the start—and I'd be obliged if you'd kindly send out those two coves as has nothing better to do than open and shut doors to fetch the poor souls here and see arter 'em a bit."

"An overset carriage? How do you know?"

"How do I know? Acos I was in it—that's how."

"You were in a carriage that overturned? Aren't you lucky!"

"Rummy notion o' luck you has," Dido said, studying her companion with curiosity. And certainly he was an unusual figure—a boy of twelve or thirteen, tall and thin, with a pale face and a mop of black hair. More singular still, he was dressed in clothes at least two hundred years out of date—the sort of clothes worn by gentry in Charles the First's day: a frilled shirt with long lace cuffs, a long-skirted embroidered waistcoat, a sword, velvet breeches, and buckled shoes. His hair was tied back with a velvet ribbon. A huge furry white dog lay at his feet; it had a pointed nose, like a bear, and the tongue lolling from its jaws was blue.

Her host, for his part, studied Dido with almost equal astonishment; he saw a sun-tanned girl, her brown hair cut untidily short; she wore long, wide trousers of dark-blue duffel, a white shirt with a sailor collar, and a tight-fitting pea jacket with brass buttons.

"Why do you wear such peculiar clothes?" he said.

"These? They're a midshipman's rig; mighty comfortable too. I jist got back from sea, that's why. Going up to London with dispatches for the Fust Lord o' the Admiralty, and our numbskull of a driver has to overturn us afore we've gone twenty miles, and poor Cap'n Hughes wounded in the Chinese wars and weak as a snail—"

"You've been at *sea*—you, a girl?" Sir Tobit stared at her round-eyed. "Why?"

"That'd be a long tale. That'd be several long tales. What about those hurt men?"

"Oh, we can do nothing for them till my grandmother has given permission," he said carelessly. "So you may as well sit down and tell me your stories till she comes. Are you hungry? Would you like something to eat?"

He pushed toward her a tray carved from some silvery foreign wood. On it were several plates, wooden likewise, containing a few wrinkled apples, some nuts, and a large lump of cheese.

"We never eat anything but fruit and cheese; my grandmother thinks it best. Cowslip wine?"

The cowslip wine, pale yellow in color, was served in an earthenware pitcher. Sir Tobit poured some into a wooden mug.

"Thankee." Dido rejected the nuts—which were wizened, strange-looking little things—but helped herself to

[23]

an apple and a lump of cheese. There had been no time for supper at the Port of Chichester, so she was glad of them. The dog snarled a little as she moved, and Sir Tobit, cuffing him lightly, said,

"Quiet, Lion!"

Glancing around the room as she ate, Dido was struck by the oddity of the contents. In a mansion this size she would have expected richness and grandeur; gold doorknobs, maybe, and crystal chandeliers, such as her friend Simon once told her were to be seen at the duke's castle in Battersea. But here everything looked dusty and worn, and seemed to be made of the plainest materials—wooden chests, straw matting, loosely woven curtains in queer, bright colors, looking as if they had been sewn by people living in grass huts on some distant foreign isle. The lights were the commonest kind of tallow candles and not too plentiful. There were strangely shaped, strangely colored clay pots, and numerous little statues and images in wood and pottery. And books were piled everywhere, higgledy-piggledy—on the chests, the floor, the chairs, and on a curious little round table which looked as if it had been carved with a toothpick from the trunk of a tree. It was rather a nasty little table, Dido thought, looking at it more closely—the top and bottom were solid disks of wood, connected by a crisscross wooden network; at every join a little wooden face grinned maliciously with white-painted teeth and eyes. The room was a large one and the farther end was almost in darkness, but Dido had an uneasy feeling that somebody was there in the shadows watching—occasionally the corner of her eye caught a movement. Perhaps it was another dog?

"Tell about the carriage accident," Sir Tobit demanded. "What happened? Were you waylaid? Was there a fight?"

"No, no, it was just an accident—nothing out o' the common."

"But how did it come about?"

"Land sakes, hain't you never seen a carriage turn topsy-turvy? The driver was a bit tossicated, that's all; I reckon he runned one o' the wheels against the bank. So over we went. And Cap'n Hughes was stuck inside. I managed to scramble out."

"Where did it happen?" Sir Tobit was asking, when the door was opened by Gusset the butler and a lady swept into the room.

Although Lady Tegleaze was plainly very old, her age was not her most striking feature. What most impressed Dido about her was a feeling of *queerness*—as if her very bright eyes were set most of the time on things that nobody else could see, as if she were listening to sounds or voices that nobody else could catch. Like her grandson, she was tall and thin, she limped slightly and walked with a stick, she wore what must surely be a wig of flowing gray curls, and had carelessly flung around her a lavender-colored satin overdress, trimmed with point lace. It was faded and slightly torn. As she came in, Dido heard a door close softly in the shadows at the far end of the room.

"Not so close!" Lady Tegleaze exclaimed, limping

swiftly toward Dido and tapping her with the stick. "Not so close to Sir Tobit—remove yourself, pray!"

The dog Lion growled softly to himself.

Rather taken aback, Dido scrambled to her feet and stepped back, ducking her head in a mixture between a bow and a curtsy. What in tarnation does the old girl think I'm a-going to do—*bite* him? she wondered, but the very oddness of Lady Tegleaze commanded respect.

"Now then," she continued, fixing Dido with those curiously bright, curiously distant eyes, "what is all this about? Who is this young person? Why is she here and where is Lady Rowena Palindrome?"

"Please, your ladyship, the young lady is Miss Twido Dite; and Frill just gave me this; he said a messenger brought it not ten minutes since." The butler handed Lady Tegleaze a note.

"Humph," she said, unfolding and reading it: "From the duchess—too late—too far—too rainy for the horses—cried off. Pish! When I was a gel horses were horses and could stand a bit of rain."

"They always cry off," Sir Tobit languidly observed. "No one wishes to come here. Why should they? You won't let *me* go to *them*."

"So who are you?" The old lady's gaze returned to Dido. Absently she took a handful of nuts from the dish and munched them.

"She had an accident to her carriage," Sir Tobit explained. "On the London road. There are two hurt men and she wants our help to fetch them. One of them's a sea captain, carrying dispatches."

"A sea captain? You have come off a ship?"

"Yes, ma'am."

"From what country? What ship?"

"A navy ship, ma'am, the *Thrush;* she was a-coming home from the China wars and stepped from her course to chase a Hanoverian schooner, and picked me up off'n the isle of Nantucket."

"*China! Nantucket!*" Lady Tegleaze could not have been more horrified if Dido had said Devil's Island. "And you come here—from such places—reeking of typhus, yellow fever, and every kind of infection! Pray stand over by the door!"

"I don't wish to stand anywhere, ma'am, if you'll only send someone to help right our coach and tend to those hurt chaps," Dido said rather aggrievedly, removing herself to the desired location.

"Gusset, have two of the men go back with this young person. But the injured people certainly cannot come *here;* that is quite out of the question. Suppose Sir Tobit caught some noxious illness from them, and it so near to his coming of age!"

"Where should they be taken then, marm?" Gusset inquired doubtfully.

"Someone on the estate can take them in!"

"There bain't many *left* on the estate now, your ladyship."

"There are some tenants in Dogkennel Cottages still, are there not? Old Mr. Firkin—Mrs. Lubbage? Very well—take them there."

Gusset looked even more doubtful, and Dido was not

too happy at the sound of Dogkennel Cottages. Still, it's only for a night, she thought; tomorrow I can stop the mail coach or summat. "Maybe your ladyship could tell me where I can get hold of a doctor?" she asked politely.

"A doctor?" Lady Tegleaze seemed vaguely surprised.

"Dr. Subito is here, playing tiddlywinks with Mr. Wilfred," the butler reminded her. "I could ask him to step along to the cottages."

"Why, yes, I suppose he *could* do so, if the child absolutely demands it; though I would not wish *him* to pick up any infection. But come, child, come along; every minute you are here increases the risk to my grandson."

Lady Tegleaze limped to the door.

"There, I said how it would be," muttered Sir Tobit sulkily. "Just when I had the chance to hear some new tales, instead of having to make up my own."

But Dido was eager to be off. "Thanks for the wine and cheese," she called back, and followed Lady Tegleaze.

At the top of the stairs, Lady Tegleaze came to a halt.

"Where is Tante Sannie?" she asked Gusset.

The butler paused a moment before answering. Then he said, in a peculiarly expressionless voice,

"She was in Mas'r Tobit's room. I reckon she be in your ladyship's room now. Would you wish for me to search?"

"No—no. I will go myself. Follow me, child."

Oh crumpet it, Dido thought; now what?

However she followed along another series of passages. Lady Tegleaze halted outside a door.

"Wait here," she commanded Dido. She opened the door and called, "Sannie?"

Through this door Dido could see another large dimly lit chamber filled with a clutter of foreign-looking furniture, draperies, and scattered clothing. A faint, sickly waft of aromatic smoke drifted out. This is a rum house and no mistake, Dido thought.

Next moment the skin on the back of her neck prickled as something small and dark scuttled from the shadows inside the room out through the door. It was too small for a person, surely? Could it be a large dog? Or an enormous spider?

Then she saw that it was in fact a tiny, bent old woman, wrapped in a kind of embroidered blanket, black and white, which covered her entirely except for two very bright eyes which peered up at Dido from under her head swathings.

"Sannie," said Lady Tegleaze. "You see this girl?"

"I see her, princessie-ma'am!"

"Look at her hand for me, Sannie!"

Dido was disconcerted when a minute, skinny brown claw shot out of the black-and-white draperies and grabbed her hand, turning it over so that the palm came uppermost. The old woman bent over it, mumbling to herself.

"This girl strong girl—much temper, much willful. Can be angry to push over a house. Can kindly love too. I see her holding gold crown in this hand—she

[29]

picking it up from ground, she putting it on someone head. I see great pink fish too—"

"Is this in the past or the future?" interrupted Lady Tegleaze.

"Past, future, princessie-ma'am—all one."

"Well, has she any sickness? Is she infectious? Will she harm my grandson?"

Tante Sannie bent over the hand once more.

"For mussy's *sake*," thought Dido, "what a potheration! All over five minutes' chat with a boy that I'll likely never see again."

"Not sick—no. Strong girl. But something strange here —tree, tree growing. Can't see clear—tree growing, spreading branches over hand. Voices talking in tree— two voices, t'ree voices? Can't see who, tree too thick, too dark. Can't see, can't see, princessie-ma'am!"

The old woman flung down Dido's hand angrily, as if it burnt her, and hobbled away, muttering to herself in a foreign language that sounded like the resentful snarling of cats before they attack one another.

Lady Tegleaze gazed after her rather blankly and stood a moment as if undecided. Then, saying to Dido, "That will do—you may go," she limped into her chamber and shut the door.

Ho, I may, may I? Dido thought crossly. There's gentry for you; full of notions and fancies one minute; then drops you like a bit of orange peel in the midst o' nowhere and leaves you to chart your own course for home.

She darted back the way they had come. Born and

bred in the alleys of Battersea, she had no difficulty in retracing her steps through the maze of passages; she found the marble stairs and ran down them.

Gusset was waiting at the foot.

"Frill and Pelmett have set out already, Missie Dwight," he told Dido. "I reckoned you'd rather they started. Be you able to find your way back to the carriage or shall I step along wi' you?"

"Thanks, mister—that's mighty kind of you. But I guess I can manage," Dido said gruffly, touched by the frail old man's thoughtfulness.

"Might I ask summat, Missie Twide?"

"O' course—what is it?"

"I heeard you say as how you were *told* you'd get help here. Might I ax *who* told you?"

"Why—" Dido began. Then she recollected the caution that had been administered by Yan, Tan, Tethera, and the others.

"It was a chap I met along the road, mister. I don't know who he was. He couldn't stop—was a-going the other way, and all in a pucker acos he was going to meet someone."

"You don't know where he was a-going, missie?"

"Why yes, matter o' fact, I do." Dido wondered why the butler was so inquisitive. "I heeard him say he was a-going to a tree—the Cuckoo Tree."

The old man paled slightly. Dido, glancing about the large, bare hall, did not notice this.

"Excuse me," she said civilly, "but would there be a chair somewheres in this here barracks, Mister Gusset?"

"A chair, missie? I'll see if I can find one for you."
Puzzled, worried, but anxious to oblige, he hobbled off,
murmuring to himself.

"She couldn't have heard wrong, could she? The
Cuckoo Tree, she said plain enough. Butter my wig, I
wish I weren't so pumple-footed."

In a little while—evidently chairs were not too plentiful on the ground floor of Tegleaze Manor—he came
slowly back, carrying a rush-bottomed ladderback with
a burst seat.

"Here you be, then, missie; was you wishful to sit
down?"

"Thankee, mister; no, it's to get back on my nag,"
Dido explained. She carried the chair out to the portico,
planted it down beside Noakes's gray, and climbed
aboard.

"Giddap, Dobbin; you musta had a good rest by now,
let's get back quick, eh? Good night, Mister Gusset,
and thanks for all you done."

"Good night, Missie Dite." Gusset untied the traces
and watched her trot off into the rainy dark. For a few
minutes after that he stood indecisively, scratching his
white whiskers; then he picked up a sack from a heap
lying out in the portico, muffled it about his head and
shoulders, closed the great doors behind him, and set
off in his turn down the pitch-black avenue.

2

By the time that Dido arrived back at the overturned carriage a dank and dripping moon was groping out from behind the rain clouds and giving a little light; she saw that the two footmen, Frill and Pelmett, had fastened a rope to the driver's box and were trying to pull the carriage up on to its wheels again.

"That's a cack-handed way o' going on," Dido muttered as, after some unavailing struggles, they stopped and blew their noses.

"What would *you* suggest, then?" Pelmett inquired sourly.

"Why, pass the rope over a tree branch, o' course!"

This was such obvious sense that the two men received it in silence; Frill, without more ado, climbed up on to the bank and tossed the free end of the rope over a stout beech bough that extended some fifteen feet above the road. With the extra purchase thus obtained, it was not difficult to right the chaise. Its only damage proved to be a snapped shaft.

"Will it go?" asked Dido.

"Reckon so. The gray nag looks a bit swymy, though. Best unharness him and put-to the bay again."

While they were doing this Dido climbed into the carriage and found that the unfortunate Captain Hughes was still unconscious.

"Hey, Mister Frill!" she called softly. "Could you help me set the poor chap back on the seat?"

As he assisted her to do so the moon came out fully and Dido was astonished to discover that the upholstery of the chaise had been violently slashed and ripped; the horsehair stuffing lay tossed in thick mounds and masses all over seats and floor.

"How in mussy's name did that come about?" she exclaimed, brushing a handful of horsehair from the Captain's cravat.

"Cushions split in the upset, o' course," Frill said rather scornfully.

Dido thought this improbable, but she made no further comment. Discovering with relief that Captain Hughes was still breathing, she spread rugs over him and then, while the two footmen searched for Bosky Dick, she went around to the luggage compartment of the chaise, opened the lid, and found, as she had expected, that their two portmanteaux and the Captain's dispatch box were gaping open, and the contents strewn about. She pressed her lips together and nodded to herself.

"Hey, miss! Where did you say the driver was a-lying?" Frill asked. "He don't seem to be noways hereabouts."

"He was in a patch of thistle just there by the road."

Dido walked up the track, now chalk white in the moonlight, to where the two men were standing. But the crushed thistle patch was empty; the driver lay there no longer.

"Musta come to hisself and wandered off," Pelmett said.

"Ah, that'll be it, I'll lay," Frill agreed, nodding wisely. "Bosky Dick allus had a larmentable hard head. Reckon he be halfway back to Chichester by now."

"Well, if you think he'll be all right," Dido said doubtfully, "there's no sense hanging about for him. He warn't no shakes as a driver, anyhows, and I want to get the poor Cap'n bedded and tended as quick as possible. Let's be off."

Pelmett went to the bay's head and they started at a cautious pace, Dido walking beside the carriage, Frill leading the lame gray horse. Captain Hughes stirred and moaned a little.

"Can you go a bit faster, Mister Pelmett?" Dido urged anxiously.

"Just so long's the wheels don't come off," Pelmett agreed, and increased the pace. They had by now reached the spot where Dido met her mysterious guides.

"How far is it to this Dogkennel Cottages?"

"Dogkennel Cottages? Jigger it, is that where we've got to take him?" Pelmett was plainly startled and not too happy at this news.

"That's what the old lady said. She said someone called Mr. Firkin or—or Mrs.—some name like Libbege —'ud look arter him."

"Mrs. Lubbage." Pelmett pronounced the name with distaste. "Well, I dessay she would if she'd a mind to; she'm a wise woman. But *I* ain't so unaccountable keen to have dealings wi' the old besom. Frill, you can do the talking."

"Not I," Frill said uneasily. "Let the lass talk for herself."

Both men quickened their pace, as if anxious to get the meeting with Mrs. Lubbage over as soon as possible. The white track, now winding between gentle grassy slopes, led into a long shallow valley at the far end of which, under a hill round and bare as a bald head, Dido could see a little row of cottages with one or two outbuildings and a couple of haystacks.

"Them's Dogkennels," Pelmett said with relief.

As they drew near, Dido saw that the cottages were flint built and looked very poverty-stricken. Some of the windows were broken; a few cabbage stalks grew in the derelict garden patches. A dim glimmer of light showed in one window; the rest of the cottages, some three or four in all, were dark.

"I'm skeered," Frill said shivering. "This is an unket place—fair gives me the twets. Can't we stop here?"

"We'd best carry the chap in," Pelmett said. "Old

Mis' is sure to ax if we did. Sides, there's the doctor's cob; while he's about she 'on't do anything twort."

A stout gray cob was tethered by the door of the cottage with the light in its window. Pelmett looked about him, picked up a rock, and as if reluctant even to touch the door, used the rock to hammer on it.

The door shot open. Plainly they were expected.

"My daffy-down-dilly!" exclaimed the man who opened to them. "What in the world kept you so long, my dear souls? Have you brought my patient? How is the sad sufferer? Let us fetch him in, *molto, molto allegro!*"

Pelmett and Frill lifted the unconscious man out of the carriage.

"Where'll we set him, gaffer?" Pelmett asked, plainly reluctant to set foot inside the cottage.

"In here, where elsewise?"

But Dido had stepped inside the open door.

"This don't smell right to set a sick man in—it smells downright horrible," she said bluntly. The little room she had entered was slightly below ground level, dimly lit by a rush dip, and it had indeed an evil smell—a damp, warm, sickly, fusty, rotten smell, of old filthy rags, and food gone bad, and burning rubbish, and a queer faint choking sweetness over all. "Ask me," Dido went on, "the air in this place is enough to *make* a body ill."

"Oh, it is, is it? And who asked your opinion, Miss Prussy?" inquired a voice at her elbow. She turned around sharply.

Beside her, studying her with hostility, stood an enormously fat woman, who wore a grubby print dress, and a grubby print apron, and trodden-down slippers. She had her arms folded across the front of the apron. Her face, with tiers of double chins, and small twinkling eyes set in folds of fat, and curly gray hair atop, should have been friendly and jolly, but although the mouth pretended to smile, the unwinking stare of the sharp little eyes made Dido feel very uncomfortable.

"N-no offense, missus," she said politely, "b-but the Cap'n there, being a sailor, is used to lots o' fresh air, and he can't abide being cooped up anywhere stuffy. Reckon he'd be better in a barn or hayloft, if you has one? 'Sides, if this is your kitchen, you won't want a sick person cluttering about in it."

He can't stay here, that's for sure, she thought, her eyes, now used to the dimness, taking in the horrible squalor of the little kitchen, the piles of soiled rags and rotting vegetables, greasy puddles on the uneven brick floor, and peeling, blackened walls.

"Eh! High-up, flarsky, and hoity-toity we are," Mrs. Lubbage said sourly. "Still, there's empty housen a-plenty; if my kitchen's not good enough for you you can take yourself next door. *I* ain't pitickler where you sleeps, it's all one to *me*. Her ladyship sends a message for me to have an eye to the poor sick gentleman; that's all *I* knows."

"Perchance it would be better to take the patient next door," Dr. Subito agreed with ill-concealed relief.

"Can you carry the poor languisher there, my good fellows?"

Not at all reluctant, Pelmett and Frill carried Captain Hughes to another of the empty cottages. The first they tried had been used for keeping chickens in, and was not much better than Mrs. Lubbage's kitchen. But the next was empty and clean enough; it even had a rickety old bedstead which Pelmett stacked with hay while Frill fetched sticks and kindled a fire in the little hearth. By the light of this, and some tapers which the men had brought with them, Dr. Subito was able to examine the Captain.

"A leg is broken, alas, which I will set," he announced, and proceeded to do so, swiftly and deftly. "Otherwise he suffers only from fever and inflammation of his head wound, that is all. The wound received at sea, I understand? Since how long? Two months? And he is recovering *con brio,* up to now?"

"Chirpy as a cricket," Dido said. "The surgeon on board his ship—that's the *Thrush*—told him how when he got to London the doctors there'd likely say he could have his bandages off. It's a plaguy shame this had to happen now. How long'll he be poorly again, mister doctor?"

"He should not be moved for two weeks—three, if this fever does not slip down very quickly. I will come back tomorrow—*subito*—meantime you will find that the large lady—Mrs. Lubbage—is a famous nurse."

"She don't look it—I'd as lief not trouble her," Dido said, wrinkling her nose at the thought of that kitchen.

"*Senti,* young lady, she has the gift of healing, she knows about herbs and charms, *molto, molto,*" Dr. Subito said earnestly. He was a small, spare man, with a sallow complexion and an anxious expression; his large black mustaches were his most lively and vigorous feature. When he spoke about Mrs. Lubbage he glanced somewhat nervously behind him and made an odd, jerky sign with two fingers. "If it were not for the intervention of Mrs. Lubbage, many, many of my patients would not have recovered!" Under his breath he muttered, "And many, many of them would not have fallen ill, *presto alla tedesca!*"

"Fire's going nice and sprackish now, sir," said Pelmett. "And I've put the lame nag in the shippen with a bit o' feed, and reckon us'd better ride the other one back to the Manor, or ol' Mis'll be turble tiffy and bumblesome, axing where we've got to."

Plainly he was dying to get away.

"I will accompany you, my good fellows, *allegro vivace,*" the doctor said quickly. "Give the patient this draught, young lady, when he awakens, and another dose at morningtide. He should have light feedings—milk, eggs, white wine. No meat. I will return *domani* —tomorrow. *Addio!* To the re-see!"

"Hey! Where am I to find eggs and wine and so forth in this back end?" Dido called after him, but he did not hear, or did not choose to.

Dido suddenly found herself left alone with the sick man; the sound of hoofs died away outside and after that, strain her ears how she might, there was nothing to be heard at all, save a distant sighing of trees.

"This is a fubsy kind o' set-out," she said to herself. "Still, no use bawling over botched butter—have to make the best of it. I'd as soon not tangle overmuch wi' that old witch next door though. Only thing is, how are we going to get summat to eat? Oh, well, maybe old Lady Tegleaze'll send some soup and jelly— or cheese and apples—no use fretting ahead. Queer old cuss *she* is, too—all those rooms in that great workus of a place, and she has to send us to a ken that ain't much bigger than a chicken coop."

She made sure the Captain was sleeping peacefully, packed the hay tight under him, and straightened the capes and carriage rugs over him. Next she brought in their valises, which would serve as tables or chairs, made up the fire, piled more hay in a corner for her own bed, and bolted the front and back doors of the cottage, which consisted of two ground-floor rooms with a loft above.

Lastly Dido pulled a packet from the front of her midshipman's shirt and carefully inspected it. It was addressed to the First Lord of the Admiralty and was covered in large red unbroken seals.

"All hunky-dory," she muttered to herself in satisfaction. "Likely enough it was *you* as whoever rummaged over the carriage was a-looking for—seeing as how nothing else was stole. But they didn't find you, and so long as we're in this neck o' the woods, or till I can lay hands on some trustable chap to take you to London, you stays right inside my shimmy shirt."

She replaced the packet, blew out the tapers, and curled up in her sweet-smelling nest.

About half an hour later she heard somebody cautiously try first the front, then the back door.

"Hilloo?" Dido called out. "Is that the baker's boy? One white, one brown, two pints o' dairy fresh *with* the top on, half o' rashers, and a dozen best pullets', *if* you please."

Dead silence greeted this request, and though Dido listened alertly for some time after, there was no further disturbance. Presently, satisfied, she fell asleep.

Early next morning, well before daybreak, Dido was wakened by the crowing of roosters near at hand. Beyond the roosters, plaintive in the dark, she could hear sheep bleating—high and low, near and far—it sounded as if the hills were covered with an immense flock of sheep, full of unappeased longing for breakfast.

"And I could do with a peck myself," thought Dido, rolling off her flattened pile of hay. "Croopus, don't they half have it noisy in the country! Still, I reckon it's time for the Cap to take another dram o' physic. Hey, Cap'n Hughes!" she said softly. "How are you a-feeling today?"

His forehead was cool and his eyes, when they opened, recognized her.

"It's the young passenger—Miss Twite," he murmured. "I will escort her to London when I carry the

Dispatch—Osbaldeston will continue in command until the end of my sick furlough. Ah, thank you, my dear—"

Obediently he swallowed down the draught which Dido had prepared for him and fell asleep at once. Satisfied that he was doing well, Dido blew up the embers of the fire and fed it with dry sticks. Now, how could she go out leaving the sick man secure from intrusion? There were bolts on both doors, and a lock on the front one, but no key.

"Nothing bigger than a cat could get in at the windows, so that's no worry," she decided. "Wonder if I could get out through the loft?"

Entry to this was through a trap door in the ceiling. She piled the cases one on another and from the top one was just able to spring up, grab the edge of the opening, and pull herself through like a squirrel.

Plainly the loft had been used in the past for housing pigeons. A number of miscellaneous oddments had also been stored up here at one time or another and then forgotten; probing about cautiously in the half dark Dido found some pewter dishes, half a dozen clay pipes (broken), a stringless lute, a box of mildewy books, an iron candlestick, a three-legged stool, some earthenware crocks, and a hip bath.

"Some o' these'll come in useful," she decided. "Now, what's out back?"

A couple of tiles had been removed from the roof to make an entrance for the pigeons. Putting her face to the hole, Dido looked out and in the growing dawn light saw that a neglected, weed-grown farmyard lay behind the row of cottages. With great care she removed another tile, enlarging the hole enough to stick her head through, and looked sideways. A big rainwater barrel could be seen to her right, just below the edge of the roof.

"Guess if I could get on to that I could climb down from it," Dido thought, measuring its height with her eye. She began taking more tiles from the hole, slipping each carefully off its pair of wooden pegs and laying it on the floor, until there was a gap large enough to climb through. Once a tile escaped her and slid down, landing with a crash on the cobbles below, but nobody appeared to have heard. When the hole was big enough she squeezed through and went down the roof on fingers and toes until she was above the big wooden cask. Prodding it first, to make sure the top would take her weight, she scrambled on to it. A broken wooden handbarrow leaned against the wall below.

"That'll do for climbing back," she thought with satisfaction, and jumped nimbly to the ground. Hardly had she done so when she heard footsteps; an old man carrying two buckets on a yoke across his shoulders walked around the corner of the cottages and across the yard away from Dido. He had not seen her but his dog, following a few yards behind, did, and gave one sharp formal wuff. The old man turned himself around —he could not turn just his head because of the yoke.

"What be fidgeting ee, Toby?" he said.

The dog barked again.

"Why, dag me, 'tis a boy. No it bean't, it be a liddle maid. Where be you from so early, darter?"

"Are you Mr. Firkin?" Dido asked. "Lady Tegleaze said you'd help me."

"Owd Tom Firkin I be, and this yer's my dog Toby."

"What kind of a dog's that? I've never seen one like him before."

Toby was a grayish sandy color, as big as a sheep, and so extremely shaggy that it was hard to tell which way he was facing.

"Old-fashioned ship dog ee be," Mr. Firkin said.

"Old-fashioned! He looks like something out o' the ark."

"Ah, he be a wunnerful clever dog wi' the ship; we ne'er loses one at lambing time."

While he was speaking Mr. Firkin continued on his way and Dido followed into a cowshed where a brindled cow stood waiting to be milked. Mr. Firkin hung his yoke over a wooden partition, took off the buckets, and sat down to milk on a three-legged wooden stool like the one in the loft, leaning his head against the cow's side. He wore a battered hard felt hat, painted gray, with a pheasant's feather in it, and a sort of jerkin and apron made of sacking over velveteen breeches and leather boots. He had a long bushy white beard, which at the moment was inconveniencing him very much; it stuck out and got in the way of the milk flow and if he pushed it to one side with his elbow it dangled into the pail.

"You want a bit o' string for that, mister," said Dido.

She had one in her pocket, with which she tied the beard, doubled up in a neat bunch.

"Nay! That's nim," he said admiringly. "I can tell ee must be a trig liddle maid. Why don't ee feed my chickens while I tend to owd Clover here, then us'll git our breakfasses."

He showed her where the hens were shut up at night "for fear o' foxy owd Mus' Reynolds" and gave her a round tin pan with a wooden handle.

"Chickens' grub be in the posnet yonder."

Outside the cottage at the far end of the row from Mrs. Lubbage's, Dido saw a kind of caldron on legs, which proved to be full of potato peelings. Under Mr. Firkin's directions, she mixed these with a measure of corn. Then she opened the fowl-house door, letting loose a knee-deep flood of brown, white, and speckled poultry into the yard, and fed them by flinging out handfuls of the mixture until they were all busily pecking and the pan was empty. Meanwhile Mr. Firkin had finished milking and carried the two full pails back to his cottage.

Dido followed and found him there carefully wringing his beard into one of the pails.

"Now then, what's all this nabble about ol' Lady Tegleaze?" he said, putting a pan of water to boil over the fire. While he cut slices off a loaf and a side of bacon and laid them in a skillet, Dido told him about the accident: how Captain Hughes, wounded in the Chinese wars, had been coming home on sick leave, when his ship the *Thrush* had become involved in another battle, against the French this time, and had captured a French frigate.

"And we was taking a Dispatch to London about it all when this roust-up had to happen."

Mr. Firkin was deeply interested in her tale.

"Yon sick Cap'n's lying with a busted leg in the empty cottage? Eh, I'll take him a posset; that'll furbish him up."

He poured milk into another pan (not from the pail into which he had wrung his beard, Dido was relieved to notice), warmed it, added sugar, eggs, and a golden fluid from a leather bottle.

"What's yon, mister?"

"Dandelion wine, darter."

The posset was yellow and frothy and smelt wonderful—like a whole field of dandelions. Dido ran back along the yard, clambered by means of the wheelbarrow on to the cask and so to the roof, through the pigeon hole, down through the loft entrance, and was able to unbolt the cottage's front door just as Mr. Firkin arrived.

Captain Hughes was stirring again, more wakeful this time, and very glad of the posset.

"Puts me in mind of the Chinese lily soup we used to get in Poohoo province," he said. It soon made him drowsy, and he slept again.

"D'you think he looks all right, mister, or d'you reckon he's feverish?" Dido asked Mr. Firkin.

"Nay, I'm bline, darter, I can't see him! Mis' Lubbage'll be the one to tell ee how he'm faring."

[47]

"*Blind? You* are?" Dido was astonished. The old man's eyes were so bright, and he was so deft in everything he did, that it seemed as if he could see better than most.

"Blinded forty year agone, struck by lightning sitting under a snottygog tree on Barlton Down. Turble fierce thunderstorms we had when I were a lad."

"How ever did you know I was a girl?" Dido asked, thinking back.

"Why, my dog Toby told me, surelye! There bain't much as my dog Toby can't tell me." The shaggy Toby wagged his tail knowledgeably and thrust his head under his master's arm.

Dido was somewhat dashed to realize that she would still have to apply to Mrs. Lubbage for sick nursing.

"Anyhows, you don't want to rouse her yet awhile or she'll be sidy," Mr. Firkin said. "She be a late lier, owd Mis' Lubbage. Come ee back and eat a rasher o' my bacon, cardenly."

Since she would be next door and within earshot of the Captain, Dido accepted.

Mr. Firkin's bacon was delicious, and so was his homemade bread-and-butter, and so was his tea "that thunderin' strong ye could trot a mouldywarp on it." After breakfast Dido washed up for him, peeled potatoes for his dinner, and swept out his kitchen, which was the same size as that of Mrs. Lubbage but exquisitely neat. Then she chopped some firewood because Mr. Firkin told her that was the one job he was sure to make a boffle of. His woodshed contained a large untidy pile of dry boughs and a small neat pile of kindling already chopped to the right size. Dido wondered who had done it.

"Mr. Firkin," she said, "if I wanted to get a letter taken to London, who'd I best ask? Is there a regular mail coach as goes by this way?"

"Once every two days Jem Hoadley takes mail so far as Petworth."

"Is he reliable? What happens to it there?"

"Nay, he's a bit shravey, Jem is; times folks's letters has gone no-one-wheres. And if the mail does get to Petworth, I dunnasay what comes to it there."

Dido resolved not to trust Captain Hughes's Dispatch to the shravey Jem until she had tried him out.

"D'you think Mrs. Lubbage'll be stirring by now? Maybe I'd best go and see her or she'll be offended?"

"Ah, she'm a taffety one," he agreed. "There's some as dassn't go anigh her, 'case she puts a mischief on 'em. Some reckons she's a wise 'ooman, others say she's downright a witch."

"What do you reckon, mister?"

"I ain't afeered o' the owd skaddle, however skrow she be. But then I wears mouldywarpses' toeses; she can't mischief me." He pulled out and showed Dido two moles' claws on a leather bootlace around his neck. "Powerful good agin the toothache they be and against the powers o' dark too. Tell ee what, darter, I'll give ee a pair; then ee 'on't come to no harm."

He picked another pair of feet from a wooden box full of very strong-smelling tobacco and threaded them on a string; Dido slung them around her neck and tucked them out of sight along with Captain Hughes's Dispatch.

Mr. Firkin and Toby then set off up the smooth steep grassy slope of the hill behind Dogkennel Cottages—which he had told her was called Barlton Down —to look after the sheep; Dido walked along to Mrs. Lubbage's cottage. Outside the door she paused with her hand upraised to knock. She could hear voices inside—or rather, one voice, very angry. It was Mrs. Lubbage.

"Show your face down here again between sunup and moonup and I'll give ee such a dose of hazel oil, ye 'on't be able to set down for a week. Hear what I say? Maybe that'll teach ee!"

There was a thud and a stifled cry.

"Now be off outa my sight," said Mrs. Lubbage's voice. There was no reply.

Dido knocked loudly on the door.

A long silence followed. Then Mrs. Lubbage—much closer to—said, "Who's that?"

"It's me, from next door," Dido called. "Come to ask you to take a look at the hurt man."

After another long wait the door opened a crack and Mrs. Lubbage's large red face peered suspiciously around it. The smell from her kitchen also came out through the crack; it seemed to have thickened and strengthened during the night.

"Oh, it's you, is it?" Mrs. Lubbage said, and opened

[50]

the door completely. Dido looked past her, but nobody else was there.

"Spose I better come along, and hob him up," the wise woman said in a surly tone. "I'll jest fetch my things."

She retired to rummage in a chest in her back room; no one else was there. But of course they might have gone out the back door. And there was a loft entrance similar to that in Dido's cottage; perhaps the other person was up there.

Dido felt sorry for anyone who lived with Mrs. Lubbage.

"Right, then, here I be," said the wise woman, emerging with a cloth bag. She glanced at Dido out of the corners of her sharp little eyes, and said, "Did ee hear me a-thumping my owd Tibbie jest now?"

"Maybe, missus," Dido said cautiously. "Why did you do that, then?"

"He be a turble owd thief, my Tib; he sucked up a pan o' milk while my back was turned, so I was a-larruping of him. He be my magico; helps me cast spells."

Dido made no reply to this, but opened the door to let Mrs. Lubbage into the Captain's sickroom. Mr. Firkin had run his fingers sensitively through a tray of oddments in his tool shed and found a pair of keys, one of which fitted the lock of her front door. She saw the sharp little eyes take note of the lock and the key.

It became plain at once that Mrs. Lubbage knew

quite a bit about nursing. She carefully removed the bandages, inspected the healing wound on the Captain's head, and dusted it with some powder from a small jar.

"What's that, missus?"

"Powdered sungreen, it be; wunnerful good for a healing cut. Now I'll put a handful o' cobwebs atop"—she did so—"and you leave them lay, and in tuthree days he'll be sprackish enough and through this liddle toss o' fever. If he gets fretful, soak these in water"—she passed Dido a handful of dried berries like raisins—"give him the water to drink, that'll ease him till he sweats."

"What are they?"

"Mortal quizzitive you be," Mrs. Lubbage said sourly. "Where I was reared, children kept their eyes open and their mouthses shut. Dried pethwine they be—if that learns you."

It did not, and Dido resolved to throw the berries away and give Captain Hughes nothing but the doctor's medicine. Mrs. Lubbage then inspected the broken leg, which she said was mending well and not inflamed.

"I'm obliged to you, missus," Dido said politely. "Can I dig your garden or do aught useful for you?"

"You can muck out my chicken house if ye've a mind to."

Dido was not enthusiastic about this task but at least it would be pleasanter than cleaning out Mrs. Lubbage's horrible kitchen. First making sure that the Captain was once more peacefully asleep and had a drink within easy reach if he were to wake, she locked him in. Whoever had searched their baggage might return for another look; besides, Dido did not trust the sly-eyed Mrs. Lubbage, good nurse or no.

Mr. Firkin's chickens had been plump, well-feathered, and lively; Mrs. Lubbage's were scrawny, mopey, and molting. You'd think a wise woman'd be able to take better care of her poultry, Dido thought, carrying baskets of shed feathers and dirty straw from the chicken coop to a pile of rubbish at the bottom of Mrs. Lubbage's muddy garden. While doing so, she observed a pony and trap trot briskly along the road and come to a halt in front of Dogkennel Cottages. Old Gusset, the butler, descended with a white-covered basket.

"Aha, there's the soup and jelly!" Dido stuck her pitchfork into a straw stack and started toward the butler, but before she reached him, Mrs. Lubbage opened her door and beckoned Gusset inside. He went after several doubtful and uneasy glances about him. The door closed. Dido, still a fair way off, then noticed another figure slip out from under the seat of the trap, look sharply around, and hurry off around the corner of the cottages.

The day was a misty, murky one; what Mr. Firkin called driply weather; but even through the damp rainy grayness this second caller, though bundled up like a chrysalis in draperies, had a familiar appearance.

"It's the funny old gal that Lady Tegleaze called Tante Sannie," Dido thought. "Why's she stealing a ride with the butler?"

In a moment Gusset appeared, looking glad to have completed his errand. He caught sight of Dido. Coming up, she noticed that he held a little carved wooden pistol, about the size of a radish, threaded on a leather thong. He pocketed it, saying in an embarrassed way, "'Tis a luck-charm," and pulled out a note, folded like a cocked hat, "I was to bring you this, Missie Twito Dide. And I've left some things for the sick gen'lman with Mrs. Lubbage. Good day to ee, missie."

He climbed back into the pony trap and drove off without apparently noticing that he had had a passenger on the ride down who was now missing.

Dido, not wishing to read her note where she could be seen from the windows, retired behind the hen house.

"Come up to the South Door after dark," she read, "follow the track, turn right at the top, across the tilting-yard, up the steps, along the terrace, through the lavender court, and I'll be waiting inside the door."

No signature—unless the smudge at the bottom was a T. And the writing was very untidy.

"Oh, that's naffy!" Dido thought. "Sposing I go all that way and nobody's there? Well, I'll wait and see what the weather's like, and how the Cap'n's fettling. Now, what about these here delicacies?"

She started back toward the cottages but before she reached them Mrs. Lubbage came out, wrapped in a man's coat and with a sack over her head. The shawled figure of Tante Sannie darted from behind a barn and joined her. The two talked together, then Mrs. Lubbage locked her door, and they set off side by side along the road away from Tegleaze Manor.

"Proper pair of old witches they be," thought Dido. "Right good company for each other. I'm not weeping millstones that old Madam Lubbage is out o' the road for a bit. But it's a cuss about the locked door."

Through the window the basket of provisions could be seen, very tantalizingly, on her kitchen table.

"What's the odds she'd never hand it over unless I ask for it? Oh well, let's have a wash and see what can be done."

The hen house being as clean as she could make it, Dido drew a pail of water from the rain butt, heated it over Mr. Firkin's fire, and had an enjoyable splash.

Then she re-entered her own cottage and climbed up into the loft.

As she had noticed before, the partition between one loft and the next was formed only of wattles. It was easy enough to push a way through this thin barrier.

But what was her surprise, when she started doing so, to hear, evidently from the loft over the empty cottage, a voice singing softly to itself in a strange little chant:

"Dwah, dwah, dwahdy dwahdy dwee
I can't see you but you can see me—
Canarack, stanarack, out of the blue
You can see me but I can't see you—"

Mystified, Dido parted two wattles and laid her eye against the partition.

Someone was sitting cross-legged in the shadows—someone about Dido's size, dark-haired, wearing ragged trousers and a shirt. That was all Dido had a chance to see, for she had made a slight noise pulling the withies apart; the singer turned a startled face toward her, sprang up, made a dart for a hole in the roof, and vanished through it. Dido heard a scrambling outside on the tiles and then a thud; evidently she was not the only one to use the water butt as an escape route.

"Drabbit it!" Dido exclaimed. "There's altogether too many mysteries around here. Now, what'd I best do—keep an eye on the Cap or go arter this here hop o' my thumb?"

Curiosity won. "The Cap'll come to no harm in ten minutes," she decided, scrambled out her own hole, and slid down the roof. As she did so she observed a small distant figure cross the field and take the chalk track that ran from Dogkennel Cottages between Barlton Down and the next big grassy hill. Almost at once the figure was out of sight in the mist, but Dido, hurrying to the chalk track, found a trail of new footprints in the white oozy mud.

"My stars," she thought, hearing no sound ahead, "whoever it is can't half cover the ground."

Luckily Dido herself was no mean runner; even so she began to wonder if she would ever catch up. The chalk road climbed steeply. High hedges on either side cut off the view. At the topmost point between the two hills, where the track started to descend, the footprints suddenly came to a stop. Dido, questing about, noticed a trail of scuffled leaves under some big beech trees to her left. She followed this clue, and came out from the trees into a wide, hammock-shaped grassy place; beyond it rose the big dome of Barlton Down. Far ahead Dido could see her quarry, running along a grass path that led around the side of the hill.

"Plague take the critter," Dido muttered, picking her way at top speed through damp knee-high tussocks of coarse downland grass. "At this rate we'll be halfway to London before I get any closer. Another five minutes and I give up!"

However once she reached the grass path, which was flat and smooth as a shelf, the pursuit was easier. On her right, the grassy slope ran steeply down into mist; a few big, dark-green bushy trees dotted the uphill slope to her left.

"All we want's a few candles and there'd be enough Christmas trees here for every soul in the country. Croopus, this is a funny sort o' place. There's so *much* of it; naught but trees and grass, and no people, and all tipped up like the side of a roof."

She was fairly out of breath, but the trail of footprints in the short, dewy grass of the path was easy to follow. As she ran soundlessly along the smooth turf she heard the voice again singing its queer little rune:

> "Canarack, stanarack, out of the blue
> You can see me but I can't see you—"

"What does the silly perisher mean?" wondered Dido. "Dunno whether he can see me, but I sure as Sunday can't see *him*."

The voice was close at hand, up the hill to her left; she stood still and then began cautiously climbing the steep slope through mist, which here was suddenly much thicker. After a moment or two the voice seemed to be straight ahead. Dido stood still again.

"There you are at last as well," the voice said in a conversational tone. "I couldn't come before; Auntie Daisy was beating me."

Silence for a moment. Dido moved another step or two. Where *was* the voice coming from?

"Why did she beat me? For coming out of the loft to get a bit of bread. It didn't matter as well—beating's not the worst."

Dido stopped once more. She had thought the voice was speaking to her; now she realized it was not. Who else was there, then? Who was answering? Where in the mist were they?

"I don't mind anything so long as I can talk to you as well."

As well? Dido thought. As well as what?

She took another step.

"*Dear* Aswell," said the voice. "I do love you."

Aswell?

Another silent step. Dido felt something tickle her nose: a gossamer-spangled sprig of yew. Peering ahead into the mist she saw that she was close to a small tree which stuck out at right angles from the steep hillside.

"canarack, Stanarack,
out of the blue
you can see me
but i can't see you"

It was a curious little stunted yew, not much more than twelve feet high; the foliage began about four feet above the ground, thick, bushy, and flattened as if the top had been chopped off, so that the tree resembled a finger with a round cake balanced on its tip. The cake was composed of close-set branches and twigs covered with dark-green yew needles and luminous red yew berries; while the finger—the trunk—was so twisted and knobbed and grooved that Dido could see it would be very easy to climb: just like walking upstairs. And the voice now came from directly above her.

"What have *you* been doing, Aswell?"

"This is getting too spooky," Dido thought. "I'm a-going up to find who's atop there."

Ducking, she edged under the branches and looked up the trunk, which was about as thick as a gatepost. The trunk turned sideways just above Dido's head, and three or four branches came out from it, like the spokes of a bent wheel. There was a gap in the greenery just big enough to climb through. Dido could see a pair of feet in very patched, broken boots, resting on one branch.

Still very silently, she set foot on the lowest knob, caught hold of two spoke branches, and with one rapid movement pulled and thrust herself up the sloping trunk, so that her head suddenly shot out through the central hole.

"*Oh!*" said the voice.

Dido found herself face to face—almost nose to nose —with the boy who had been in the loft.

"Blimey, he's thin!" was Dido's first thought. Then she looked around. They were sitting—it was impossible not to sit at once—in a kind of soup bowl of green yew needles—the foliage was so thickly massed that it held them like a cushion, with their feet in the middle, resting on the central spokes.

The boy would have bolted again, but Dido was in his way—he could not escape. Besides—

"*Please* don't skedaddle!" Dido said. "Croopus, I can do with a bit o' company in this wilderness! I'm lonesome! What d'you think I've bin a-chasing you for?"

The boy took a deep breath. It was plain that Dido's sudden appearance had frightened him badly—she could almost see his heart thumping under the thin torn shirt. He looked nice, though. He was amazingly dirty —smeared with grime, wet from the drizzle, wrapped in a filthy matted old sheepskin jacket. His dark hair was cut raggedly short and festooned with cobwebs, as if he spent most of his time in the loft. But he looked far, very far, from stupid.

"Who are you?" he brought out presently.

"I'm Dido Twite. I'm stopping in one o' those Dogkennel Cottages with a hurt chap—Mrs. Lubbage is tending him."

"Please," said the boy earnestly, "*please* don't tell Mrs. Lubbage that you saw me!"

"*Course* I won't." Dido was affronted. "I ain't a blobtongue. What'd happen—would she beat you?"

"I don't mind being beaten. She does worse things than that."

He looked as if he would rather not discuss it. Dido asked instead,

"Is she your auntie Daisy?"

"Not really. All my family are dead. I used to live with another old woman in Suffolk—I think she was Auntie Daisy's cousin. She wasn't any kin of mine. Then she died—that was last year—and Auntie Daisy fetched me here. She said no one must ever find out I was living with her. I don't much like it here. It was better in Suffolk. Sometimes the rector used to teach me."

"Why mustn't anyone find out?"

"I don't know. Maybe she's not allowed to have children because she's a witch."

"Is she *really* a witch?" Dido asked.

"*She* thinks she is."

"Are you scared of her?"

The boy pondered, his gray eyes fixed on distance. "I'm more scared of the other one," he said at length.

"Which?"

"Her friend. Tante Sannie." He looked a little impatient—as if, Dido suddenly thought, he expected her to know all this already. She glanced around her at the bushy little dark-green tree, which could have held about two more people as well as themselves, but did not, and asked,

"Who were you a-talking to when I climbed up?"

He looked still more surprised. "I was talking to Aswell, of course."

"Who's Aswell?"

"My friend. Can't you hear him? He's talking now."

"No I can't," Dido said crossly. Was the boy touched in the upper works?

"No you can't," the boy agreed, after listening again. "Aswell says I'm the only one who can hear him."

"Where is he?" Dido asked rather disbelievingly.

The boy frowned, getting his thought into words. "In a way he seems to be here. Sometimes when we first start talking I can feel him—feel him put his hands between mine. But it's hard for him to do that—it only lasts a minute. *Really* he's thousands of miles away."

"Where—in the *sky?*"

"I suppose so. He'll come when I call. Not always but sometimes. And more often here in the Cuckoo Tree than back in the loft."

Dido was suddenly enlightened.

"You fetches him by singing that funny rhyme—canarack, stanarack?"

"Of course." He seemed as if he found Dido dreadfully slow-witted, and she felt a little forlorn.

"What's your name?" she asked.

"Cris."

"Well, Cris, why don't you run away from Auntie Daisy? Croopus, I would, if I had to live in the loft all the time."

"They'd find me," Cris said. "Even if Auntie Daisy couldn't, Tante Sannie would be sure to find me, wherever I went. And I couldn't bear that. She can do things." He shivered. "Besides, Aswell says it's better

[63]

if I stay. Aswell knows much more than I do. And I can help the old man—Mr. Firkin."

"Does he know you're there?"

"He doesn't *let* himself know—I expect he guesses Auntie Daisy would be angry," Cris said, thinking again. Dido suddenly realized that he was not at all *used* to having a conversation—it took him a minute to translate her questions into his thoughts and back again. "But I think he does know. He leaves food for me. And Toby knows, of course."

Dido nodded. "Don't you see *no* one else?"

Cris looked puzzled. "Who could I see? I'm supposed to stay in the loft while it's light. But Auntie Daisy's too fat to come up, so most days I come here."

"It's nice." Dido leaned back against a spicy, springy cushion of yew. "Reckon you could just about *live* in this tree. Can you eat the berries?"

"The red squashy part you can—but it's not very nice, it's sickly. The green seed in the middle is poisonous."

"Do cuckoos build their nests here?" asked ignorant Dido.

"Cuckoos don't build. They lay their eggs in other birds' nests."

"Then why's it called the Cuckoo Tree?"

Cris listened a minute.

"Aswell says it's always been called that—since Charles the First's time. Because it's such a funny shape."

At this moment the sun, which had been battling with the mist for the last ten minutes, suddenly burst through. The clouds lifted in a great spongy, steamy mass, melting skyward into the blue.

"Saints save us!" exclaimed Dido.

She had not realized how high up they were. Below the Cuckoo Tree the wooded hill shot steeply down for six hundred feet, and at its foot flat country began which stretched away—field after field, wood after wood —into the far blue distance. There were villages, churches, a town with a tall steeple, a pair of lakes not far off, reflecting the color of the sky. On either hand the downs rolled away, one behind the other, like green grassy waves. And the beech trees in the woods down below blazed red and gold in their autumn plumage.

"Where's London?"

"You can't see that from here—it's over fifty miles."

"Not that town there?" Dido was disappointed.

"No, that's Petworth."

The name reminded Dido of Captain Hughes and his Dispatch.

"I'd best be getting back," she said regretfully. "What about you?"

"I daren't come back now the mist's lifted. I'll have to wait till it's dark."

"Don't you get hungry?"

"Used to it. Maybe I'll find some blackberries or nuts left."

Dido felt in her pockets and discovered a couple of eggs which she had picked up in Auntie Daisy's hen house. One of the eggs had broken.

"Ugh!" She pulled out her fingers slimy and dripping. "Lucky the other one ain't bust. Sposing it's not addled, that is. You could build a little fire and roast it."

"Thanks." Cris took the egg. His thin, serious face broke into a smile which made Dido wonder if he had ever smiled before.

"My stars!" She suddenly remembered. "The doc's sposed to be coming at noon to look at my Cap'n. I'd best scarper. Tooralooral, Cris. See you in the loft, maybe."

Cris turned rather pale. "You'll be careful? If Auntie Daisy heard you up there—"

"Mum as a mouse in a mad cat's ear," Dido promised, and climbed nimbly backward down the trunk. It was like going down the companionway of a ship.

At the foot she noticed an odd thing: a corkscrew, which somebody had screwed several turns into the reddish, flaky bark. A small piece of green ribbon was tied to the handle.

"Daffy idea to leave a corkscrew in a tree trunk!" Dido thought. "No bottles hereabouts? Wonder why Cris has it there?"

It was not until she had started the steady jog trot back to Dogkennel Cottages that she remembered Yan, Tan, Tethera, and the rest. They too had been planning to come to the Cuckoo Tree. Could the corkscrew belong to them, rather than to Cris? And did Cris know about them?

She reached the top of the hill and started running down the slope toward the little row of cottages. Away to her left she could see Mr. Firkin, with his dog Toby, sitting in the middle of a huge flock of sheep.

"Ask me," said Dido to herself, "Mr. Firkin and Toby are about the only two around here that ain't muxed up in some kind of havey-cavey business. Blight it, there comes old Sawbones Subito on his nag; I'd best hustle."

3

The doctor's verdict on his patient was favorable.

"Another two weeks," he declared, "and we shall have him *con moto, allegro assai!* It is a strong constitution, fortunately—*fortissimo!* Continue with the treatment along the lines I have laid down. The *signora* Lubbage—she has seen him?"

"Yes," said Dido, "she put these here cobwebs on him. She ain't home just now."

"Ah, that is good—I mean, that is good she has seen him. *Eccolo,* I will return on Friday," said Dr. Subito, and made off at top speed, casting wary glances along the road in either direction.

Captain Hughes was wakeful, after the doctor's inspection, and somewhat fretful.

"I could eat a sturgeon, bones and all," he announced, and Dido glanced around the bare little room.

"We're clean out of prog, Cap," she said. "Wait a couple o' minutes and I'll see what I can fetch in."

Mr. Firkin still sat out in the hillside with his sheep, a couple of miles away, but the basket from Tegleaze Manor was close at hand, temptingly in view through Mrs. Lubbage's kitchen window.

"I spose she did lock the door?" Dido said to herself. She walked along to the witch's cottage carrying Captain Hughes's clasp knife, with which she thought it would be easy enough to force the door. She tried it to make certain: yes, locked. Just as she was about to insert the knife blade between door and doorpost she experienced a curious prickling sensation in her hands; at the same time a small buzzing voice—where? inside her head perhaps—said, faintly but audibly,

"This is a hoodoo lock. Beware. Do not touch it."

"Eh?" Dido looked sharply behind her. Nobody was there. "Have I got a screw loose?" she wondered, and approached the knife blade to the crack once more.

Again she heard the voice, distant but distinct, impossible to locate, like the drone of a loud mosquito:

"This is a hoodoo lock. Beware. Do not touch it."

"Rabbit me!" Dido, thoroughly discomposed and uneasy, stepped back, eying the door as if it might fly open and thump her. "This is a right mirksy set-out! Talking doors—I spose when I goes to lay hands on the basket of grub it'll get up and walk away! Well, the old crone may have hoodoo'd her front door, but I'll lay she didn't think to set one o' her spooky booby traps in the attic—blow me if I don't fetch the vittles out that way just to serve her right for her nasty suspicious nature."

Somewhat to the surprise of the Captain she returned to his room, piled up their luggage, and climbed into the loft. Then she made her way along through the series of lofts until she reached that of Mrs. Lubbage, whose trap door was open. Jamming a broomstick across the hole, Dido tied a length of cord to it, and slid down.

Mrs. Lubbage's kitchen smelt even worse with the door shut; the smell was like a solid, threatening presence in the room.

Just our luck if it's turned the grub sour, Dido thought, moving carefully and warily across the greasy bricks toward the table on which stood the hamper of provisions. A label on the handle reinforced her courage: it said in large clear print:

FOR THE SICK GENTLEMAN
AT DOGKENNEL COTTAGES

Bet we wouldn't a-seen a crumb of it if I hadn't come to fetch it, Dido thought, grasping the handle. Next moment, with a startled gasp, she almost dropped the whole supply on the bricks for, sitting on the table close by and revealed when she picked the basket up, was the largest rat she had ever seen, brindled, with a tail that must have been fully two feet long. It did not scurry away, as an ordinary rat would have done, but turned its head slowly and gave her a steady look; Dido felt a cold sensation between her shoulder-blades.

However she returned the look boldly.

"You'll know me again, Frederick, that's for sure," she said to it. "And I just hope you've kept your long whiskery nose out o' the Cap'n's cheese. Now, how'm I going to get yon basket up the rope?"

She solved this problem by attaching the basket to the end of the rope and pulling it up after her; watched, meanwhile, by the rat, "as if," thought Dido, "he was learning how so he could do it himself next time."

The rat was not the only creature that seemed to be watching her; she noticed, in a corner of Mrs. Lubbage's kitchen, a small carved wooden table exactly like the one she had seen at Tegleaze Manor, with little black faces and white-painted eyes that seemed to follow her.

"If I never go back into that boggarty place again it'll be soon enough," she thought, scrambling back into her own loft; "blest if I know how Cris can stand *living* there. No wonder he seems a bit out o' the common.

"Anyways, we got the grub."

She lowered it down into Captain Hughes's sick-room, jumped down herself, and unpacked the hamper with exclamations of satisfaction.

"Bread—butter—cold roast chicken—flask o' soup—cheese—red currant jelly—grapes—oranges—and a bottle o' wine. Couldn't a done you better if you'd been Admiral o' the Fleet," she told the Captain, and proceeded to heat up some of the soup for him and toast some of the bread.

"I've poured in a dram o' wine as well, so it's right stingo stuff," she said, giving him a bowlful. She herself ate an orange and a leg of chicken to hearten her for the scene which she felt certain must follow Mrs. Lubbage's return and discovery that the basket was missing.

Sure enough, at about sunset there was a tremendous thump on the door.

"Hush! You'll wake the Cap'n!" Dido hissed, opening it.

Outside stood Mrs. Lubbage, brawny arms akimbo, little black eyes snapping with rage.

"Evening, missus," Dido greeted her politely, slipping out and closing the door. "Guess you was wanting to ask about the basket o' prog Lady Tegleaze sent down for us. Cap'n Hughes was fair clemmed wi' hunger, and you hadn't left word when you'd be back, so I jist nipped along and helped myself—hope that was all hunky-dory."

The witch stared at her for a moment, started to say something, and then changed her mind.

"How did you get in?" she asked at length, in a surly tone.

Dido could not mention the loft, because of Cris, so she opened her eyes wide and innocently replied,

"Why, how d'you think? Down the chimbley?"

Mrs. Lubbage seemed annoyed but baffled by this answer and was about to ask another question; luckily at that moment a distant bleating, which had been drawing closer, became so loud that no further conversation was possible; Mr. Firkin had arrived home with his flock. Mrs. Lubbage stumped off angrily to her own cottage; Dido ran to help Mr. Firkin and Toby persuade the sheep to file through a gap between two hurdles and so into the pasture at the rear of the farmyard.

As they passed through the gap, Mr. Firkin touched each sheep with his white crook, and Dido could hear him counting,

"Yan, Tan, Tethera, Methera, Pip—"

Each time he came to *Den* he moved his hand down the crook, which had notches in it.

"Mr. Firkin," said Dido, when the sheep were all safe in the field, and she was scrubbing potatoes in the old man's kitchen, and setting them to bake among the glowing logs in his fireplace.

"Yes, darter?"

"What was that you were saying when you counted the sheep?"

"I was a-counting of them, darter."

"Yes, but what were those words—Yan, Tan, Tethera—"

"That be ship-counting lingo. Lingo for counting ship," Mr. Firkin explained kindly.

"Oh, cranberries! We're a-going round like a merry-go-round! Well, suppose I was to meet some chaps as called 'emselves Yan, Tan, and so forth; I'm not saying I *did*, but suppose I was to—"

Mr. Firkin's old brown face took on a cautious expression.

"Nay, I'd say let well alone, darter. Mebbe 'tis all talk but I've heard tell as how there be folk called Wineberry Men as 'tis best not to meddle with."

"Smugglers, maybe?"

"Hush! Nay, more like kind o' civil service gentry," Mr. Firkin said hastily. "Best not to talk about 'em, darter. Wallses do have earses."

Deciding that the Wineberry Men almost certainly were smugglers, Dido returned to Captain Hughes and found him wakeful and fidgety.

"What about our Dispatch?" he demanded. "Do you have it safe, child?"

"Yes, yes, Cap'n. All rug. Right here." Dido tapped her chest, which crackled reassuringly.

"We must get it to London somehow," the Captain fretted. "What day is it today?"

"Fust o' November, Cap. All Saints' Day."

"And the coronation next week! It is desperately important that the Dispatch should reach the First Lord before then."

"Doc says you mustn't be moved afore two weeks," Dido pointed out.

"Then we must find a reliable messenger."

Dido bit her thumb. "I knows that," she said gloomily. "But trying to find a reliable cove in these parts is about as likely as picking up a pink pearl in Piccadilly. Everyone's up to the neck in summat. There's a carrier called Jem; today's his day to call, seemingly; but Mr. Firkin says he's shravey. Best not give him the Dispatch. What I thought I might do, Cap, if you're agreeable, is send a note by Jem to a cove I knows in London asking him to step down and help us."

"Is your friend reliable?" the Captain asked, pressing a hand to his aching head.

"Sure as a gun, he is!"

Since Captain Hughes, who was beginning to feel weak and feverish again, could think of no better plan, he agreed to this.

Dido sat down to the unaccustomed task of writing a letter. Borrowing the Captain's traveling inkhorn and quill, using a bit of paper the cheese had been wrapped in, she wrote:

"Dere Simon. I doo hop yore stil alive. I am all rug—wuz piked up by wailing ship an hadd Grate Times abord her. Brung home in Man 'o' War like Roilty. Wil tel more wen I see yoo. I do hop yore stil alive. Iff yoo can pleez cum hear wear I am stuk at preznt or send relleye relible cove. I badly need sum wun. I doo hop yore stil alive. Lots ov luv. Dido."

She folded it and addressed it: "Simon as used to livv in Rose Alley, Care of Doc Furniss, The art Skool, Chellsey, London."

She had scarcely finished this when voices were heard outside, there came a knock on the door, and Mr. Firkin ushered in a lank, greasy-haired individual in a moleskin cap and gaiters.

"This yer's Jem Mugridge, as'll take your letter to Perroth, darter."

One glance at him was enough to make Dido thankful she had not planned to entrust Captain Hughes's Dispatch to the shravey Jem; he looked about as reliable as a stoat.

"That'll be five-and-a-tanner," he said, receiving the letter, his little pink-rimmed eyes meanwhile darting into every corner of the room.

Dido was fairly sure that a letter to London should not cost so much, but Captain Hughes counted five shillings and sixpence out of a purse which he brought from under his pillow, Jem's eyes following every movement and every coin.

"I thankee sir and missie. That'll be in Pet'orth by breakfast time."

"So I should hope, if Petworth is but five miles distant," the Captain remarked testily.

When Jem had departed on his flea-bitten mare, Dido asked the Captain if he would have any objection to her stepping up the road to Tegleaze Manor.

"There's a cove there as asked to see me, and it seems only civil to go, seeing they sent us the basket o' prog. Mebbe I'll find someone as we can trust there; you never can tell."

Captain Hughes agreed to this; but since he seemed rather low-spirited at the prospect of being left alone, Mr. Firkin was easily persuaded to come and keep him company. Mr. Firkin's brother, it turned out, had been a seafaring man and a great singer; the two men were soon absorbed in discussing sea shanties and comparing tunes. Leaving them to it, Dido slipped off.

As she left the cottage some animal scuttled away, quick and quiet, along the wall. It might have been a rabbit or a large rat.

"I'll be glad when we can shift out o' this hurrah's nest," she thought with a shiver. "You gets the notion someone's everlastingly a-peering over your shoulder."

However, nothing else seemed to be stirring in the cold, moonshiny night. She walked up the beech avenue toward the Manor, turned right at the top as instructed, and found herself on the edge of an enormous sunk lawn.

"Guess this must be the tilting-yard," Dido thought. "The sides is tilted, anyhows; it's like a dripping pan." She scrambled down the steep grassy slope and walked across turf that was silver with icy dew. Black yew trees, once clipped to resemble giant pineapples, but, from neglect, grown into many strange shapes, were placed about the lawn in pairs, like sentries. Dido slipped from one pair of shadows to the next and ran softly up a flight of steps toward the house. She passed along a terrace above the lawn, through a wicket gate, through a small walled garden, and so came to a side door, half hidden under a great vine. While she was wondering whether to knock, the door opened.

"Hallo! I saw you come up the steps. Make haste—after me. Isn't this capital!" breathed Sir Tobit. Dido felt her hand taken; she was pulled into the dark; the door shut quietly behind her. She allowed herself to be led up a narrow flight of stairs, along a passage, and so presently found herself in the room where she had been before. It was just as dusty and untidy as it had been on the previous evening.

"Now we can talk," said Sir Tobit, throwing himself comfortably in a chair. "Grandmother is in bed with one of her headaches, so she won't trouble us."

"Talk, what about?"

"You can tell me your adventures. I've read all my books. So the only way I can amuse myself now is to make up stories—and that's very boring because I know what the end is going to be. Well, go on—begin!"

Dido was not eager. However she felt some sympathy for Sir Tobit's solitude and boredom, so she obliged with a brief account of how she had been shipwrecked, picked up by a whaler and carried to Nantucket, and brought home by his majesty's sloop *Thrush*.

"And I must let someone in London know that Cap'n Hughes is stuck here with a broken gam," she finished. "I've sent a letter to a pal o' mine, but I don't trust that carrier Jem above half; is there any reliable cove you can suggest?"

"There aren't many men left on the estate," Tobit said. "We're so poor, everyone has left, except Frill and Pelmett, and I wouldn't trust *them*."

"Poor? In a place this size?" Dido was surprised.

"You see, Grandmother has a great fondness for betting on the horses. When she was a girl she loved riding; then she was thrown and broke her leg. So now as she can't ride, she bets instead; since I've been living here I believe she has gambled away, oh, hundreds of thousands of pounds. Yesterday she gave FitzPickwick her last diamond ring to sell. That's why I have to wear these clothes; we can't afford to buy new ones. But luckily there are lots of old ones about the house."

"How long *have* you lived here, then?"

"Oh, ever since I was a baby. I was born in the West Indies, on Tiburon Island; we have—used to have—estates there. Papa and Mamma lived there, but they were killed in a hurricane, so Tante Sannie brought me here. I don't remember that. Sannie didn't know what it would be like here; she's homesick, but there isn't enough money to send her back." He spoke indifferently, but Dido felt that, since he was lonely himself, he ought to have more sympathy for the old woman's plight, stuck here in this great dusty cold house, so far from her own warm island.

"I'd better be getting back." She prowled restlessly about the untidy, shadowy room. "Is that you?"

A picture on the wall showed three children, dressed in clothes such as Tobit wore. The boy in the middle, holding hands of the other two, who stood slightly behind him, might have been Tobit at a younger age.

"No, that's three ancestors—two brothers and a sister who lived in Charles the First's time. They were triplets—all the same age."

"It'd be grand to be a triplet—you'd never be lonely then," Dido said, studying them with some envy. "What happened to them?"

"They quarreled," Tobit said coolly. "One fought on

the king's side, one on Cromwell's, and the third one went overseas and vanished. The other two lost all their money in the Civil War, so ever since then triplets have been thought unlucky in our family."

"Have there been many more?"

"No, none; but we've had bad luck just the same. . . . Come along; I'll show you Cousin Wilfred's dolls' house."

He pulled the reluctant Dido—croopus, dolls' houses at his age! she thought—out of the room, along passages and downstairs into the main hall—empty tonight; and through an open door into a small room at one side of it.

"Come on—old Wilfred isn't here, he's playing tiddly-winks with Sawbones Subito. Look—isn't it queer!"

Cousin Wilfred's room was as shabby as Tobit's, but in a different way. The furniture here was old, and had once been handsome, but was now falling to bits: the wood was worm-eaten, the satin upholstery faded and torn. Only the dolls' house looked well-cared-for. It was a faithful copy of Tegleaze Manor, beautifully made, furnished to the last detail with curtains, carpets, plates on the tables, pictures on the walls, even a carriage in the stables. There were no dolls, but tiny suits of clothes like Tobit's hung in the closets.

"He made it all himself, from old prints of the house as it used to be," Tobit said, carelessly throwing open the front.

"Even the pictures?"

These were oval miniatures, carefully framed, no bigger than postage stamps.

"No, those are real. Some ancestor collected them.

[80]

Some of them were quite valuable, but Grandmother sold those—all except one, which isn't here. She'd like to sell *that*, but it belongs to me—or will when I come of age."

"When's that?"

"Next week—on my fourteenth birthday."

"Where's the picture now?"

"At the lawyers'—they don't trust her. Come on." Tobit was restless—nothing seemed to interest him for long. He moved to the window. Dido took a last look at the nursery with its three white-spread beds, box of tiny toys, hoop leaning against the wall, and dappled rocking-horse which might just have stopped swaying, as if three children had rushed out of the room, slammed the door, and gone their different ways.

"Hey!" whispered Tobit. "Look!"

He beckoned Dido to the window. They were looking out on the moonlit tilting-yard. Two figures paced across it and vanished into the shade of a pair of yew trees.

"It's old FitzPickwick—wonder what *he's* doing here at this time of night. And who that is he's talking to. Tell you what—let's go out and stalk 'em, that'd be famous fun. Wait, have I got my peashooter on me?"

Tobit rummaged in his black velvet pockets.

"I druther have a word with your butler—is he any-wheres about?" Dido said, impatient at the prospect of such a childish sport.

"*Gusset?* Why? Anyhow, you can't, it's his evening off; he goes to see his son. Ah, two shooters and lots of peas. Here, have one." He thrust a slender pipe into her

hand and poured into the pocket of her duffel jacket
what felt like about a pound of heavy little dry objects.

"Ain't we a bit old for sich goings-on?"

"What else is there to do in this moldering barracks—
except make up stories? I'm a dead shot," he boasted.
"With a sling I can hit a hare at a hundred yards. Only
there aren't any hares. Oh, *do* come along."

"What's that?" Dido asked, as they passed a large
chart on the wall.

"Family tree—all the way back to the Saxons." He
pulled her along yet another dark passage.

"Who's old FitzPickwick?"

"Our bailiff—he's a toffee-nosed sort of fellow. It's
my belief he's feathered his nest handsomely out of
Tegleaze Manor," Tobit said, sounding all of a sudden
surprisingly shrewd. "He sells Grandmother's jewelry
for her, and places her bets."

"Doesn't give her very good advice, if she always
loses."

"Hush!"

They had come out into a brick-paved stable-yard,
like that of the dolls' house. A gate and a flagged path
brought them back to the terrace overlooking the tilting-
yard.

"When Jamie Three had *his* coronation," Tobit muttered discontentedly, leading Dido down the steps and
along in the shadow of the high yew hedge that bor-
dered the lawn, "Granny and Grandpa had a pageant
here, with champagne and roast peacock for all the
tenants. But now there are hardly any tenants, and no

cash—not even enough for me to go up to London to *see* the coronation."

"Would your gran let you?" Dido asked. "I thought she was so set agin your going out in case you catch summat nasty?"

"Oh, she won't care what happens to me once I come of age—and my birthday's before the coronation—I'm fourteen on Monday, the coronation's on Wednesday, I daresay you didn't know, just home from sea? Old Jamie Three died, and now it's going to be his son. He's always been called Prince Davie but he's going to be Richard the Fourth. And there's going to be fireworks on Ludgate Hill, and oxes roasted in Stuart Square, and processions, and all sorts of high jinks—don't I just wish I was going."

Mention of the coronation reminded Dido of her own worries. "If Gusset isn't here I guess *I'll* be going, back to Dogkennel," she said. "Please to thank your gran for the prog."

"The what?"

"The grub—the basket o' vittles."

"Oh, *she* won't have sent anything—far too mean. No, if some food came, I daresay Gusset sent it. Hush—there they are!"

He dragged Dido into an alcove in the yew hedge, where they lurked in the shadow.

Low voices gradually became audible as the two men paced across the immense lawn.

"Oh, *I* won't expose your little g-games—don't think it, my dear f-fellow. It's n-nothing to *me*, believe me, if you've pocketed a rent roll as long as the M-Mississippi River. Money is of s-small interest to me."

The speaker's voice had a curiously deep, grating quality, broken by his occasional stammer.

"What is, then?"

"That's old Colonel FitzP," whispered Tobit in Dido's ear. "But I'm blest if I know who the other one is."

"The name! The place! You d-don't understand what it means—when one has s-spent all one's life in a lumber camp as n-nobody—Miles Tuggles—pah! To change that I'd commit any c- any crime. As to your peccadilloes—what's the old lady to me? Or the b-brat either? I give you my word, my research into your d-dealings was solely to effect an introduction so that we could meet on equal t-terms—"

[84]

"I wonder?" Colonel FitzPickwick's soft mutter was overheard only by the two eavesdroppers.

"But harkee now," the first man went on. "I hold you in a cleft stick. I know so much, I promise you I could c-cook your goose with six words, dropped in the right quarter. S-so it is in your interest to help me. I n-need a pretext for remaining in the neighborhood—"

The two men moved away. The word "puppets" was all that Dido could catch of the next remark.

"Puppets!" muttered Tobit discontentedly. "Old Fitz-Pickwick's mad about puppets; they're his hobby. He's always boring on about them."

"—be a first-rate cover," FitzPickwick was saying, when the two men next strolled in the direction of the watchers.

"That will do. Now tell me the rest—you have n-no choice. This Godwit you mention—"

They turned and paced away again.

"Let's go after them!" breathed Tobit, and tweaked Dido's hand; the two listeners slipped from their hiding place and crossed to the shadow of a pair of yews.

"—rollers," they heard Colonel FitzPickwick say. "They are fixed already. And the diamond will pay for half. But the rest of the money—" The two men passed behind a tree and their words were lost. "—still to come," the Colonel was saying when they reappeared. "If Lady Tegleaze—" another pair of trees cut off his words—"certain His Highness Prince George would lend a favorable ear to your claim."

"Rot it, so I should hope! But as to these rollers—"

the stammering man was beginning, when Dido heard a soft hiss beside her, a phtt! and Colonel FitzPickwick raised a hand to his cheek.

"Strange! I could have sworn I felt a hailstone. Yet there's not a cloud in the sky."

"Oh, famous!" Tobit breathed in Dido's ear. "I got him fair and square."

"'Twas a m-mosquito, I daresay. Rollers, now: rollers are all very fine. But where's your motive power?"

"A mosquito? You forget you are in England in November, my dear sir. If the weather's breaking I must be off. My mare's a thoroughbred—she has an aversion to hail."

"You shoot now!" whispered Tobit. "Go on—I dare you!"

"I druther listen," Dido muttered crossly. "Hush! I've a notion—"

"Motive power yet remains to be found. Godwit thinks a system of levers. Now, if humans were as easily moved as my mannikins—Devil take it! That was certainly a hailstone. It hit me on the ear."

Tobit was suffocating with suppressed laughter.

"Got the old windbag again. Him and his mannikins!"

Colonel FitzPickwick turned and walked off decisively, his companion following with reluctance, turning back for many glances at the house.

The shadows of the two men followed them like long black-velvet trains.

"Now we ain't sure what it was all about," Dido complained when they were out of earshot.

"Oh, pho, what does it matter? Just old Pickwick's usual hocus-pocus about puppets."

"But it seemed to be about your grandmother and this place."

"What do I care about this place? As soon as I'm of age I shall run off to sea and turn pirate. Yo, ho, ho, and the jolly black flag," said Sir Tobit, and aimed a broadside of peas into the yew tree. "Come on, we'll spy on old Wilfred and the sawbones." He tugged Dido at a run along the yew hedge, up the steps, and around the end of the house. They looked through a window into a small room where, by the light of one dim candle, two men were crouched over a tiddlywinks board. Dido recognized the doctor; the other was a little tiny gray-haired old fellow like a water rat in a velvet robe and nightcap.

"Pity the window's shut," Tobit muttered. "I'd like to give old Wilfred a fright, in return for all the games of tiddlywinks he's bored me with. D'you dare me to break the window?"

"O' course not! What a mutton-headed notion."

Dido, becoming more and more impatient, was about to take her leave, when a sudden fierce whisper from behind startled them both.

"Bad, bad boy! What you doing, what you about?"

Like a black, angry dragonfly the tiny figure of Tante Sannie darted from a patch of shadow, hissing reproaches at Tobit.

"You not allowed out after darkfall, you know that!

Spose a memory bird hear you, spose the Night Lady catch you in her claws?"

"Oh, stuff. Don't talk such nonsense, Sannie," Tobit said, but he glanced behind him uneasily, then put a couple of peas in his mouth. "Anyway, I'll be of age next week and can do as I please!"

"Also, who is *this?*" Sannie peered up at Dido. Over the black-and-white draperies muffling the lower part of the old woman's face, her tiny eyes glittered like the points of nails. "Hah! I know you! You little bad sickness girl, Sir Tobit not allowed to play with you. Lady Tegleaze be very angry when she hear."

"We weren't playing," Sir Tobit said sulkily. "I was showing her the grounds by moonlight."

"Don't you false-talk me, boy! What this?" Sannie twitched the peashooter from his hand. "Ho! You be of age next week, be you? You got no more sense than baby picknie. Out after darkfall, shooting Joobie nuts! Spose hit somebody in him eye, sent to prison? Then you never come of age, you know that!"

"Oh, fiddle. Nobody gets sent to prison for shooting with a peashooter. I shall shoot as many as I like." Rebelliously he snatched back the tube and blew a pea at the window. It bounced off the glass with an audible ping, but the two men inside, absorbed in their game, never even lifted their heads.

"Oh, so brave little feller!" Sannie's tone became silky as syrup. "So brave to shoot Joobie nuts. But don't you dare swallow nut!"

"I'll do that too, if I want!" He swallowed the two

nuts he was sucking, eying the old woman with defiance. But almost at once a curious change came over his face. He glanced behind him again, twice, and gave a violent shiver.

"Is cold, my little thingling? Is hearing some noise in bushes, memory bird, maybe?"

Tobit shivered again, glancing about with dread.

"Come along then, come in quick before the Night Lady fly over. Come along, little thingling. Old Sannie make you cup of thistle tea."

She took his hand and led him off; Tobit followed meekly.

"Croopus!" muttered Dido, when they were out of sight.

She was so startled by the change in Tobit that she remained where she was for several minutes, pondering. "It was those peas—Joobie nuts, or whatever she called them. What the blazes can they be?"

She pulled a handful of the heavy little dry things from her duffel pocket and eyed them suspiciously. In the moonlight they looked gray, wrinkled, harmless enough; about the size of nasturtium seeds; they felt faintly gritty, as if they had been dusted with salt. Warily Dido tried one with the tip of her tongue. It did taste salty. She spat, and glanced behind her, suddenly overcome with an almost irresistible urge to duck: it seemed as if she could hear the whizz of giant wings overhead. Out of the corner of her eye she thought she saw a huge shadow flit over the moonlit grass. But when she turned and looked there was nothing.

"Shiver my timbers!" She stared again at the peas in her hand; was about to throw them on the ground; but in the end, tipped them back into her pocket and ran fast and quietly away from the house. Suddenly the night seemed full of noises: a cold, liquid call, some bird maybe; a soft drumming tick; a rattle—or was it a chuckle?—coming from the yew hedge. Dido darted across the tilting-lawn, where the pairs of yew trees seemed to be shifting just a little, changing their positions after she passed them; she did not look back but had the notion that they were moving together behind her, perhaps coming after her, as in the game Grandmother's Footsteps.

"Rabbit me if I ever taste another o' them perishing Joobie nuts," Dido muttered. "No wonder Tobit and his granny both seem a bit totty-headed, if they keep a-chawing o' the nasty little things."

Ahead of her now lay the beech avenue, with its bands of moonlight and shade. She felt some reluctance to go down it, but shook herself angrily and ran on at top speed. Then, coming toward her, she saw a black figure. It seemed to vary in size—wavered—grew tall—shrank again.

Dido gulped.

"This here's nothing but a load o' foolishness," she told herself, and went on firmly. The figure seemed now to have no head and three legs. But of course when she came closer she saw that it was merely old Gusset, hobbling back from his evening off, wearing a sack over his head, helping himself along with a stick.

"Hey there, Mister Gusset!" Dido greeted him warmly when they were within speaking distance. "I'm tickled I didn't miss you—wanted to say thanks again for the basket o' vittles—Tobit said as how likely you'd sent 'em your own self."

"Oh, no trouble, missie." The butler seemed embarrassed. "Glad to do it for the poor sick gennleman— I heeard tell as how he's a naval captain? And you've been a-visiting Mas'r Tobit, have you, missie? That's good, that is—he can do with a bit o' young company."

"That he can," Dido agreed. "Ask me, he has his head in the clouds most o' the time, he's got some right cork-brained notions. And that old witch as sees arter him—Sannie or whatever she calls herself—it's a plaguy shame she couldn't be shipped back to Thingummy Island, her and her Joobie nuts."

Gusset glanced around him warily. "You're right there, missie," he said, sinking his voice.

"What are those Joobie nuts, anyways?"

"Summat she brought with her from Tiburon, Missie Twido. She grows 'em from seed, up where the old asparagus bed used to be. She allus has a plenty of 'em. Don't you go a-swallowing they hampery things, missie— they'll give you the hot chills, don't they give you wuss."

"What happens when Tobit comes of age next week?"

"Why, nothing much, missie. I reckon things'll goo on pretty much as usual."

"He doesn't come into any cash, so's he could go off to school?"

"No, missie. Only the heirloom."

"What's the heirloom?" Gusset had spoken as if every-one would know of it.

"It be a liddle painting, Missie Dwite. Only small, smaller than the palm of your liddle hand, but it be painted on ivory, and I've heeard tell as it be worth thousands and thousands—enough to put everything to rights round here."

"Fancy! What's it of?" Dido asked curiously.

"'Tis a picture o' the Tower of Babel, missie. 'Tis painted by a famous painter, I've heeard tell. Anybody can see it—they keeps it at Perrorth, at the lawyers', a-set in a glass case in the wall."

Mention of Petworth recalled Dido to her own prob-lems.

"Mister Gusset, I've got to get a message to London, urgent. How can I send it? I gave a letter to that Jem, but he don't look reliable to me."

"Jem Mugridge, missie? No, he ain't noways re-liable."

"Well, then, what'd I best do? The message has to get to London before the—before the end o' next week."

"Best to goo yourself, missie."

"But I didn't oughta leave Cap'n Hughes while he's sick."

Gusset pushed back the sack in order to scratch his white head. He reflected.

"Well, missie," he said at length. "There's some chaps I know as gooes up and down to London regular. Trad-ing chaps they be. Some mightn't say as how they was reliable, but I speak as I find, and I've allus found 'em trustable."

"D'you reckon they'd help me, mister?"

"I'd hatta ask," Gusset said cautiously. "I couldn't promise, see?"

"When will you see them?"

Gusset seemed unwilling to commit himself, but said he'd see them by Friday, maybe, and would try to let Dido know on that day.

"Now I'd best be getting in, missie. 'Tis turble late."

"Good night, then, Mister Gusset, and thanks."

The old man hobbled off, and Dido ran on down the avenue toward Dogkennel Cottages. Her talk with Gusset had cheered her and the queer visions and sounds that had troubled her before seemed to have died away; she whistled as she ran, and jumped over patches of shadow in the chalk cartway. But just this side of the cottages she came to an abrupt stop. Something—*surely* it was a dragon?—lay on the weedy grass in front of the little row of houses. Its eyes glittered. When it saw Dido it stretched slightly, and spread out its wings.

Dido bit her thumb, hard. Then she stooped, picked up a sizable chunk of flint from the track, and hurled it at the monster, which broke into about seven different sections. Three of them were sheep, which trotted nervously away. Two or three more were chickens, flapping and flustered. One, which might have been a rat, scurried into the shadow of Mrs. Lubbage's cottage.

Mrs. Lubbage herself was sitting by her door on a

[93]

broken-backed chair, gazing, apparently, into a pail of water.

"Evening, missus," Dido said civilly as she passed.

The wise woman lifted her head and gave Dido a long, expressionless stare. But she said nothing.

"Utchy old besom," Dido thought, taking her key from under a stone, where Mr. Firkin had left it. "Anyone can tell as manners weren't thought much of where *you* was reared!"

Rather more clumsily than usual, she fitted the key into the lock.

And all the time, as she turned it, opened the door, and let herself in, she could feel Mrs. Lubbage's malevolent stare boring into her shoulder blades.

4

"Consarn it!" exclaimed Dido, as the bucket of chicken food slipped out of her hand, falling heavily on her toe.

"What's to do, darter?" mildly inquired old Mr. Firkin, coming out of the cowshed with his two pails of milk.

"I dunno why it is—my fingers is all thumbs today. I spilt a bowl o' hot water on the Cap'n's bed, and I dropped our breakfast eggs in the fire, and hit my thumb with a hammer when I was a-fixing the leaky window, and caught the other one in the rat trap you lent me, and broke my tortoise-shell comb that a friend in Ameriky gave me, and now I've bin and dropped the hens' grub all over my feet—not that the hens care."

Dido was standing in a sea of chickens, who were vigorously pecking her toes and ankles.

"My hands feel greasy all the time," she grumbled. "I wash and wash, and it don't right 'em."

"Sounds to me like Mrs. Lubbage overlooked ye," Mr. Firkin said gravely. "Have ye got on the mouldy-warpses' clawses?"

Dido clapped a hand to her neck and remembered that she had taken off Mr. Firkin's protective charm when she went to bed.

"My stars! Do you really think—"

But she remembered the wise woman's long, angry stare as she sat before her door in the moonlight.

"I'll fetch those claws right away," Dido declared, and did so, before sitting down to breakfast with Mr. Firkin. And whether it was because the claws gave her more confidence, or really had power against bad wishes, her run of ill luck seemed to have ended for the time; she gave the Captain his breakfast, made up his bed, and had the satisfaction of hearing him say that he felt somewhat better and thought his leg was mending.

"I fancy that by tomorrow or the next day I could walk with a crutch, if one could be procured," he said.

Mr. Firkin, when asked, said he could fettle one up, but it would take him two-three days. Or there was a chap in Petworth, Godwit by name, who generally had one or two crutches and such gear in his shop.

"The lame gray coach horse is a-mending, too," Dido said. "Reckon if the doc agrees it's all rug for Cap'n Hughes to walk a bit, I could ride in to Petworth, tomorrow maybe, and see what this Godwit has in stock." Godwit, she thought; I heard that name some-wheres just lately; where was it now?

Dr. Subito did not come that day, however, and meanwhile the Captain, really not as strong as he made out, was glad enough to lie and doze, wake for a short time, eat or drink a little of the invalid fare provided by Gusset, and sleep again.

During the afternoon, when the invalid was in a sound slumber and seemed likely to remain so for some time, Dido, first carefully locking him in, slipped away to the Cuckoo Tree, taking a roundabout route in case anybody was watching. Mr. Firkin was off with his flock at a distance, Mrs. Lubbage nowhere to be seen. There had been no sight or sound, either, of Cris all day, though Dido had once or twice stuck her head through the loft opening and listened intently. She could not help feeling a bit anxious about Cris. Mrs. Lubbage had seemed so very angry about the basket of food—and Cris was the nearest scapegoat at hand, unless you counted the brindled rat.

But when she at length reached the Cuckoo Tree, on its steep slope of grassy hillside, Dido thought at first there was nobody in it.

"Cris? Are you there?" she called softly.

No sound came from the dark, thickly massed foliage above.

"Might as well climb up, though," Dido thought, noticing that the corkscrew with its bit of ribbon had been removed from the trunk. "Looks like someone's been here."

Up she went, quick as a squirrel—and found Cris, lying in a bushy hammock of yew needles.

"Hey, didn't you hear me—" Dido began, and then

saw that Cris was fast asleep, curled up, knees to chin, one cheek pillowed on a fold of dirty sheepswool jacket, which he had thrown around him, and clutched like a comforter. His cheeks were streaked with tears and one had a mark on it, half bruise, half cut.

"Blame it," Dido thought angrily, "that old scrow has been a-larruping of him, and it's my fault, partly; I ought to a waited till she came home, 'stead o' taking the basket. But the Cap'n was *that* hungry—how's a body to act?"

Troubled, uncertain what to do for the best, she sat and watched the sleeping Cris. Time passed, and the pale November sun moved toward a furry shoulder of hill behind which it would soon dip. "Hadn't I best wake him?" Dido wondered. "It'll be right parky soon— and the Cap'll be stirring presently. But Cris does sleep *so* sound."

Presently, though, the sleep began to be broken by little whimpers and twitches; letting go of his sheepswool jacket, Cris started to suck his thumb; a tear trickled from the corner of his closed eye; then the eyes opened, and he was awake, and terrified.

"Easy there; easy!" Dido arrested his first frantic scramble for the trunk. "It's only me—Dido, remember? We was talking here afore. I brought you some vittles. Mr. Gusset fetched some down from the Manor, and I reckoned as how you might be glad of a bite. Here— it's only bread and cheese, but it's good."

She went on talking calmly while she pulled out the packet of food and handed Cris a large slice of brown bread and hunk of cheese. "You get that inside you, you'll feel better. There's apples, too, for afters; I didn't like to carry a bottle o' drink in case old Madam Lubbage was a-looking out her back window."

Cris took one or two cautious bites and then bolted the food down ravenously, eating all the cheese first, and the bread next; his trembling quieted and presently he gave a deep sigh.

"Did the old girl beat you much?" Dido asked quietly.

Cris nodded. "She was in a rage last night when I got home. She asked me where I'd been and I wouldn't say, so she beat me. Being beaten's nothing. But she said she was going to listen to my dreams all night and then she'd know where I'd gone. I don't know what I'd do if she found this place."

"Croopus," muttered Dido. "D'you reckon she *could* listen to your dreams?"

"I don't know," Cris said. "I stayed awake. I stood up all night and pricked my arm with a bramble thorn so I wouldn't fall asleep. That was why I was so tired today. Auntie Daisy went off at noon to physick someone's sick cow, so as soon as she left I came here."

Between sentences Cris was taking bites from the second apple; he finished by chewing and swallowing the core. Then he sighed again.

Dido gulped and said gruffly, "Cris, it was my fault the old girl beat ye, acos I nicked a basket o' groceries outa her nasty dirty kitchen and that riled her. So I feel right bad about it and this is to say I'm sorry. Well, go on, take it: it's for you!"

Cris stared wonderingly at the little object that Dido held out in the palm of her hand. It was a tiny whale, carved from ivory.

"I brought it back from Ameriky," Dido explained. "The sailors make 'em on the whaleboats when they've nowt else to do."

Timidly Cris took it and turned it over and over. "It's pretty."

"You could wear it round your neck on a string—there's a loop on the tail, see? Maybe it'd keep off back luck—like Mr. Firkin's mouldywarpses' claws."

Cris made no answer.

Dido, rather hurt, was beginning to wonder if he didn't think much of her gift—which she had really hated to part with—when he suddenly said,

"It *is* lucky. Aswell says so. It will help me find—something I never knew—that I had lost."

He spoke in a dreamy, listening way, as if he merely passed on the words of someone else, and then lay back, relaxed and peaceful in his thickset hammock, smiling at the twilit sky. "Thank you for coming, Aswell! I was afraid you wouldn't today, I was so tired."

Dido shivered. All at once the place felt unchancy to her.

"Guess I'd best be going," she mumbled.

"Isn't the sky beautiful up there," Cris went on without heeding her. "Look, there's the first star. When I lie here I seem to be looking *down* into the sky, not up—it's like a huge well, don't you think? I feel as if I could jump right into it."

"Cris!" Dido exclaimed. "You hadn't oughta talk that way! It's not sensible."

"What is sensible, then?"

Cris turned his filthy, bruised face inquiringly toward Dido, who found herself at a loss.

"Oh, I dunno! Ask me, this is a right spooky part o' the world—*nothing's* sensible round here. Well, don't get downhearted, Cris, anyhows—if the old baggage wallops you any more, holler out, and I'll come and give you a hand—the two of us oughta be a match for her."

With a sad smile, like the wind ripple over a field of long grass, Cris said,

"All right. I'll remember."

Dido slithered down the trunk. "Powerful scent o' honeysuckle or summat round hereabouts," she thought. "Didn't know you got honeysuckle at this time o' year, but there's no telling what you'll get in these cockeyed parts. The mischief is, there's too many wrong 'uns and not enough right 'uns. And what right 'uns there is, is blind, like Mr. Firkin, or in poor twig, like my Cap, or too old to be very spry, like Mr. Gusset. And the *young* 'uns is next door to addle-pated, Tobit a-playing with them unnatural peas, and Cris a-talking to somebody in the sky. There's hardly an ounce of sense betwixt the pair of 'em. Pity they couldn't meet, they'd deal together like porridge and cream."

Thinking about them, as she trotted over the hill, she was struck by the similarity between the situations of Tobit and Cris: both of them forced to live so lonesome and mopish, their lives made a burden to them by queer-natured old crones. "And that spooky Tante Sannie is friends with Mrs. Lubbage—wonder if she knows about Cris? If I hadn't enough to worry about, getting Cap'n Hughes's Dispatch to London," Dido thought, "there's an awful lot wants setting to rights round here."

Mrs. Lubbage had returned from her cow doctoring, and was picking herbs from a tangled, nettle-grown patch under her kitchen window.

"Oh. So you're back, are you?" she said, giving Dido a hard stare with her little sharp eyes. "Well? Do ye want me to have a look at the sick chap or not? 'Tis all one to me."

Dido conquered an impulse to refuse. Best be polite, she thought.

"Yes, please, missus."

"I'll get my things, then."

While Mrs. Lubbage was dressing the Captain's wound, Dido noticed the brindled rat slip through the open door and along the angle of the wall and floor. Without pausing a second, Dido grabbed a heavy beech root from the firewood heap and slung it hard at the rat, which squealed indignantly and scurried out, limping.

"What was that?" exclaimed the Captain, startled.

"Jist an old rat, Cap; if he shows his snout in here again I'll pepper his whiskers," Dido said cheerfully. Mrs. Lubbage darted a black look at her but said nothing.

When she had finished her doctoring—it took less time today, for the wound was better—she said to Dido, "You step outside with me, missie!"

"Back directly!" Dido told the Captain.

Outside it was quite dark. A ray of lantern light from the doorway illuminated Mrs. Lubbage's broad face. Dido did not care for its expression.

"Now, harkee, gal," said the wise woman. "And pay heed, for I don't reckon to say things over. You crossed my path twice already, you went spanneling into my kitchen 'thoughten leave, and you hurted my old Tibbie-rat."

"*Your* rat, missus? How was I to know?"

"Don't aggle at me, gal! I'm warning ee, if I have any more mizmaze from ee, I'll make things right skaddle for ee, *and* for that chap in there. 'Twouldn't take but a pinch o' naughty-man's-plaything to set his wound into a mortification. And as for you—you puny little windshaken emmet—I could make you wish you'd never been borned."

Dido was silent. Mrs. Lubbage evidently took her silence for defiance; she went on,

"And I hear you bin upalong to Tegleaze, where you've no right nor business, making a sossabout, upsiding Mas'r Tobit. You leave that boy be! Do he land hisself in trouble before he come of age, then he won't noways inherit his grandpa's luck-piece."

Mrs. Lubbage might have said more, but she was interrupted at this moment by Gusset, in the trap, who came to a halt by them.

"Evening, Missis Lubbage," he greeted the wise woman politely. "Evening, Missie Twido Dight. I brought ye some more stuff for the sick navy gennleman."

With a surly jerk of her head, Mrs. Lubbage retired to her own house.

Dido would have taken the heavy basket from Gusset, but he insisted on carrying it in. As he did so, Dido's quick eye caught sight of Sannie, as on the previous occasion, slipping from the back of the trap and darting off to visit her friend.

"Don't I just wish I was that flea-bitten rat for five minutes to hear what the old crows is a-talking about in there," Dido thought. "I bet it's nothing good."

Gusset, it turned out, was dying to have a word with Captain Hughes.

"I did hear, Cap'n, sir," he quavered politely, "as how your ship was the *Thrush?*"

"You heard right," answered the Captain who, propped against rolled-up sheeps' fleeces, was drinking barley soup.

"I've a nevvy on that vessel," explained Gusset. "Able seaman Noah Gusset. Did ee e'er come across the boy, Cap'n, sir? Do 'e still be live and kicking?"

"Why, certainly! He is a fine fellow—will probably end up as Master Gunner. I have often spoken to him," the Captain said cordially. Old Gusset's face lit up at this news. "My brother Ed'ard'll be in a rare proud scarrifunge when I tell him!" he said, and could not do too much for the Captain; he bustled about, toasting bits of bread and warming up a mixture of wine and spices which he said would make the Captain "sleep like a juggy."

Dido, seeing that she was not needed for a few moments, said quietly to Gusset, "I'm jist going aloft a minute, mister, to see arter summat; shan't be long," and nipped up into the roof. Using the utmost caution she crept along to the loft over Mrs. Lubbage's kitchen. The moon had risen by now and slivers of light, finding their way through cracks between the tiles, showed that Cris was not there; most likely, Dido guessed, having had his hunger stayed with bread and cheese, he had gone back to sleep, and would not return all night in case Mrs. Lubbage should listen to his dreams.

"Blest if I'd want her a-listening to mine. Though I dessay it's all rubbish," Dido thought.

Mrs. Lubbage's trap door was closed, but Dido lay with her ear pressed against the crack, through which came a faint gleam of candlelight.

"Tell me about it again," she heard Mrs. Lubbage say.

"I done tell you many, many time!"

"Aye, but I had dunnamany things go caterwise on me today. The cow died, and my Tib-rat got hurted, and yon flarksy little madam nabbling at me—I could do wi' hearing summat brightsome."

"Is all green and warm," Sannie said. "Green and warm from east to west, from north to south. Orange trees, mango trees, love apples, sweet grass and honey flowers, all a-blowing and a-blooming. The sea she do sing by day and by night, white sea a-breaking on the black rocks. Old Fire Mountain, he up above, a-muttering in he sleep but never waking. And in that island, isn't no rudeness, isn't no mocking of old people; old

people paid proper respect, is loved, is given the callum drink and bonita bread, quilt stuffed with happiness feathers, wherever they do fancy to warm they bones."

"That's the place for me," Mrs. Lubbage said. "Round hereaways they treats you like dirt, even if they *is* scairt of you. Treats you like dirt and owes you money. If they gets to owe you too much, then they takes and drowns you in Black Pond."

"Never mind—never mind! Old Sir Tobit's luck-piece going to bring us luck, going to change all that. In three weeks—maybe two weeks—us'll be on a great white ship, a-sailing, sailing—"

"Over the white waves and the black waves—"

"A-wrapped in silk satin and treated like two queens—"

Plainly this was a conversation the two friends had held many times before.

"Until we comes to Tiburon Island—"

"Till we steps ashore and they cries, 'Is Tante Sannie come a-home! Is dear old Tante Sannie!'"

"And her friend what's come to live with her!"

"And they give us the callum drink and bonita bread and wrap us in quilt stuffed with happiness feathers!"

"All on account of Sir Tobit's ivory luck-piece."

What the dickens is all *that* about? Dido wondered. She stuck her eye to the crack. Down below she could see the top of Mrs. Lubbage's table, on which were a bottle, a saucer, and two teacups, which were removed, emptied, and refilled at regular intervals. Sometimes she could see the rat's pointed, whiskery snout drinking wine from the saucer.

But do they reckon to *steal* Tobit's luck-piece? Dido wondered.

She crawled back silently to her own loft and dropped down. Gusset had heated up a quantity of water in the hens' breakfast pan and was slowly but expertly shaving Captain Hughes, who appeared to be greatly enjoying this attention and was meanwhile relating all he could remember about the life and exploits of Able Seaman Noah Gusset.

Dido put away the provisions and squatted down by the fire on the three-legged stool.

"Mister Gusset," she inquired presently. "This little ivory painting you was a-telling me about, is that what they call Sir Tobit's luck-piece?"

"Why, yes, missie, acos the first Sir Tobit brought it back from furrin parts a couple o' hundred years agone, in oughteen sixty-summat. He reckoned it'd bring him luck, see?"

"Did it?"

"No, miss, it didn't. Some say as 'twas because it was stole—but I dunno if that be a true tale."

"What'll happen when this Sir Tobit gets it?"

"I reckon 'twill be passed over to his gran to take care of, like the rest o' the property."

Dido would have liked to ask if Gusset thought the old lady would get Colonel FitzPickwick to sell the heirloom and use the money for bets, but this did not seem a very polite question.

"And that happens next week?"

"Yes, missie. Unless Sir Tobit should die or go to prison first wards."

"Go to *prison?* Why in the name o' judgment should he get sent to clink?"

"Oh, no reason, Missie Twido; only it says in the will that if the heir be thrown in jail afore coming of age, then he loses the right to the heirloom."

"I see. Who gets it then? Lady Tegleaze?"

"No, missie. The next heir 'ud get it if there was one. But, being as there ain't, I believe it do go to some museum."

"No wonder Lady Tegleaze is in such a twit to see Tobit don't get in bad company."

Captain Hughes had been silent for the last few minutes and was now found to be asleep, so Gusset took his leave. Dido had wondered if he bore any message from Tobit, but none was forthcoming, so it seemed probable that the heir was still subdued by the effects of Sannie's scolding, or the Joobie nuts.

Two days passed quietly. Captain Hughes continued to mend, though slowly; Dido took care not to offend Mrs. Lubbage, and did various odd jobs for her and Mr. Firkin; Cris was not seen, but gifts of food that Dido left for him in the loft were taken. Mrs. Lubbage did not leave her cottage and so Dido, who would have liked to go to the Cuckoo Tree, did not think it safe to risk leading the witch to Cris's retreat.

On Friday Dr. Subito returned for another of his brief, nervous visits, and pronounced Captain Hughes well enough for a little gentle exercise on crutches if they could be obtained.

"Don't you reckon I'm well enough to hire a coach and go on up to London, doctor?"

"*Non tanto*—never, never! It is not to be thought of! The jolting—the swaying—*piu mozzo*—*doppio movimento* —*furioso*—it would inflame the head injury—bring on a syncope—a cataclysm—if not death itself! No—no, slowly we return to health, *poco a poco.*"

"Don't set yourself in a pelter, now, Cap," soothed Dido. "I'll be off to Petworth this very arternoon and get you a pair o' crutches."

But she herself was decidedly restless and uneasy; four days had passed and there had been no word from her friend Simon. Was he no longer living in London, or had her letter gone astray?

Addio! To the re-see," said the little doctor. "I return next week. In the meantime—*legato, non, non troppo!*"

He placed his finger to his lips, bowed, and departed at speed.

Not long after his departure, Gusset arrived with more provisions. After chatting a little to the Captain he glanced around cautiously and drew Dido away to the middle of Mr. Firkin's paddock, where they might be seen but could not be overheard.

"About that message you wanted sent, missie."

"Yes?" said Dido eagerly.

"Those chaps as I spoke of is willing to meet you and

talk it over. They be a darksy lot, see, they 'on't carry for every which-who, they're pitickler."

"That's all rug," said Dido. "The Cap's pitickler too; this is a very pitickler message."

"Ah!" said Gusset. He looked around again, advanced his mouth closer to Dido's ear, and murmured, "Do ee have the letter right, tight, and safe, missie?"

"That I do!" replied Dido, curbing an impulse to feel for the Dispatch inside her jacket.

"That's good," said Gusset. "Acos I did hear as how yon coach upset of yourn were fixed by somebody as wanted to lay hands on that there bit o' scribing. I dunno if 'tis true, but that's what I did hear."

Dido nodded. She was not surprised, having come to the same conclusion.

"Have you any notion who mighta done it, Mister Gusset?"

He came so close that his white whiskers tickled her ear dreadfully.

"That I dassn't say! But be that letter anywise connected wi' guvment business?"

Dido nodded, warily.

"I reckoned so!" said Gusset triumphantly. "I could tell as Cap'n Hughes must be a jonnick guvment man. Well, missie, round Tegleaze there be a pesky lot o' them Georgians."

"Hanoverians? The ones as wants to get rid o' the king?"

"That's the ticket! 'Twas one o' they fixed the accident."

"But how about these chaps o' yours? *They're* all hunky-dory?"

Mr. Gusset was affronted. He drew himself up. "My boy Yan's a true-blue king's man," he declared proudly. "Why, didn't he carry Gentleman's Gargle and twisty-corks every month for Jamie Three his own self—aye, and Oil o' Primroses for Her Majesty, bless her sweet face?"

"Your boy Yan? Why then—"

"Eh, massypanme! What have I bin and said?" Mr. Gusset was dreadfully upset. "Now, Missie Twido, don't ee let on as how I told ee that, don't ee, please! My boy Yan'd be turble taffety if he knew."

"Why, Mr. Gusset, I wouldn't dream of such a thing arter you been so kind to us and brought us all these vittles."

"Promise, do ee? Well, then, I was to tell ee, when ee be in Perrorth 'sarternoon, to go to a pub called The Fighting Cocks—at the end o' Middle Street, it be—don't ee go into the pub, now, but go ee round up a little twitten lane to the back, where they holds the cock-fights. Go ee there roundabout four o'clock. And there prensly a chap'll come up to ee and say, 'Larmentable scuddy weather we be having.'"

"And what do I say?" Dido inquired briskly.

"Don't ee say nowt, but goo along o' him, missie, and he'll talk over about taking yon message. And ee won't let on as I by-named my boy Yan?"

"No, no, Mr. Gusset, o' course I won't."

After Dido had reassured the old man several times he took his leave, still very shocked at his lapse.

Dido ran back to the cottage with a lighter heart.

"Things is looking up, Cap, I reckon. As far as I can puzzle it out, old Mr. Gusset's friendly with a set o' they moonshine men, what the folks round here calls Gentlemen. And this lot is a mighty high-up crew, seemingly; used to carrying stuff to the king hisself."

"Never?" exclaimed Captain Hughes, much shocked. "His Majesty buying smuggled goods?"

"Well," said Dido, "I did hear tell as how the corkscrew tax was perishing stiff; I dessay old Jamie Three had better things to spend his dibs on. Corkscrews! O' course! What a muttonhead I am!"

"I beg your pardon, my child?"

"Nothing, nothing, Cap!" said Dido hastily. "Anyways, if they really takes run stuff to the palace, and all the nobs, they're the boys for us, ain't they? You want your Dispatch taken to the Fust Lord o' the Admiralty—like as not he's on their list for Organ-Grinders' Oil, or his lady for Parsley Face-powder."

Captain Hughes was obliged to admit the truth of this.

"Well, child—see what you think of them. Do not decide rashly. If you have the least doubt as to their trustworthiness, take no further steps. So much is at stake! Confound it—I wish my head did not still ache so—I wish I were not so wretchedly weak."

"Now don't you fret, Cap! If I can, I'll get one o' the chaps to come back here and have a word with you."

"Do. Do, child."

"I'm to meet 'em in Petworth at four this afternoon. Come to think," said Dido, rubbing her brow, "how did old Gusset know so quick that I was a-going to Petworth?"

Captain Hughes supposed the doctor must have mentioned it. "Does he not spend most of his time at Tegleaze Manor?"

"He does, that's so," agreed Dido thoughtfully. "Jist the same, I wish news didn't travel quite so fast in this back end."

When she had given the Captain his dinner she went out to the shippen and untethered the gray coach horse.

"Come on, Dapple, you lucky old prancer; you're a-going to have a change of air."

Since she had been giving him his feed all week and fomenting his lame leg with potato poultices under Mr. Firkin's directions, the gray had become very friendly. He allowed Dido to put on his bridle and to strap a sheepskin for a saddle around his barrel-shaped middle; she climbed on him from the water butt; and they were off. It was no use waving to Mr. Firkin, sitting with his flock on the hillside, but Toby wagged his tail amicably as they passed, and so Dido waved to *him;* her spirits rose as she left the quiet little valley.

"Pity the weather's so misty and murky; but anyways, it's grand to be out on the gad."

5

Mr. Firkin had told Dido the way to Petworth. It lay first down an exceedingly steep descent, on which Dapple slipped and snorted and complained. Above, on the misty hillside, dim glimpses of great beech trees in their flaming autumn colors reminded Dido of red-hot embers hidden under a layer of ash.

The road then twisted through a small hamlet of thatched houses: Duncton, Mr. Firkin had said this was called.

Growing accustomed, by the time they had left Duncton behind them, to Dapple's jerky trot, Dido rode thoughtfully, pondering about Tegleaze Manor and its inhabitants, and the conversation they had overheard between Colonel FitzPickwick and the other man, Miles Tuggles. What was all *that* about? Tobit had not seemed in the least interested, but Tobit was a totty-headed boy;

wouldn't know an egg from an Austrian. Nonetheless it seemed to Dido that the talk concerned Tobit quite closely; so far as *she* could make out, Colonel Fitz-Pickwick had been doing something he shouldn't, stealing money from old Lady Tegleaze, like as not—maybe that was why she never had any luck with her bets, maybe they never got placed at all—and the other fellow had got to know about this somehow and was threatening FitzPickwick with exposure unless he assisted in some further plot, something connected with Tobit and Lady Tegleaze and the Manor itself—otherwise, what had he meant by "the place—to get all this I'd commit any crime?"

Havey-cavey goings-on, without any doubt whatsoever.

Goodness knows what all the talk of rollers and motive power was about; but at that point the two men had been a little farther away; perhaps Dido had misheard them.

Well, she thought, if Yan, Tan, Tethera, and their mates will take the Cap'n's Dispatch to London so *that*'s off my mind, I reckon I oughta do something about old gravel-voice Miles Tuggles. Dear knows what, though. Tell the Bow Street officers? That'd mean going to Bow Street; can't do it till the Cap's better. Warn Tobit? No use, he'd only start on about pirates or peashooters. Warn Lady Tegleaze? She'd never heed *me*. Maybe the lawyers in Petworth, the ones as looks after the heirloom, maybe they'd have some sense? Might be worth talking to them. Anyways, I'd like to see old Sir Tobit's luck-piece.

It had taken her the best part of an hour to reach Petworth; as she rode up the long straight track that led into the little walled, red-roofed town, she wondered at the lack of people; all the houses seemed shut and empty. But when she reached the sloping central market place this fact was explained: a fair was in full swing there.

It was mostly a farming fair: stalls around the sides of the square and overflowing into the streets nearby offered every kind of produce—eggs, butter, cheeses, apples, red and gold, bunches of late roses and purple daisies, farming tools and equipment; there were pens of cattle and sheep, crates of poultry; girls with pails offered their services as dairymaids, Dido saw shepherds with smocks and crooks and carters with whips. But as well as these there were various entertainments and peep shows, a band playing country dances, and a central merry-go-round, which had horses gorgeously painted in red, gold, and white.

"Better-looking than you, poor old Dapple," Dido told her steed. "Guess we'd better find somewhere to leave you out of all this mollocking."

Following Gusset's directions she located The Fighting Cocks Inn at the end of Middle Street, and asked permission to tie up Dapple in its stable-yard. Then she returned to the central square on foot, for at one side of it she had seen a shop window containing scythes, fowling pieces, wooden hayrakes, stools, ladles, and copper cooking pots. Sure enough, when she approached it more closely, she found a small painted sign over the door which read: Godwit & Son, Ironmongers & Conspirators.

"Humph," said Dido, considering this. "Well, I reckon the two things does go together, so it's kind of handy having 'em under the same roof; I spose they can fettle you up a riot, weapons, trimmings, and all, at wholesale rates."

She walked in, and demanded of a thin, wizened little man in rimless spectacles if he had any crutches in stock. He did have a pair, slightly too long for Captain Hughes (whose measurements Dido had taken before setting out); he promised to shorten them, put leather padding on the arm rests, and have them ready for her in an hour's time.

"I daresay you can amuse yourself at the fair meanwhile," he said with a meager smile.

Dido, who had decided that he was a soapy-faced fellow, replied that she had plenty of errands to occupy herself, and asked if he could direct her to an apothecary's, and also to the lawyers who had charge of the Tegleaze heirloom? At which Mr. Godwit (for it was he) raised his thin gray eyebrows and darted a very sharp glance at her indeed through the rimless glasses, but told her, still smiling gently, that she would find Wm. Pelmett, Chymist & Chirurgeon, on one side of his shop, downhill, and Messrs. Pickwick, FitzPickwick, and Wily, Solicitors and Attorneys-at-Law, on the other side, uphill.

Dido did not care for the sound of this. Still, I guess

as it's to be expected they'd all be cousins or kindred in a small place like Petworth, she reflected.

She went downhill first, and bought some ointment which the doctor had recommended for the Captain's wound, and a roll of bandage, since, even in Mrs. Lubbage's exceedingly dusty house, the supply of spider-web was running low. Wm. Pelmett, Chymist, bore a strong and unprepossessing resemblance to Pelmett the footman.

Next Dido turned uphill toward the lawyers' office, but before she reached the doorway she was startled to observe, set in a glass-fronted case in the wall of the building, what must surely be the Tegleaze luck-piece itself.

"But that could never have hung in a dolls' house," she thought. "It's far too big." Then she realized that the whole front of the case was in fact a powerful magnifying glass; the oval picture painted on a piece of ivory mounted in the case, though appearing to be about the size of a man's face, was really not much bigger than a gull's egg.

"It's a right naffy bit o' work, I will allow," Dido thought, studying it with interest. "I still don't see how it could be worth such a *deal* of dibs, but whoever done it put plenty of elbow grease into the job, I can see that, special considering how tiny it is. Musta been at it for hours."

The picture showed a very high tower, encircled by a spiral ramp. Hundreds of little people were rushing up and down the ramp, were occupied in building the tower, climbing ladders, at work with trowels and buckets of mortar; others were setting bricks, wheeling barrows, or consulting plans; but many others were just arguing, or even fighting, presumably about how the tower should be built; and in any case the tower had been struck by lightning and was falling down, so a great many people were trying to escape from it and trampling over each other in the process; some devils, down below, were finding the whole affair very funny indeed, and some angels, up above, seemed sad about it. The picture was painted in very bright, beautiful colors, reds and greens, browns and yellows; it seemed even gayer than the merry-go-round horses. The faces of all the little people were done with wonderful skill, no two the same, each with something strange, unexpected, yet lifelike about it; the painter's name, P. Bruegel, was neatly written in one corner.

"Fancy just leaving it there, where anybody might bust the glass and walk off with it," Dido murmured wonderingly.

"Oh, there's no risk of *that*. For one thing, the glass is specially strong: you'd need a diamond to cut it; for another, everybody round here thinks it's unlucky; no one would buy it from the thief."

Dido looked around in surprise at this unexpected reply; for a moment she thought that it was Cris standing behind her; then she recognized Tobit in what he plainly considered to be disguise; he had abandoned his black velvet and ruffles; instead he wore a frieze coat

and pantaloons. The lower half of his face was concealed by a red muffler.

"Tobit! What the plague are you doing here?"

Dido was not best pleased to see him; his presence would make it difficult to go into the office of the family lawyers and say she suspected a plot against the family; they would probably think it was just some of Tobit's romancing.

"Anyway, how in the world did you get leave of your gran?"

"Oh, I took French leave," said Tobit boastfully. "Pelmett told me Petworth fair was on, and I didn't see why, as I'm not going to the coronation, I shouldn't at least come to *this*; so I put a lot of minced-up Joobie nuts in Grandmother's gruel, and she's gone to bed with one of her headaches; and now I'm going to have a fine time, I can tell you."

"Did Sannie know?"

"She kicked up a bit of a dust, but I didn't pay any heed. After all, I'm nearly of age."

"How did you get here?"

"Came with Frill in the trap; he's doing some errands for Colonel FitzPickwick. Come on—let's go and look at the shows." He grabbed her hand.

Dido went with some reluctance; she glanced back toward the offices of Pickwick, FitzPickwick, and Wily; but at this moment the heavy black outer door opened and two very elderly gentlemen came out, followed by one somewhat younger; the first two were so extremely old and frail that they could get along only by leaning against one another; they looked like ancient hairless mice; while the younger one, presumably Mr. Wily, had such an extremely villainous, untrustworthy countenance that Dido at once decided there would be no sense in going for advice and entrusting her suspicions to *him*.

"All in whatever it is, hand and glove together, like as not," she thought.

Tobit did not wish to go on the roundabout; he said it would most likely make him sick; but he spent a good deal of money at the shooting gallery and the houp-la stall; it did not seem to occur to him to treat Dido, who had no cash for such amusements, but he liked her to watch him.

"This time I really will get it over—you'll see—I am a prime shot, once my eye is in! Oh, confound it! All the stands are just too big for the hoops, if you ask *me*. That wasn't my fault. Can I have another six shots for ninepence?"

"How did you come by all the mint sauce?" Dido asked, noticing his pockets heavy with coins.

"Frill lent me some; said he'd just been paid. He's a good-natured fellow. Now—this time I'll *certainly* get it over—you just watch, you'll see."

But he did not. Presently he became bored with the houp-la and moved on to a skittle stall.

Dido, tiring of his unjustified optimism, wandered along to the next booth, which was a kind of Punch-and-Judy show, apparently. A crowd was collecting in front of it. Weird and melancholy music was being played on a hoboy, somewhere behind the booth, by an

unseen performer; to Dido there was something tantalizingly familiar about this music, but she could not
name it.

"Walk up, walk up, ladies and gentlemen: watch
M-Miles M-Mystery's amazingly M-Mysterious Mannikins; what m-makes them move about? See the g-grandest
show of its kind in the world—the *only* show of its kind
in the world! And it's all f-free—free, gratis, not a penny
to pay. Watch the M-Mystery of the Miller's Daughter;
the M-Macbeth Murder case; the Strange Tale of the
Loch N-Ness Monster; see the dragon s-swallow St.
George!"

Since the show was free, Dido stood on the outskirts
of the group and waited. After a while the red-and-
yellow curtain was pulled up, letting out a cloud of
tobacco smoke, and revealing the little stage, lit by a
baleful greenish light. There were some bits of painted
wooden scenery and a backcloth representing a millhouse
with a large water wheel.

"The Mystery of the Miller's Daughter! Ladies and
gentlemen, you will now be the first spectators of this
amazingly blood-curdling drama, the only one of its
k-kind!"

The hoboy played a melancholy and off-key version
of the "Miller of Dee."

"L-ladies and gentlemen, if any of you should have
the m-misfortune to suffer from weak nerves, p-palpita-
tions, sympathetic vibrations, digestive disorders, heart-
burn, high t-tension, low spirits, vapors, or m-melancholy,
you will be p-pleased to hear that soothing refreshments

are on s-sale, at the extremely reasonable price of six-pence a packet."

Sure enough, a boy was going around with a tray containing little paper twists. Dido had not sixpence to spare, nor did she suffer from any of the ailments mentioned, but she looked with curiosity to see what the refreshments could be that would cure so many different troubles: so far as she could make out, each packet contained a small quantity of Joobie nuts.

The Mystery of the Miller's Daughter was heralded by an extra-loud flourish of hoboy music; then two puppets came hopping on to the stage: Rosie, the Miller's Daughter, and her sweetheart.

"Why," Dido thought scornfully, "they ain't but glove puppets; *I* can see what makes 'em move."

She had to admit, though, that they were unusually large, lifelike glove puppets, with something eye-catchingly strange and wild about their appearance. "I know what it is: the bloke as made them had been studying that picture, Grandpa Tegleaze's luck-piece."

The play was very comical at first: all about the efforts of Rosie and her sweetheart to escape the vigilance of her stern father, the Miller; they hid in all sorts of ingenious places—behind the mill wheel, up the apple tree, in the copper—while the Miller, completely bamboozled, rushed about the stage hunting for them, puffing and panting with fury.

But Dido soon became more interested in watching the audience than the play. The people in front nearly split their sides at the funny scenes; they staggered about and bumped into each other, bawling advice to the Miller which he always followed just too late. In their enthusiasm most of them had swallowed down all their Joobie nuts, and the boy with the tray, going around again, did a brisk sale; the sixpenny packets, Dido noticed, had been replaced by slightly larger ones which cost a shilling. Having swallowed a few more, the audience became almost hysterical with excitement, shouting, clapping, and screaming, as if they had before them the finest actors in the world. It seemed as if they saw more than was actually taking place on the stage and Dido, remembering what she had seen after merely tasting a Joobie nut, was not surprised.

She glanced at the church clock, set high on a tower, just visible over the red roofs: ten minutes to four. Time to go and meet Mr. Gusset's boy Yan.

Tobit, luckily, was absorbed in front of a stall where the game was to swing an iron ring hanging on a long cord so as to hook it over a peg on a panel at the back. It looked easy enough, but was evidently not so, judging by his lack of success. The prizes were goldfish, swimming in little semi-transparent bags made of pigs' bladder filled with water and tied up with twine. Wonder if Cap'n Hughes would like a goldfish to keep him company, Dido thought. But then I dessay it'd hate the coach trip up to London presently. Anyway, Tobit's happy enough and he won't notice if I skice off; hope Frill takes him home afore he notices the puppet show and starts stuffing down Joobie nuts.

She made her way back to The Fighting Cocks Inn,

and, following Gusset's instructions, turned under a low archway at the side, around a corner, and up a steep and narrow cobbled alley. This brought her into a little courtyard, where twenty or thirty men were standing in a circle, apparently waiting for a cockfight to begin. Two, in the middle, were taking their birds out of baskets, looking them over, strapping them into their fighting gear, and talking to them encouragingly, while the crowd laid bets and shouted advice. Dido had seen cockfights in London and did not like them, but this one made a good excuse for loitering in the court, so she stood at the back of the crowd and pretended to be examining her purchases.

In a minute she heard a familiar voice.

"Arternoon, maidy! Larmentable thick weather, 'tis!"

"Right fretful," Dido agreed politely.

The speaker was a well-set-up young fellow in a shepherd's smock; he had curly dark hair, cut rather short, a brown weathered complexion, and very bright observant brown eyes; he gave Dido a friendly grin and jerked his head, indicating that she should follow him in an inconspicuous manner. Everyone's attention was fixed on the cockfight, now starting, so they slipped away. He did not lead her back into the street; they went up a flight of steps from the alley into a big, bare, barnlike upper chamber, where there were two or three long trestle tables and a quantity of benches and stools.

"'Tis the inn banquet hall," Yan explained. "My uncle Jarge, he owns the inn. There'll be grand junketings here, come Coronation Day."

He sat down on a stool and Dido perched on another; she noticed that he smelt powerfully of clove pinks and orange blossom.

"It be the perfume," he explained apologetically, noticing her sniff. "Do what us may, *some* of it leaks out. And the mischief is that they Bush officers are training special hounds, now, to goo arter it; like truffle hounds they be."

"Couldn't you disguise it with onions or summat? Or strew pepper, to go up their noses?"

"Pepper costs terrible dear, lovie; but 'tisn't a bad notion. I can see my old gaffer's right—a nim, trustable little maid you be. So now, how can us Wineberry Men help ee?"

One look at Yan Wineberry in daylight had assured Dido that here was the right person to help her; she explained that she needed a letter taken to the First Lord of the Admiralty.

"Oh, no trouble about *that*, my duck. Us takes grog to old Lord Forecastle regular. Next trip Sunday night. He'll get it Tuesday maybe, Wednesday for sartin."

"Not before?"

"Us travels slow, you see, love; for one thing it 'on't do to joggle the grog, the old Crozier of Winchester created turble one time when the sediment got shook up in his pipe o' port wine; then there's deliveries along the way—us has a private way, slow and sure, what the Bush officers don't know about."

"Oh well, guess the Cap'll be agreeable, so it's

Wednesday for sure. Could you come and see my old Cap? Just so he'll feel easy about it?"

"I'll need to wait till arter dark, then, lovie. I'll come Saturday night—Dogkennel Cottages, ben't it? Owd Mis' Lubbage, therealong, be a terrible untrustworthy woman, no friend o' mine. Dunked in Black Pond she'd a bin, long agone, done she hadn't bin so thick wi' the Preventives and the Hanoverians."

"What are the Hanoverians doing mixed up with the Preventives?" Dido asked, puzzled. "I thought as how the Preventives were government revenue officers? And the Hanoverians are *agin* the government, surely? My pa used to be one; he was in a plot to blow up Battersea Castle; but he got found out and run off and no one's seen him since."

"Oh, it be simple enough," Yan said. "Nobody likes the Preventives—always clapping gurt dratted taxes on grog and twistycorks that honest folk has taken trouble to fetch over from France; and nobody likes the Hanoverians either, allus a-trying to blow up poor old King Jamie, and now his son, that's a-going to be Dick Four. So as nobody liked *either* lot, they just nature-ally set up together."

"I see. Now, how about the letter—will I give it you tomorrow night?"

"That'll be best," he agreed. "Now—if you wants to get in touch with me afore then—do ee know the Cuckoo Tree?"

"Yes I do."

"Well, if you wants me, just ee stick a twistycork in the Cuckoo Tree trunk and come back there the next noon or midnight arter—someone'll meet ee. Right?"

"Right."

"Us'd best leave by onesomes—I'll goo first and when you hear me whistle, you follow."

He gave her ear a friendly tweak and slipped down the narrow steps, quieter than a shadow. Dido waited until she heard his soft all-clear whistle from the street, then silently followed him.

Even more silently, when she had gone, a tiny figure unfolded itself from under one of the trestle tables and stole away in a different direction: Tante Sannie, aged, bent, frail as a bunch of cobwebs, quick as a spider.

Dido went back to Godwit & Son, Ironmongers & Conspirators. Mr. Godwit had the crutches ready, neatly tied up with cord so that she could sling them on her back. She paid, and was leaving his shop when she heard a disturbance from the upper end of the square, where Miles Mystery had his Mysterious Mannikins. People were shouting, "Stop thief!" and a portion of the crowd had broken away and was racing up a small cobbled lane that led in the direction of the church.

"What's it about?" Dido asked a fat man.

"Some lad nicked a couple o' goldfish off of the goldfish stall. Got caught red-handed—or rather, wet-pocketed," the man said, with a loud laugh at his own wit. "They're arter him now—they'll catch him soon enough." Too fat to run himself, he filled his lungs with air and shouted, "Stop thief! Catch the pesky ragamuffin. Stop thief!"

By now all the upper portion of the square had emptied; Mr. Mystery's theatre was empty and unattended. Dido took the opportunity for a quick examination of the puppets, which had been left, lolling and lifeless, on the stage. "They ain't bad," she thought critically, "but they're no better than what Pa used to make, when I was little."

She turned back in the direction of Middle Street; the ground hereabouts was white with the little twists of paper in which Joobie nuts had been wrapped. Suddenly her eye was caught by something familiar in the look of one of them: she picked it up and read her own handwriting: "Dere Simon. I doo hop yore . . . I am all rug . . . an hadd Grate Times." The paper had been torn into four; scuffling with her foot she found another piece. So much for the shravey Jem! No wonder her letter had not been answered. It had traveled no farther than Petworth Square. But how had it come to be wrapped around a packet of Joobie nuts?

"I jist hope Yan, Tan, and co are a bit more trustable," she thought, greatly cast down by this discovery.

She walked on feeling thoroughly uneasy, she could not think why. After all there was no reason to suppose that the boy who had stolen the goldfish—

But as she reached the top of New Street the hue and cry, which had swung in a circle around past the church and back toward the center of the town, came surging in her direction.

Ahead of the crowd, but only just, she was horrified to see Tobit, gasping and wild-eyed. Half a dozen yards from Dido he tripped and fell, as a tall man sprang forward and tackled him.

"Got the little varmint!" shouted the crowd.

Tobit was on his feet again, fighting frenziedly.

"I didn't take it, I tell you I didn't!"

"Ah, how did it come to be in your pocket, then? Why did you run off?"

> "Little Tommy Tittlemouse
> Went to the skittle-show
> Lined his breeches
> With other men's fishes!"

somebody sang derisively.

"Someone must have slipped it in my pocket."

"A likely tale! Tell that to the magistrate!"

A constabulary officer, conspicuous with his truncheon and top hat, was making his way through the crowd.

"What happened?" he asked.

"Why, it was l-like this, officer," said the man who had caught Tobit. Dido studied him curiously. He was very tall, very thin, with a long, flat face, not ill-looking but very yellow in complexion; his hair was dusty dark and his eyes, big, yellowish-gray, and slanting, were strangely like those of a goat. Dido noticed that his hands, though they retained a vicelike grip on Tobit, shook all the time; it seemed that he could not control their shaking. "I r-run the m-mannikin show in the square—Mr. M-Mystery, you know. I was just coming to

[132]

the end of my M-Miller's Daughter play when, l-looking out at the crowd through a slit in the curtain, I s-saw this boy steal a couple of g-goldfish from the next stall and slip them into his p-pocket."

"That's a lie!" shouted Tobit. "I never did any such thing! Why, if I wanted, I could easily buy a goldfish—I've plenty of cash."

He brought out a handful as proof—it was wet, and bits of pig's bladder were mixed up with it.

"Stole the money too, like as not," somebody commented.

"Did anybody else witness this?" the constable asked.

"Yes, I did!" Somebody was shouldering his way to the front of the crowd; Dido was shocked to recognize Frill the footman. "With my own eyes I saw him," Frill went on sorrowfully. "Oh, Mas'r Tobit, how could ee do such a thing, boy, bringing down your poor old grandma's white hairs?"

"I never did, I tell you! Someone must have planted it on me."

"He's right!" said Dido, angrily coming forward. "It's all a plot against him, so he'll be sent to prison and won't come into his luck-piece. *You* know that," she said accusingly to Frill. "I bet your tale's naught but a pack o' lies." He gazed at her as if he had never laid eyes on her before.

"Oh, and did *you* see the occurrence, miss?" said the officer.

"Well, no, I didn't, but—"

"Just a-wanting to keep your playmate out o' trouble,

eh? Well, my advice to you, maidy, is, don't poke your liddle nose into matters as don't consarn you, or you'll be in trouble too. Come along you," he said sharply, grabbing Tobit's arm. "We'll see if a night in the stone jug'll cool you down and make you more biddable— then tomorrow you'll go afore the beak."

The crowd followed as he hurried Tobit away. Frill and Mr. Mystery strode alongside.

Dido started after, but a hand on her arm checked her.

"You'll never do no good that way, lovie," said a warning voice. "Best not get imbrangled."

She looked up into the eyes of Yan Wineberry.

"But it was all a put-up job—" she began indignantly.

"Whisht! O' course it was. That Amos Frill is as crooked as one o' my twistycorks. But no sense in making a potheration now, or what'll come of it? You'll be run in too, for nabbling at a constable in pursoot o' his dooty."

"What'll I do then?"

"Best tell old Lady Tegleaze first. The magistrate's a friend o' hers—old Sir Fritz FitzPickwick. Reckon she'll be able to put matters right wi' him."

"D'you reckon so?" Dido said doubtfully. "What if that don't work?"

"If that don't work us Wineberry Men'll see what we can do."

Somewhat comforted by this assurance, Dido fetched out her nag, mounted him from the steps in front of The Fighting Cocks Inn, and made for home as fast as possible. But Dapple had no great turn of speed, and as she passed through Duncton in the misty twilight she was overtaken by a trap bowling rapidly along. It was driven by Frill, who passed her without a sign of recognition; the trap's other passenger, bundled up like a sackful of shadows, was not visible to Dido.

"Blame it!" she thought. "Now he'll get home first and tell his tale."

She delivered the crutches to Captain Hughes, who was delighted with them, gave him a hasty summary of the afternoon's events, including the satisfactory interview with Yan Wineberry, and explained that she must hurry on to Tegleaze Manor.

"That you must," agreed the Captain. "Not a doubt but the boy's been framed, by the sound of it; makes one's blood boil. Why, when I think how I'd feel if my own boy, Owen, got into such a fix—I've a good mind to come along with you and talk to this Lady Tegleaze."

However his indignation and the effort of attempting to leave his bed made his head swim so badly that Dido was alarmed and begged him not to overexert himself.

She prepared him a hasty meal, explained her intentions to Mr. Firkin, who promised to keep the Captain company and, observing that Mrs. Lubbage's house was in darkness, remounted the dismayed Dapple and continued on her way.

As she neared Tegleaze Manor she saw one faint glimmer of light in an upstairs window, and when she pounded on the door, Gusset presently appeared with a candle.

"Oh, Missie Dwighto Tide!" he exclaimed dolefully. "There be desprit tidings of Mas'r Tobit—caught a poaching goldyfishes and clapped in clink!"

"I know, I was there! But it's all a pack o' lies, you know, Mister Gusset—he didn't do it." As she said this, though, a sudden doubt assailed her. Tobit was such an unaccountable, impulsive boy—supposing he had done it? But no, why should he? "I've come to tell Lady Tegleaze the truth," she went on stoutly.

"Oh, that's good, that's good, Missie Dide—I'll take ee to her directly," Gusset quavered, and escorted her upstairs so slowly and shakily that he scattered great drops of candle grease on every step.

In Lady Tegleaze's dim, dusty bedroom, Dido found a conclave assembled. Frill was there, looking thoroughly hypocritical; the corners of his mouth were turned down as far as they would go, and his hair had been parted in the middle with a wet comb. Dr. Subito was there with a finger on the pulse of Lady Tegleaze, who lay on a couch looking pale and haggard; Sannie, wielding a large ostrich-feather fan; old Cousin Wilfred in his dressing gown, holding a bottle of smelling salts and looking somewhat bewildered; Pelmett stood with an untouched plateful of nut cutlets; and another member of the group, greatly to Dido's astonishment, was Mrs. Lubbage, whose solemn expression did not disguise a gleam of excitement and malice in her twinkling little eyes. Tobit's big white dog Lion had crept in and was lying in the middle of the room with his head on his paws, flattened out, like a thick white fur rug; every now and then he let out a mournful whimper.

"Who is *that?*" demanded Lady Tegleaze as Dido entered; then, recognizing her, added fretfully, "Why, it's that quarantine child who forced her way in once before. I daresay she began all the trouble, putting ideas in the boy's head. Tell her to be off, Subito; she is not wanted, specially at such a time as this."

"But my lady," pleaded Gusset, "she be come about Mas'r Tobit; says as how it be all a pack of lies that he took the fish."

"Nonsense, man! Frill himself saw the incident. A devoted family servant would hardly lie, would he? Oh! to think I should have to suffer such a blow. My own grandson convicted of poaching, three days before his coming of age. Such a vulgar crime, too. It is crushing—entirely crushing."

"But ma'am—I am sure that it is all a plot."

Dido wished that some of these people would go away, so that she could talk to Lady Tegleaze in private.

"Who would plot against me—and why, pray?"

"Colonel FitzPickwick—" began Dido, but at that moment the Colonel himself entered the room. Seen in daylight his hair and mustaches were so white that Dido wondered if he dipped them in bleach; they formed a decided contrast to the whites of his liver-brown eyes which were a blood-veined mud color; his teeth, when he showed them, looked as if inside some-

[137]

where they must be labeled "Best Staffordshire porcelain."

"Dear lady—who speaks of me?" he said, coming forward.

"What news?" Lady Tegleaze demanded. "What news of my grandson?"

"He will appear before the magistrates at ten tomorrow; my cousin Fritz presiding; let us hope that as it is a first offense, Fritz will be lenient; ten years in Lewes Gaol, perhaps, rather than a life sentence in Botany Bay."

"Oh, what difference does it make to me where he gets sent?" Lady Tegleaze said pettishly. "Or for how long? The main thing is that we lose the heirloom. When I think of the trouble I have wasted in rearing that child—and all for this! Stupid, ungovernable boy! Well, I wash my hands of him—I wish now I had kept the other instead."

"Other?" twittered the mouselike Cousin Wilfred, evidently much startled. "What other, Catherine?"

"Why, surely you remember that there were twins? Or rather, triplets, but one died at birth. Sannie brought the other two from Tiburon when their parents died. But *I* said that it wasn't to be expected that I should have the trouble of looking after *two* grandchildren; one would be quite enough work; so I kept only the boy."

"And I said, princessie-ma'am, two-baby twins bring always bad, bad luck in family, almost as bad as three-baby; better get rid of one, better keep boy, just."

"Good gracious! Mean to say you just *disposed* of one?" mumbled Cousin Wilfred, really shocked.

And Dido thought, "Well! I allus did say she was a queer old trout but, ask me, that's downright heartless! Fancy tossing out your own grandbaby like summat you'd give a rag-and-bone man."

"Oh well, Sannie said she'd find a home for it somewhere, in an orphanage or something; you'll just have to find it again now, Sannie, and double-quick too, now Tobit's no use to me."

"That's not easy," said Tante Sannie, wrinkling her leathery, monkeylike forehead under its sparse silvery hairs. "Not easy, that! Who know, who know where that baby be now? Far, far away, daresay; cost a much, much money to find her. Hundred, t'ousand pound."

"Well, the money'll have to be found somehow," snapped Lady Tegleaze. "FitzPickwick, you'll have to arrange it. Sell one of the chimneys—or the portico, that's made of marble, isn't it?"

Dido, meanwhile, had been struck by a blinding flash of inspiration. Without pausing to listen to anything else she turned hastily toward the door, noticing two faces only on her way: Gusset's, full of reproach at her supposed desertion; and that of Colonel Fitz-Pickwick who looked as if he had received an utterly staggering blow; his jaw had dropped in disbelief, his large porcelain teeth stuck up like Dapple's, and he was directing a look of pure fury at Tante Sannie, who took no notice whatsoever.

6

Back at Dogkennel Cottages, Dido briskly approached that of Mrs. Lubbage. It was unlit, as before, and the door was locked. When she tried it, the little voice buzzed in her ear:

"Beware! This is a hoodoo lock."

"Oh, be blowed to that," thought Dido impatiently. "If old Sannie and Mrs. Lubbage are hoping to squeeze a thousand quid out o' Lady Tegleaze before they'll produce Tobit's sister, they're liable to be pretty riled with me anyways, sposing I spile their game; busting the old crone's witchlock can't make matters much worse, I reckon."

She found a lump of rock and gave the ramshackle door a vigorous thump; it burst inward.

From up above an alarmed voice cried, "Who's that?"

"Cris? It's me—Dido!"

She walked into the kitchen—which smelt even worse than on her last visit—and looked up. Framed in the black square of the loft opening was a pale, scared face.

"I thought it must be people coming to duck Auntie Daisy," breathed Cris. "She said once that some day they will do. But, Dido, you won't half catch it when she finds you here! And so shall I! Breaking down the door, too—didn't her hoodoo lock work on you?"

"Yes, a bit," said Dido, crossly rubbing her hands. "My fingers tingles as if I'd been pulling stinging nettles. But I don't believe in such stuff! Anyways, come down, Cris; I wants to talk to you."

"Where's Auntie Daisy?"

"Up at Tegleaze Manor."

Encouraged by this, Cris jumped lightly down.

"Why did you let on you was a boy?" Dido snapped out.

"I—I—Auntie Daisy said I must, always. For *goodness'* sake don't tell her you found out," Cris gasped, looking frightened almost to death.

"That'll be all right—don't you worry. What's your real name, then?"

"It is Cris—Cristin. She said if anyone got to know, she'd put a freezing spell on me, so I was shivering cold to the end of my days. She can too—she did to old Mrs. Ruffle at Open Winkins."

"Rubbidge. Mrs. Ruffle probably had the ague. Now, listen, Cris—I've lots o' things to tell you. But there's no time to lose, so you come along o' me, and I'll explain as we go—agreeable?"

"Go where?"

"I'd as soon not say till we're farther along," Dido said cautiously.

"Supposing Auntie Daisy comes back?"

"I don't reckon she will jist yet."

"I can't go without asking Aswell!"

"Oh, croopus," Dido thought. But she felt some sympathy for Cris—plainly the unusualness and suddenness of her arrival had thrown the girl into such a state of fright and indecision that she was almost paralyzed. She stood trembling, huddling the ragged sheepskin jacket around her thin shoulders, her huge dark eyes fixed hauntedly on Dido.

"All right, go on, ask Aswell then," Dido said patiently. "But I think we'd best get outside, hadn't we? Shouldn't think Aswell'd fancy coming into a murky den like this."

They went out into the little weedy front yard, dark now, and misty; Cris sang or chanted her curious rhyme:

"Dwah, dwah, dwuddy dwuddy dwee—
I can't see you but you can see me—"

Dido perched on the yard wall. Cris stood with her eyes shut and hands stretched out. There was a long pause, of expectation and strain; then Cris gave a short sigh.

"It's all right. Aswell says I ought to go."

"Well, so I should hope!" Dido muttered to herself, but aloud she merely remarked, "Come along, then—can you trot? That's the dandy—" catching hold of Cris's hand. She had stabled Dapple, who had certainly done his part for the day, before coming to find Cris.

The two girls ran along the chalk track at a steady pace, and Dido said,

"Right, listening, are you? Now, Cris, do you know what twins are?"

"Brothers and sisters the same age?" Cris said doubtfully.

"That's it. Now, how'd you feel, Cris, sposing I was to say you had a twin brother nobody'd ever told you about?"

There was a long silence. Then Cris's voice came hesitantly out of the dark.

"Could you say that again?"

Dido said it again.

"Dido?"

"Yes, Cris?"

"Do—do you mean that I really *have* got a brother?"

"Yes, Cris. His name's Tobit. He's in pokey at the moment, but we'll get him out someways."

"Pokey?"

"Jail. Prison."

"Why?"

"Someone fadged up a tale against him o' summat he hadn't done."

"I've got a brother called Tobit." Cris was trying

[143]

over the words to see how they sounded. "I have a brother. Do you know—everything seems *warm* all of a sudden. As if the air was warm and I could swim in it like a fish. I've got a brother," she said again.

"Hey, hold on!" Dido became a bit anxious. "He's jist an ordinary boy—not an angel!" Leastways he's not all *that* ordinary, she thought; but anyway I reckon Cris would take to him if he had three legs and a sword on his snout.

"Now, there's lots more to tell you, Cris, so pay attention; that ain't all by a long chalk."

"What else?" But Cris sounded vague as if, in spite of Dido's caution, her attention was not fully engaged.

"It's like this. As well as Brother Tobit, you've got some grand relations up at Tegleaze Manor. Old Lady Tegleaze is your granny. And there's Cousin Wilfred. They're a-going to be right pleased to see you," she added thoughtfully, "acos now Tobit's been in jug he's lost his right to the luck-piece. At least I spose he has; jail's jail, even if it's on a skrimped-up charge."

"Lady Tegleaze is my grandmother?" Cris murmured dazedly.

"That's right. Mind, don't go running off wi' the notion that life up at Tegleaze Manor is going to be everlasting sherry cobbler and larks on toast—it ain't so. Lady T has gambled away all her dibs on the races. But at least it'll be a whole heap better than life with Mother Lubbage. You won't have to lurk up in the loft and live on spud scrapings. And old Auntie Daisy'll hatta treat you civil from now on."

"Sannie's there," Cris said, half to herself. "I'm scared of Sannie."

Dido frowned. She too had thought about this.

"Well, we just got to find a way to put a damper on that old spider monkey. And, whatever you do, Cris, *don't* you go eating of those Joobie nuts; you lay off 'em."

"Will I have to stay up at the Manor always, now?" Cris was sounding more and more doubtful.

"Now, Cris! Dido began scoldingly. In her heart, though, she was uncertain enough. Would Cris be happier up at the Manor with all those funny old things? But *surely* it was better than life at Dogkennel Cottages?

There was another pause, then Cris sighed again.

"Aswell says I belong there."

Thanks a million, Aswell, Dido commented inwardly. You're a real pal.

Five minutes' more trotting and they reached the Manor. Dido walked in without knocking. No one was about; she guessed that everybody was still assembled upstairs.

"Come along; this way. Crumpet, Cris, don't gawp so—you'll hatta get used to the place."

She led Cris over the marble paving, up the stairs, and then turned in the direction of Tobit's room. "Here, this won't take but a moment and I reckon it'll help—"

Rummaging in Tobit's untidy apartment she found several of his black velvet suits.

"Put one o' these on, it looks to be just your size.

[145]

Lawks, gal, you're nought but skin and bone, it surely is time we got you outa that old devil's clutches. Now, where does the boy wash?"

Investigating, Dido found a dressing closet and washstand with pewter basin and ewer. She soaped a cloth and briskly scrubbed the inattentive face of Cris, who had found the picture of the three children and was standing riveted in front of it.

"That's *Aswell!*"

"You said you'd never seen Aswell," said Dido, buttoning cuffs.

"No, but that's how I imagine him."

"It's *you*. Here, look at yourself—" Dido wheeled her to face the looking glass over the mantel. Cris gazed in astonishment.

"Is that me? I never saw myself before."

"Croopus, Cris, you ain't half got a lot to learn," Dido muttered, hard at work with a molting silver hairbrush. "Right! We're ready, come along."

She led Cris through the maze of passages to Lady Tegleaze's room.

The conclave was still assembled, but now something mysterious was going on. Sannie and Mrs. Lubbage, evidently at the request of Lady Tegleaze, were doing a bit of conjuring. Another pewter washbasin had been filled with what looked like ink. Sannie had lit a lot of incense sticks which, stuck about in egg cups and toilet jars, were filling the room with white choking smoke. Frill, Pelmett, Gusset, the doctor, Cousin Wilfred, and the Colonel were standing in a ring looking nervous and ill at ease; Lady Tegleaze still reclined on her couch; Mrs. Lubbage was gazing into the basin of ink while Sannie chanted foreign words in a shrill unearthly tone.

"Ah, now I begins to see clear," Mrs. Lubbage was saying, as Dido poked her head around the door. "Yes, I can see a face. Yes, it be the face of your granddaughter Cristin, my lady. . . ."

"Where is she?" Lady Tegleaze asked eagerly.

"Wait a minute—wait a minute—the driply mist be a-thickening again. Ah, now 'tis clearing. Cristin be a turble long way from here, my lady—over hill and dale, over bush and briar, over sand and swamp and sea. Far, far away, she be; 'twill cost a power o' money to fetch her home."

"Now, *that's* a funny thing," Dido said, stepping in briskly and dragging the nervous Cris behind her. "I'd a notion she was no farther away than right here, and it'd cost nothing at all to fetch her!"

Three things then happened simultaneously: Lady Tegleaze shrieked, Colonel FitzPickwick let out a fearful oath, and Mrs. Lubbage, startled almost out of her wits, upset the basin of ink, which poured in a black flood all over the carpet.

"My granddaughter!" Ignoring the fact that her lavender satin was trailing in the ink and that her wig was awry, Lady Tegleaze rose, swept forward, and enveloped Cris in a bony embrace from which the latter, looking somewhat taken aback, freed herself as soon as she could.

"Knavery! Arrant deception! Dear lady, do but think! What possibility can there be that this come-by-chance brat could be your grandchild? It is a piece of barefaced imposture!" Colonel FitzPickwick had recovered and strode forward, casting looks of rage at Sannie and Mrs. Lubbage.

"Imposture?" snapped Lady Tegleaze. "Nonsense! Look at the child's face. Besides—look at the dog."

The dog Lion, who would go to no one but Tobit, was standing on his hind legs, with a paw on each of Cris's shoulders, crying with joy, and licking her face with a large blue tongue. She put her arms around his white furry neck and hugged him back.

"Pity I washed her face," Dido thought regretfully. "It would a been prime to have it come plain when the dog licked it. Never mind, she's *in*, that's the main thing."

For it was plain that by Lady Tegleaze, by Cousin Wilfred, and by Gusset, Cris had been unhesitatingly accepted. The two witches, biting their lips with chagrin, were quarreling in furious undertones. Frill, Pelmett and the Colonel, pale and angry, were on the point of quitting the room when Lady Tegleaze said to Cris,

"Now, tell me, what do you want, dear child? What do you need? Food, clothes—er, toys?"

"Nothing, thank you, my lady," Cris said politely, "only—"

"Call me Grandmother!" snapped the old lady. "Only? Well, what?"

"Only to see my brother Tobit."

"Oh, *that* is quite out of the question. He has done for himself. I've washed my hands of *him*."

"But, Lady Tegleaze," said Dido, "I'm sure as ninepence he didn't steal those fish. They was palmed off on him. Arter all, who in the name o' thunder would be so totty-headed as to stick a pair o' goldfish in his britches pocket?"

"Whether he stole them or not, it is all one. If he had not disobeyed me and gone to Petworth, he would not have exposed himself to such a risk. I have no more interest in him. If he is sent to Botany Bay it is no concern of mine."

"But, Grandmother—" Cris began.

"No more, miss!"

Botheration, thought Dido. What an old tarmigan. This alters the look o' matters.

She had expected that, in gratitude for the production of Cris, Lady Tegleaze would be prepared to exert herself on Tobit's behalf, but plainly that was not going to happen.

Murmuring, "Well, enjoy yourself, Cris, see you Turpentine Sunday," Dido slipped away, following the Colonel who, without noticing her, had walked rapidly to the back stairs, down them, and out along the path to the tilting-yard.

The pale moon was beginning to struggle out, throwing long spindly shadows on the mist. Dido saw another shadow, with its owner, move out from one of the yew trees.

"Well?" Dido recognized the grating tone of Miles Mystery. "How did it g-go? Will the boy get a stiff sentence? How did the old lady take the n-news?"

"Oh, as expected. But—"

"But what?" Mystery said sharply.

"Our plans are overset. Another grandchild has turned up."

"Devil take it! What are you telling me? How can there be another grandchild?"

"It seems there was a twin sister of Tobit, mislaid or farmed out in infancy. Those two old hags, Sannie and Mrs. Lubbage, have been playing deuce-ace with us—they knew of this other child all along, and planned to demand a handsome sum from Lady Tegleaze as the price for producing her when Tobit was knocked out of the game."

"Wait till I lay my hands on the d-double-dealing old witches! They'll reckon that money hard-earned!"

"But they never got the money!"

"S-so? Why not?"

"That strange child—the one who is lodging at Dog-kennel with the navy captain—*she* suddenly sprang the plot and produced the missing grandchild."

"How in Lucifer's name did she know about it?"

"Lord knows. We shall have to do something about her. She may know too much for comfort."

"Not only her. We shall have to get rid of the other grandchild."

"How?"

"If she was lost once—she m-must be lost again."

Dido's blood ran cold at the calm way in which Miles Mystery uttered these words. Plainly the Colonel also felt a qualm for he said,

"No violence, Tuggles. You know I draw the line at violence. It's too dangerous."

"Oh, call me Tegleaze! It is my name, after all. Hark, what was that?"

Dido held her breath. Had they seen her, crouching by the hedge? But then she saw Mrs. Lubbage and Aunt Sannie, still bickering angrily, come down the steps and start to cross the lawn. They had not noticed the two men, and appeared somewhat confused when Colonel FitzPickwick accosted them.

"A f-fine trick you played us, you miserable pair of old scarecrows!" Mr. Mystery exclaimed angrily. "You needn't think I'll stir myself to send you to Tiburon Island *now*. Pretending to help us with Tobit and the old lady—and all the time you had another grandchild hidden up your sleeves!"

"Is not pretending!" Sannie said fiercely. "*Is* helping! Number two grandchild—pooh! T'ousand pound in pocket, why not, then get rid, easy as Tobit."

"Only you didn't get the thousand pounds," Mr. Mystery pointed out unkindly. "And *I'm* not weeping millstones—you deceitful pair of old crows! Well, you can whistle for your great white ship to Tiburon after that—you'll not get it from me, even when I come in to the estate."

"Just you bide a minute, you fine Mr. Mystery!" hissed Sannie, scuttling after him like a scorpion as he turned away. "You cast us off now, you fine fellow, you be sad and sorry, afore long soon, when the ground gape black under you foot, when the water snatch you in she claws, when the luck-piece hang over you head and you can't reach!"

"Best keep the old beldames in a good humor," Colonel FitzPickwick urged in a low tone.

Mystery jerked his head reluctantly. The two men and the two old women were slowly moving away, their unnaturally long shadows trailing behind them on the mist like black wings.

"Drat!" said Dido. "I wish I could a heard a bit more."

She ran softly across the lawn, but the two couples had separated, and the men were mounting horses in the stable-yard.

Slowly and thoughtfully, Dido made her way home. As she neared Dogkennel Cottages she recalled Mrs. Lubbage's make-believe dragon, and quailed a little at the thought of what might be in store for her tonight. But whatever it is, I'll just throw a rock at it, she decided.

Tonight there was no dragon, nor was Mrs. Lubbage herself to be seen. Suspicious of the silence and darkness, remembering Mrs. Lubbage's broken lock, Dido approached her own cottage and looked for the key under the stone. But the key was not there. A glimmer of candlelight showed in the window and the door was open. Surely it was late for Mr. Firkin still to be sitting with the Captain.

Dido pushed the door back and went in.

Mr. Firkin was not there. Instead, Mrs. Lubbage and Tante Sannie were sitting in silence, one on either side of the Captain's bed. He did not stir as Dido entered; he appeared to be sleeping.

A dreadful apprehension filled her; she darted forward to the bed and leaned over it.

"Cap'n! Cap'n Hughes! Are you all right?"

He neither moved nor stirred. The sharp eyes of Tante Sannie and Mrs. Lubbage moved up and fixed on Dido like pins in a map.

"Cap'n Hughes! Please say summat!" She shook him a little, but he did not answer. He breathed, but only just; his mouth was a little open, his face deadly pale, what could be seen of it under the bandages.

"If you've killed him, you old—" burst out Dido, choking with grief and terror, "if you've hurted him— Oh, what have you *done* to him? What'll happen to him?"

"Wait and see, Miss Prussy! Wait and see!" Mrs. Lubbage gave Dido a look of malignant satisfaction. "And maybe this'll teach ye a lesson not to be so quick to meddle in other folks' concerns! Come, Sannie; us'll leave, eh, now the fine young lady's come a-home. *She* can look arter him."

Dido hardly noticed when they left. She was frantically rubbing the Captain's cold hands. She filled a stone bottle with hot ginger ale and put it to his feet; she mixed a mustard plaster and laid it on his stomach; she fetched in a bundle of chicken feathers and set light to them, filling the room with foul-smelling fumes; she tickled his feet and held a warm flatiron to them, and sprinkled snuff under his nose. None of these remedies had the least effect; the Captain continued to lie still as a log, hardly alive, yet not quite dead.

In despair, Dido went and roused Mr. Firkin who came quickly when she had made him understand the gravity of the case. He felt the Captain all over with careful, wise old hands.

"Arr; she've overlooked him, surelye. Deary me, darter, that *is* misfortunate, just when he was a-coming along so nimbly."

"Is he dying?" asked Dido, gulping.

"Nay, I wouldn't say that, darter, not here-an-nows. But die he may, don't she take the spell off'n him again. He can't eat, see, not while he be thisaway; he be like to starve."

"What'll I do?" Dido muttered, half to herself.

"Ee'll have to eat humble pie, darter; I dunno how ee harmed owd Mis' Lubbage, but ee'll have to undo it, and ask her to take off the overlooking."

"She never would. And *I* never would," said Dido flatly. "It didn't even *advantage* her any to hurt the Cap'n; she just did it out o' pure malicefulness. I'll cure him somehow. Or I'll *make* her take the spell off. Anyways, I don't believe in spells!" She was half crying.

"Well, darter, us'll try this and us'll try that. A drop o' Blue Ruin wi' red pepper in it works wonders for my old ewes, time they suffers from the sheepshrink; I'll see how that gooes down."

It did go down; and the Captain blinked, as if it had given him a lively minute's dream; but it did not rouse him.

"Anyhows, that shows we can feed him," said Dido, recovering, and rather ashamed of her loss of control. "Why, when I was in a swound on board the whaler they fed me for nigh on ten months with whale oil and molasses. I'll get some molasses in Petworth tomorrow."

"Music," muttered Mr. Firkin. "Music be a powerful strong tonic agin sorcery and spells. I dunno why but so 'tis. I'll sing the Cap'n a shanty or two."

"Just afore you gets going," said Dido, visited by a sudden idea, "Mr. Firkin, does you have sich a thing as a corkscrew?"

Mr. Firkin, who had opened his mouth to sing, paused in midbreath.

"A twistycork, darter? Surelye. Look ee in the chest in my tool shed, ee'll find one there." He filled his lungs again.

Dido found the corkscrew, whispered to the Rio-bound Mr. Firkin that she would be back in twenty minutes or so, and set off at a fast run for the Cuckoo Tree.

The next day dawned gloomy and lowering. Dido awoke very dejected. Captain Hughes still lay in the same stupor; his condition had not changed despite all Mr. Firkin's songs; and she could not help blaming herself bitterly. Supposing he *never* recovered? And what other forms might Mrs. Lubbage's ill will take? Suppose the witches made Cris's life miserable at Tegleaze Manor? Suppose they prevented the Dispatch from reaching London?

Trying to shake off these thoughts, she gave Dapple an extra handful of feed.

"Eat up, old mate, us has to go into Petworth and get some spermaceti and treacle."

Just before she left, Gusset arrived with more provisions and a bottle of blackberry wine.

"Old Lady Tegleaze be rare and spry," he told Dido. "Reckon she thinks a granddaughter be a better bargain than a grandson."

"How's Cris settling?"

"A mite peaky and homesick; it do all seem turble big and grand to her, poor young maidy. How be the Cap'n?"

When Dido told Gusset what had happened he shook his head in an anxious and gloomy manner, and promised to send Dr. Subito as soon as possible.

"Though I doubt he'll not be able to do anything, missie; old Mis' Lubbage's spells be desprit powerful when she's roused. 'Tis better to keep on the right side of her, or she can do deadly harm. I know, who better." A shadow passed over his aged face.

"I've got to get him away from here," Dido said, biting her lip with anxiety. "You don't think Frill or Pelmett'd help—I could borrow the trap and take him to an inn—he can't be wuss off than he is here."

"Pelmett's gone, missie."

"Gone? When?"

"Said he had an offer of a sitiwation wi' better pay and took his bundle and went off last night."

"Sounds a bit havey-cavey? What about Frill?"

"I doubt he be going to follow. We shan't miss 'em, they warn't much use."

Gusset took his leave, casting a wary eye in the direction of Mrs. Lubbage's house, and promising he would ask about the trap. But, he said, he thought it very unlikely that Lady Tegleaze would be willing to lend it.

Dido left the Captain in the care of Mr. Firkin, who usually spent Saturday cleaning his cottage. Dido promised to do this when she returned, and also to buy him some provisions.

When she reached Petworth, she could not help noticing that it seemed to be in an extreme state of turmoil and uproar. People were rushing hither and thither, up and down the streets, in what seemed a purposeless way, like ants when their nest has been disturbed.

Dido stopped a man and asked him in which street the Magistrates' Court was to be found. He gave her a blank stare and replied,

"What's the use o' that, pray? It's gone. No use locking the stable door arter the horse has skedaddled," and strode away.

When she inquired of another he replied, "They sat early. The Court's closed now."

"Why? They was due to sit at ten; 'tis only quarter to, now."

But the man had not waited; he was roaming up the street, peering into every cranny as if he expected to find an emerald brooch there.

Dido noticed a remarkable number of constables about, too, whose behavior was of the same wandering kind; they stopped, they started, poked with their staffs in flower beds and window boxes, rummaged in the baskets of goods exhibited for sale outside shops.

Out of patience at last, Dido went to the apothecary's, bought a pound of spermaceti and a gallon of treacle, and asked Mr. Pelmett what the mischief was the matter with everybody, and why had the Magistrates' Court sat early?

"Constabulary was needed elsewhere," Mr. Pelmett said curtly. He looked, Dido thought, put out about something; had a face as long as a rolling pin.

"What for?"

"Every man jack of them's out looking for the Tegleaze heirloom."

"W-what?" gasped Dido. "You mean—"

"It's been stolen."

"But I thought the glass case was burglar proof."

"It was cut by a diamond. Expert cracksmen have been at work."

"My stars," muttered Dido. "Here's a fine flummeration. I spose that perishing Mystery decided he better get his paws on it right away, without waiting for any more hocus-pocus over grandchildren. I'd dearly like to know who that Mystery *is*—a-calling of himself Tegleaze and a-reckoning to polish off heirs right, left, and rat's ramble—it's plain he's close connected with the family someway."

There was no sign, today, of Mystery's puppet theatre; the whole of the fair had been expeditiously tidied away.

Dido could get no information from anybody about what had happened at the Court session, and she did not dare linger in Petworth asking questions for fear the doctor should arrive before she returned. She urged Dapple back at what he considered a most unreasonable speed for an animal with a gallon can of molasses banging about on his withers.

In fact the doctor did not arrive until half past eleven and Dido was becoming wildly impatient before his cob drew up at the gate. Furthermore, he seemed very reluctant either to come in or, when he did enter, and saw the Captain's condition, to advise anything at all helpful.

In answer to all Dido's questions as to whether the patient needed new medicines, or new treatment, or new diet, he merely reiterated,

"*Tranquillamente—lusingando—amabile—poco a poco!* Only the utmost care will save him."

"But can't you advise anything, Doc?"

"*Non troppo*—I think not," replied the doctor, casting a hunted glance in the direction of Mrs. Lubbage's quarters.

"Don't you reckon it'd be a good thing to shift him from here?"

"*Largamente*—yes; yes I *do* think so." Dr. Subito made this answer in an undertone, finger on lips, and the moment after, took his leave, going off so fast that he forgot to pocket the five-shilling fee Dido had laid ready for him on the table. Oh well, he had hardly earned it, she decided.

It wanted but twenty minutes to noon by the Captain's chronometer. Dido flew to Mr. Firkin's cottage, swept, mopped, and set all to rights; laid out his groceries on the dresser where he could feel them over; and then, telling him she would be back as soon as possible, ran off in the direction of the Cuckoo Tree. No time to take a roundabout way; she hoped that she was not observed.

Behind the little tree, stretching away around the far side of the Down, was a thickish yew wood; as Dido approached the Cuckoo Tree from one side, a figure slipped quietly through the wood on the other, and they met by the Cuckoo Tree trunk, from which Dido's corkscrew still protruded.

"Well, love; what be the trouble?" said Yan Wineberry.

"Old Ma Lubbage has overlooked my Cap'n," Dido gulped out. "He's struck speechless; so there ain't much sense in your coming to see him tonight. And I dunno what to *do* about him."

"Humph," said Yan. "Things is tolerable troublesome all round then, for *I* found out that the magistrates had a private session this morning and sentenced that young Tobit to ten years' transportation. Which is as much as to say a lifer."

"But that's wicked!" Dido was horrified. "How could they—with no one there to speak up for him?"

"Well, they did." Yan was somber. "But," he added more cheerfully, "that's no skin off'n our nosen, for we're a-going to break into Petworth Jail 'sevening, for to fetch out Pip, my number five, who got hisself buckled up by mistake, and we'll fetch out young Mas'r Tobit at the same time."

"Oh, Yan, that's prime!" Dido hugged him. "Can I come too? So Tobit knows it's friends?"

"But what about your Cap'n?"

"Yan, is there any lodgings in Petworth where I could get him fixed up? I jist can't abear leaving him alongside that old fiend any longer."

"Well, reckon Uncle Jarge might have him," Yan said, scratching his head. "That is, if he's not a Scotchman; Uncle Jarge can't abide them."

"No, he ain't a Scotchman; he told me he comes from Pennygaff in Wales, and got a boy there called Owen. Is that your uncle Jarge as owns The Fighting Cocks pub?"

"That's right, lovie. My aunt Sary, she'm a wonderful comfortable woman; I dessay she'd take tolerable good care of the Cap'n if he be that sick; she'm a famous nurse."

"How could we get him there?"

Yan seemed to have unlimited relatives.

"My cousin 'Tholomew, over to Benges, guess he'd lend his haycart. Put the Cap'n on a bit of hay, he won't feel the jounces so bad."

Dido could hardly speak, the idea of getting the Captain away from Dogkennel Cottages was such a relief. She picked a sprig of yew and carefully stripped off all the tiny dark-green leaves. When she had her voice under control she said,

"What time should I have the Cap ready to shift? When are you breaking into the—"

"Hush! Who's that?"

They had been speaking very softly, but now he dropped his voice to a breath and laid a finger on her lips. Above them a voice began to sing:

> "Dwah, dwah, dwuddy, dwuddy, dwee
> I can't see you but you can see me—"

"*Cris!*" exclaimed Dido. "What in the Blue Blazes are you doing up there?"

A silence followed, then a timid voice said,

"Dido? Is that you?"

"Well, o' course it's me, gal! But why the plague are you here, 'stead of up at the Manor, eating your dinner with a silver spoon? I call that downright ungrateful!"

There was another long pause, then Cris slid down the trunk. Her face was pale, and there were traces of tears on it; she had the old sheepskin jacket huddled over her velvets.

"Aswell won't come to me at the Manor," she said miserably.

"Oh, botheration," Dido muttered.

"Who be this, then?" Yan asked in an undertone. He had been even more startled than Dido by Cris's sudden appearance.

"Tobit's twin sister," Dido explained in the same tone. "Old Ma Lubbage had her hidden away all these years in her attic, ready for a bit o' blackmailing tick-tacks when Tobit got put away."

"Have you been up yonder tree afore, ducky?" Yan asked Cris.

"Many times. More than I can count," she told him.

"Then that explains a power o' puzzlement. Some o' my Wineberry Men would have it that there was a liddle Pharisee lived up the tree," said Yan, grinning.

"But, listen, Cris," said Dido, who was anxious to get back to the Captain. "You can't run off from Tegleaze Manor, you gotta give it a fair trial. Why, gal, you're in clover there, in the lap of thingummy—all found, four square meals a day—"

"It's lonesome!"

"Oh, crumpet it—"

"It would be different if my brother was there."

"Well, we're a-going to rescue him from quod this very arternoon. Though what us'll do with him then—"

"Are you?" Cris's face lit up. "I'll come too!"

Disconcerted, Dido and Yan stared at one another. At this moment another voice broke in.

"Well!" it said gloatingly. "So I found ye out at last, did I? This is where ee went skrimshanking off to outa my loft, was it? The old Cuckoo Tree, eh?"

Mrs. Lubbage stood before them, arms akimbo, her face red with hurry and triumph.

Cris turned white as her ruffles, Dido drew a sharp breath.

"Make a slap-up liddle nestie for to play hide-and-seek in, did it? Well, I'll soon tell Amos Frill abouten it, time he'll bring his scoring axe and chop it down!"

"No!" cried Cris, and laid her hand protectively on the trunk.

"Ah! But I say yes, my young madam. And ee'd best come back to Tegleaze with me now; Sannie an' me'll put ee to bed with a shovel, I can tell ee!"

"Hold your tongue, you sidy old witch, or by the pize I'll give ee summat that'll misagree with ee," interrupted Yan angrily. "Let's have none o' that moonshine about cutting down the Cuckoo Tree. You know well, if ye was to lay a finger on it, there'd be no roof over your head by nightfall."

Mrs. Lubbage seemed to swell like a slug with rage; she darted an evil look at Yan.

"Moonshine is it, Yan Gusset? I know a thing or two about moonshine too! If ee have the roof off my head, I'll give ee neighbor's fare."

"There's nought ye could do wuss than ye done already," Yan said bitterly. "You poisoned my mum, putting nightshade in her morgan-tea, I know full well."

"Prove it! Ye can't!" Mrs. Lubbage grinned spitefully.

"I can too." The smile vanished from her face. "I've a witness. That wouldn't bring my mum back, though. But you'd best mind your ways, you old canker-moll. Go

[165]

back to your crony. Tell her the Tegleaze luck-piece is stole, you can mumble your jaws over that together."

Mrs. Lubbage's jaw did indeed drop at this piece of news. Without another word she turned and waddled away as fast as she could over the steep hillside.

"That'll give 'em summat to worrit about," Yan said with satisfaction.

"Who stole it, Yan, d'you reckon?" Dido asked.

"Ah, that's a black mystery, that is."

"I'll lay it *was* old Mystery. Croopus, time's a-wasting —I must get back to the poor old Cap. Cris, are you going to come along o' me, then?"

Cris nodded; she was still pale and speechless from the scene with Mrs. Lubbage.

"I'll send my cousin 'Tholomew round with the hay-cart, come cock-shut time then," Yan said with his friendly nod, and slipped away into the yew wood.

Dido and Cris returned to Dogkennel Cottages—not without some terror on the part of Cris in case they should meet Mrs. Lubbage. But Mrs. Lubbage was no-where to be seen—doubtless she had hurried off to take counsel with Tante Sannie.

"I hope she'll stay away till we've gone," said Cris trembling.

Dido considered her thoughtfully. "What are we a-going to do with Cris," she wondered. "If she won't go back to the Manor, and wants to be with Tobit—and if we rescue Tobit—he'll have to stay hid somewhere till we can find a witness as'll say his arrest was a put-up job—where can we stow the pair of 'em? Oh well—no sense getting into a sussel about it yet."

She fed the unconscious Captain some treacle and spermaceti, gave herself and Cris something more substantial, and then packed up their things in readiness for departure. What food remained she took around to Mr. Firkin and told him they were leaving.

"Nay, that be ernful news, darter," he said sadly. "Mind, I ain't saying you're wrong—I dessay the Cap'n'll do better if he bain't anigh that old grummut—but ee've been brightsome company and I'll grieve to part from ee."

Dido grieved too. She had grown fond of the kind old man.

"Spose old Mother Lubbage gets swarly with you when we've flitted?"

"She 'ont harm me, darter; I ain't afeered of her, see?"

Just the same Dido felt a pang when, after Cousin 'Tholomew had turned up with his wagon and they had loaded the Captain and their boxes on to the layers of hay inside, they drove off leaving Mr. Firkin with Toby beside him, standing at his cottage door, listening, listening, and waving as long as he could hear the sound of the wheels. He looked so old and so frail to be left there alone.

"You oughta have him to live up at the Manor, Cris," she said, swallowing, "when we've got Tobit out of jug and—and things is all settled."

Cris looked as if she thought it unlikely that such a time would ever come.

Cousin 'Tholomew was a red-faced, silent, curly-headed giant who drove them to Petworth at a slow walk, with Dapple harnessed alongside his own cart horse, and refused to accept any payment.

"Nay, 'tweren't no manner o' trouble. I had to come anyhows, to get a new Canterbury hoe," he said gruffly, and made his escape as soon as he had left them at the inn.

Uncle Jarge and his boy Ted received them kindly at The Fighting Cocks, and Captain Hughes was carried upstairs to a little white-walled room at the very top of the house, "where," said Miss Sarah Gusset, "he won't be disturbed by the street noises or the cockfighting."

Dido only wished he *would* be disturbed; he lay so pale and silent. But plump, smiling Miss Sarah seemed a kind and resourceful nurse; she had a bed so stuffed with hot bricks that it was like a Roman bathhouse, a whole tub full of aromatic vinegar, and a great quantity of hickory pepper, to make him sneeze. So he lay warm and sneezing, and at least by this they knew he was still alive.

"Now," said Miss Sarah, when the Captain was settled, "I had a message for you from that scamp, my nevvy Yan. I'd best not miscall him, though, had I? George gets all his corkscrews and Blue Ruin and Dutch Stingo and Calais Cordial from Yan—mum's the word! He surely is a member, that lad! Anyway, you're to meet him under the arch at six sharp, so you'd best have a bit of supper first, by the kitchen fire."

Miss Gusset's kitchen fire blazed in a huge open hearth by which hung hams and dried fish and bunches of herbs. Dido and Cris sat on stools in the hearth itself and were given earthenware pipkins of the best soup they had ever tasted and bread fresh out of the big oven, while Miss Sarah bustled about getting supper for the customers, and Uncle Jarge looked after the bar, occasionally putting his head through a little hatch to tell them the latest gossip.

"Harwood's pig be loose again! Foxhounds to meet here, Saturday's a fortnight. That Mr. Mystery, as he calls hisself, is still in the town, lodging with Hoadleys at the Angel; going to give another show. Asked could he lodge here and give his show in our yard, but I said we were full up."

Croopus, Dido thought, that was a near squeak!

"We'd best get you out o' them velvets, Cris, they're too noticeable. I've a notion old Mystery means no good by you; anyways you're too like Tobit by half; anyone might pounce on you thinking you was him. You'd best wear my spare midshipman's rig."

The midshipman's gear included a canvas smock, like enough to a shepherd's smock so that Cris would pass unnoticed in the street; and besides this, Miss Sarah rummaged out a sheepskin cap from a collection of odds and ends left behind by visitors to the inn. This covered up her dark hair.

At a minute before six they slipped out the back door and found Yan already waiting under the arch, with a couple of other men, muffled up like carters in sacking. They carried long brushes, a ladder, and bags of soot.

"Naught better than to look like a chimbley-sweep

when you're fixing to break into a jail," whispered Yan cheerfully. "It's a good reason for having the ladder with you, likewise for blacking your face; and if things comes to a roughhouse, a handful o' soot's wonderful boffling does it hit the other chap in the face."

He nodded approval of the girls' dark-blue rig, gave Dido a large sheet of very sticky paper to carry, and led off up the alley in the direction of the jail.

When they were halfway along, a man slipped silently past them, going in the opposite direction. It was too dark to see his face, but Dido gave two or three sharp sniffs after he had passed by.

"What's amiss, my duck?" whispered Yan, who was amazingly quick to notice anything that happened near him.

"The smell o' that chap's tobacco," Dido whispered back. "I knowed someone afore who smoked that kind—Vosper's Nautical Cut." She stopped to unstick the paper which had caught against itself—it was spread with treacle, Yan explained. He remarked that with a sniffer like hers, Dido was wasted outside the scent trade, and then they had arrived at the jail, a small brick building that stood beside a windmill on the outskirts of the town. It did not appear as if the jail were put to very frequent use; grass grew over the doorstep. There were bars on the ground-floor windows, but not on the upper ones. A watchman was seated on the mounting block outside the jail, drinking something from a leather bottle. Yan stole up behind him and gave him a brisk, deft thump with a sock full of soot; he toppled silently off the block and the contents of his bottle spilled on to the grass.

"Organ-grinder's oil," said Yan, sniffing; "wonder where he got it? Why, 'tis Sam Pelmett, I thought he was in service up to Tegleaze."

"He left there this morning," Dido said.

"We'd best put his head in a bag and tie him up middling tight."

This done, Yan took the treacled paper from Dido, ran up the ladder as nimbly as if chimney-sweeping were really his profession, smoothed the paper against a windowpane, and then tapped it with his soot-filled sock. The pane broke, but stuck to the paper, which he passed down to his mates. He then put an arm through the window, found the catch, opened it, and disappeared inside.

Five minutes of somewhat uneasy silence went by. At last one figure, two figures, suddenly and softly appeared around the corner of the building.

"It's us!" whispered Yan. "Came out the back door—dang me, it wasn't even locked."

"But where's Tobit?" Dido asked anxiously, for Yan's companion was a grown man.

"That be the mischief of it, ducky—he ain't there."

"Are you *sure?*" Dido made a movement toward the jail, but Yan grabbed her arm.

"Sure as Sunday—we went over the whole place, there's not another soul inside. But Pip here, who was in the next cell, says that not half an hour agone he heard some chaps come along, mouching and mum-

[171]

chance, have a word wi' the watchman, open up the boy's cell, and take him off wi' them. What d'you make o' that?"

"Oh my stars!" said Dido. "I reckon that there Mystery's gone and kidnapped him!"

7

Tobit had been horribly bored in jail. He was shut into a little upstairs room that looked out on to a pigsty with three pigs in it. Beyond that lay a grass-grown yard in which there was a well. The well appeared to be dis-used: it was covered by a millstone with moss on it; the wellhead was weatherworn, the handle and chain rusty. A pile of old farm implements lay in a corner of the yard, half grown over with brambles. On the other side of the yard was a windmill with some doves on its roof.

Tobit had plenty of time to study all these details. For a while he tried to amuse himself by firing Joobie nuts through his peashooter at the pigs, but their hides were so thick that they didn't notice; it was very poor sport and he presently gave up. For a while, too, he tried to cheer himself by hoping that his grandmother would send to have him released, or that some witness would come forward to say that he had been wrongfully arrested, but time passed, and his hopes sank lower and lower. Night fell. When he had been sitting in the dark for a couple of hours somebody opened his door and thrust in a rush dip, a loaf of brown bread, and a mug of weak beer; he had no more visitors that evening. It took him a long time to go to sleep; he made up dozens of different stories about how he was rescued by highwaymen, by Hanoverians, by outlaws; how he managed to escape by tearing his sheets into strips and climbing out of the window. But nobody rescued him, there were no sheets, it was a long drop to the ground, and then there were the pigs underneath; Tobit had a great dislike of pigs.

He thought of swallowing a Joobie nut. When he was little, Sannie had given him Joobie nuts to suck for toothache and there had been a fearful fascination about the things they made him see—trolls, giant bats, griffins. Then Sannie had forbidden Joobie nuts, which of course added to the excitement of sucking them. But now Sannie was not here to provoke, and he didn't fancy the kind of visions that Joobie nuts might produce in the little dark prison room. He counted sheep instead and at last fell asleep.

Next morning, not particularly early, the door opened and he was surprised to see Pelmett, who brought a loaf of brown bread and a cup of watery milk. Tobit's heart leapt up.

"Has Grandmother sent to have me let out?"

Pelmett dumped the cup and loaf on the floor, then stood regarding Tobit with folded arms and a scornful smile.

"Old Lady T? Not middling likely! You've cooked your goose with *her,* my boy—she've cut you off. There'll be no more airs and graces, Mas'r Tobit now! Yes, Sir Tobit, no, Sir Tobit, what can I fetch for you, Sir Tobit—ugh, you spoilt young twort! You'll be pulled afore the Beak this morning, and you'll be given a lifer in Botany Bay, and serve you right. All for a couple of fourpenny shubunkins!" He laughed in a sneering manner as if he knew more than he was prepared to say, picked up the empty beer mug, spat into it, and retired, slamming the door.

Presently two constables appeared and hustled Tobit into a downstairs room.

Three gentlemen were already seated there, behind a table. He recognized the Tegleaze family lawyers, and hope rose in him again. But the two old gentlemen, Pickwick and FitzPickwick, stared vacantly about as if they had not noticed him come in, while young Mr. Wily flipped through a bunch of papers, stood up, and proceeded to read aloud in a rapid gabble:

"Accused was seen to steal two shubunkin fish, worth fourpence-three-farthings, property of Miss Betsy Smith; fish were subsequently discovered in accused's pocket."

"Shocking, shocking," mumbled the two old gentlemen. One of them asked, "Where is Miss Smith now?"

"She has left town."

"Names of witnesses?" croaked the other old gentleman. They seemed half asleep, and as if they were unable to distinguish objects more than two or three feet away.

"Mrs. Aker, Mrs. Baker, Mr. Caker, Miss Daker, Mrs. Eaker, Mr. Faker—all ratepayers; a Mr. Twite, and a Mr. Mystery, who happened to be passing through the town, and Amos Frill, footman at Tegleaze Manor."

"Ah yes, mumble mumble; very respectable, Tegleaze Manor. Mumble mumble," said one of the two old men.

"And the culprit's name?"

As the younger lawyer read out Tobit's name, both constables fell into such a fit of coughing that it seemed almost impossible the old gentlemen should have heard it, but this did not seem to make any difference.

"Guilt clearly proved then," said one. "I think we are all agreed on that? Mumble mumble."

"Indeed yes, mumble," said the other. "And the sentence? Are we agreed on that?"

"Ten years in Botany Bay, I think we decided before coming in?"

Here it was young Mr. Wily's turn to cough in a reproving way.

"Did you hear, young man?" said old Mr. FitzPickwick, blinking in Tobit's direction. "You are sentenced to ten years' transportation, and we hope you are duly grateful for the leniency of your sentence."

Tobit's mouth was so dry with astonishment and dismay that he was incapable of making any reply, but nobody noticed; young Wily snapped out,

[177]

"Constables, remove him!" and he was hustled back to his cell.

"You'll be taken off on Tuesday, when a gang goes down to the convict ships at Pompey," one of the constables told him. "Ah, and am I thankful I'm not in *your* shoes!"

They dumped down his dinner—more brown bread and a bowl of weak pea soup. After that, nothing happened for a number of hours and Tobit was left to his own miserable reflections. He tried to tell himself stories about how he escaped on the way to Portsmouth; how he was rescued by smugglers, by French privateers, by pirates from the convict ship—but none of the stories rang particularly true, and even if they had, they left a lot of time ahead of him which would have to be spent in a very disagreeable manner.

By five o'clock that evening it is probable that he was the most unhappy boy in Petworth.

He was sunk in a sort of melancholy daze when he became aware of low voices having a conversation just outside his door, and the sound of coins chinking. Then the door was softly opened. Tobit, who had been staring gloomily out at the pigs, turned his head, but before he could see who had come in a neckerchief was whipped over his eyes and a noose was drawn tight over his hands. Something pricked him between the shoulder blades.

"D'you feel that?" inquired a voice in his ear. "If you want it to go another six inches in, just holler! It'd go in as easy as a knitting needle into a ball o' yarn."

Tobit prudently remained silent and was half pulled, half pushed very rapidly and, as far as he could make out, by at least two men, downstairs, out into the frosty night, a short distance over cobbles, a shorter distance over grass, and into a building that seemed large, to judge by the echoes, and had a strong, not unpleasant odor of bran, sacking, and grain. He could near a regular creaking, and the mutter of distant voices. A door slammed behind him and a bolt rattled. The cloth was removed from his face and he discovered that he was in a large, round, dimly lit room; sacks, some full, some empty, were piled against the walls; in the center was an arrangement of ropes and pulleys leading up through a hole in the high ceiling. The floor was thick with dust or flour. He realized that he must be in the windmill; the creak was the regular noise of the great sails as they went around.

A small oil lamp burned on a trestle table about ten feet from where he stood; beyond the table sat a man whose face could not at the moment be seen because he was leaning forward, looking down intently at a small object that lay between him and the light.

Presently the man raised his eyes from their gloating scrutiny and peered past the lamp. Tobit recognized the puppet master.

He spoke harshly and abruptly.

"Where's your sister, b-boy?" he demanded.

Tobit remained silent, thinking the question could not have been addressed to him.

But the man repeated impatiently.

"You have a tongue—use it, or b-by the powers, I'll d-drag it out of you. Where's your sister? Where will she have hidden herself?"

"I—I haven't got a sister!" gulped Tobit.

Here another man, who had been standing in the shadows, moved forward. So low were Tobit's spirits that he was not particularly surprised to recognize Colonel FitzPickwick. The Colonel remonstrated.

"What difference does it make where the girl is, Tegleaze—since you have the heirloom?"

These words made Tobit start forward, but he was dragged sharply back by the cord around his wrists; Pelmett and another man still stood behind him.

"I tell you, I'll have no contenders for the title!" said the man addressed as Tegleaze. "When the Hanoverians come to power I want my claim clear. The boy is to be transported—very well, *he's* out of the running. But where's the g-girl? Where has she run off t-to?" he snarled at Tobit.

"I don't know what you are talking about!"

"He never met his sister," interposed FitzPickwick again. "He did not even know she existed. But doubtless we can soon track her down. She was friendly with the pair who have just decamped from Dogkennel Cottages —she may be with them. They'll not have gone far."

"She m-must be found."

"What will you do then?" the Colonel asked uneasily.

"Ship her overseas t-too, perhaps—back to Tiburon. Or m-marry her, maybe! How can I tell till I find her?"

"I don't understand you, Tegleaze!" the Colonel exclaimed. "You are so changeable. First you were going to wait till the boy came of age so that his grandmother would get her hands on the heirloom; I could have persuaded her to part with it as with all her other geegaws, for gambling money."

"Are you so sure?" interjected the other man. "The old lady is afraid of the luck-piece—Sannie told me so. She may be too willful and scatterbrained to scruple over gambling away family jewels and money, but the heirloom is something different. She believes, Sannie told me, that it has some uncanny power—that when it is in her hands it will bring her *luck*."

"But *you* do not believe such superstitious nonsense?"

"N-no." Tegleaze seemed to hesitate. "But perhaps I do not altogether t-trust you, FitzPickwick! You might, after all, if you *had* succeeded in getting it from her, have kept the luck-piece for yourself! After all, those two old hags of yours were playing a fine double g-game. If it had not been for their suddenly producing this precious girl, I could have made my claim as heir, once Tobit was out of the count. B-but that won't be so s-simple now—even if we get rid of the g-girl people might ask awkward questions; you can d-dispatch *one* rival heir without arousing suspicion, but if there are *two*, you have to be more c-careful! Until King George is on the throne and our c-cause has triumphed I'll stay in the b-background—now I have the luck-piece I c-can afford to wait. Our f-friends will see I have my rights after we have dealt with the Wren's N-Nest."

"Well—very well. Shall I deliver the luck-piece to the

Margrave of Bad Fallingoff? He will give all the jewels in his crown to see it safe!"

"Thank-ee, FitzPickwick," the other man said dryly. "I'll take care of that little m-matter myself!"

"What about Godwit—what about payment for moving the Wren's Nest?"

"Have no fear—you can trust *me!* Tell him to set his wits to work on the matter—he will receive f-funds within the w-week."

The seated man picked up the little object that lay before him; it was slung on a thin black cord, which he proceeded to tie in a knot. His hands, while doing this, shook so violently that two or three times he nearly dropped it; it swung crazily from side to side and Tobit could not get a clear view of it, though he could guess what it was.

"I wonder you care to part with it—since it is the family treasure?" Colonel FitzPickwick said inquisitively.

"The *family?* The family that does not even know of my existence? Pah! I should like to c-crush it to dust!" the other man said with such violent anger in his voice that the Colonel took an instinctive step forward. "S-set your mind at rest, however—I shall n-not do so! After all, this little t-trifle is going to pay for our t-triumph—it will set your humble servant back in his rightful place as well as K-King George. But, C-Colonel, I detain you —you have other engagements, I am s-sure. Pray don't let me inc-inconvenience you."

The Colonel seemed reluctant to leave.

"What about the boy—you'll not harm him?"

"Pelmett and Twite shall take him back to jail—ready for export. I see you were right. He c-can tell us nothing useful. G-good night, my dear sir."

He stood up and stepped to escort Colonel FitzPickwick from the place, carelessly slinging the black cord around his neck as he did so. But the cord, insecurely tied, came unknotted, and the pendant slipped off it and fell without a sound on to the dusty floor. They exchanged a few last words at the door, then the Colonel went out and mounted a horse, which could then be heard trotting away.

"Now," Tegleaze said briskly returning. "Give Fitz-Pickwick a few minutes to get clear, then dispose of the b-boy."

"Back to the lock-up, eh?" Pelmett said with a meaning wink.

Tegleaze did not reply; Tobit felt a sudden oddness in the atmosphere.

"Who are you?" he blurted out.

"Found your t-tongue, eh?" Mr. Mystery gave Tobit a long, strange, chill stare. "Well, it won't do you much good now. And it won't do you much good to know who I am. But I'll tell you—I'm your cousin—your cousin Miles Tegleaze. Our great-great-great-grandfathers were brothers, back in Cromwell's day. Yours fought on the king's side and prospered; mine went overseas to the Americas and f-fell on hard times. So did his son and his son's son. But n-now it is *my* turn to crow."

He swung away as if the sight of Tobit fidgeted him, and studied some plans that lay on the table. "Right," he said presently without looking around, "t-take him out."

Pelmett and the man called Twite grabbed Tobit's arms again and urged him toward the door. But he tripped over an iron bolt that fastened a trap entrance in the floor and, unable to keep his balance with his arms behind him, fell flat on his face.

Just before he hit the floor he saw something to his left in the thick, floury dust: a small, round, brightly colored object—the Tegleaze luck-piece. By pushing himself sideways, as if struggling to get up, Tobit was just able to gulp it into his mouth—along with a lot of dust—before the two men dragged him upright again.

Once outside the mill they did not, as he had expected, take him back toward the jail. Instead, Twite held him, while Pelmett moved a few feet away.

"Dark as the inside of a cow," Tobit heard him mutter. "Where is the plaguy thing—Ah—" There came a strange grinding creak as if heavy metal or stone had been slowly opened or dragged to one side. With an indescribable pang of terror Tobit remembered the disused well in the windmill yard.

"Too bad about this, young feller-me-lad," muttered the man called Twite. "But orders is orders—that Mystery knows enough about me to have me strung up by the heels from Temple Bar. I'll undo your hands though —you can swim if you've a mind to."

Tobit felt the noose gently slipped from his wrists— next minute he was pushed violently forward—trod on nothing—and fell, gasping with shock and fright. The luck-piece flew out of his mouth as he fell. Something struck his arm and he made an instinctive clutch at it, first with one hand, then with the other. It was the well rope, which burnt and scraped his palms as he shot helplessly downward. Another loud grinding creak overhead told him that the well's lid had been shut above him; at the same moment his fall was checked; he came to rest on something cold and sharp that cut and bruised his knees and shins: the bucket. Tobit and the bucket together dropped a few more feet; then, apparently, the rope caught, or had come to the end of its length.

Dangling in the dark, Tobit reached out with one hand; he could feel the circular brick wall of the well all around him, nothing above or below. He found a Joobie nut in his pocket and dropped it, but could hear no splash; either the well was dry, or the water was too far down for the sound to be audible. Up above, he could see a tiny circle of night sky, about the size of a button, with a single star in it. This must be the round hole in the middle of the millstone.

"I am hanging on a bucket in a well," thought Tobit very slowly and carefully. "I don't know how deep it is, but it may be *very* deep. I daren't shout for help because the nearest person is probably that man who says he is my cousin, and he wants me to die, I suppose so he can be sure of getting Tegleaze Manor. I have lost the luck-piece, which is at the bottom of the well. The only other people who know where I am are Pelmett and that man who undid the rope. Everybody else will think

I have escaped from the jail. Grandmother has cut me off. No one will care what has happened to me."

With a tremendous effort he managed to wriggle up so that he was half kneeling on the bucket. It was difficult because the bucket swung about and tipped, and when he had changed his position the metal rim hurt his legs, but at least some of the weight was off his arms. He wondered if the rope would break.

After a while he tried to make up a story about how he was rescued from the well, but no possible story seemed to meet the case.

He began to feel painful cramps in his arms and legs, but there was no way that he could move to ease them; he could find no comfort, either for mind or body.

He had thought himself to be miserable in jail, but in comparison with his present situation the jail seemed quite a cozy, homelike place. He wondered if he could be dreaming—having a nightmare—but it was all so unlikely that he was sure it must be real. The dreams from Joobie nuts were nothing like as frightening as this.

Joobie nuts. He felt them rattling in his pocket like heavy little peas. He could chew a couple and give himself a different kind of dream—but then he would go to sleep and fall off the bucket and that would be the end of him.

Presently, for no better reason than to distract his mind from the hopelessness of his plight, he began puzzling over the talk between Tegleaze and Colonel FitzPickwick.

"Where's your sister?" Tegleaze had asked. And Fitz-Pickwick had said, "He didn't know she existed."

What could they have meant? Surely they were not talking about him?

"I haven't got a sister," Tobit repeated obstinately. After another very long pause he added,

"Have I?"

Dido, Cris, and the three Wineberry Men stood in dismay, at a loss, out by the jail, until Pip said in an urgent whisper.

"Butter my wig, boys, let's scarper! Us doesn't want to be picked up by the constables spannelling around outside the lock-up."

"He's right," said Yan. "You two liddle maids'd best get back to The Fighting Cocks, smartish. If there's kidnappers abroad 'tis time for honest folk to be under cover."

"But what'll us do about Tobit?" said Dido worriedly. "I don't trust that Mystery—*he*'d pinch the birdseed from a blind canary. What'd he want to kidnap Tobit from jail *for*?"

No one could answer this.

"I'll nip round to the Angel, where he was staying, and have a word with the landlord," said Yan. "He be my great-aunt Gertrude's godson. He'll tell me if old Mystery's stirred out lately and where he's been. You two lads, Tan and Pip, quick yourselves out o' town and get to work on tomorrow's load, I'll see you presently.

And if I pick up any news at the Angel I'll leave word with Aunt Sary."

They separated, going in three different directions. Dido and Cris started down the alley, back toward The Fighting Cocks. But Cris went slower and slower, presently stopped altogether.

"What ails you, gal?" Dido said in an impatient whisper. "Bustle on, can't you?"

"I—I feel as if Aswell were trying to say something," Cris whispered back. "But I can't quite hear—can't make out what it is. Wait—wait just a minute!"

She stood still, then turned slowly back the way they had come, like a water diviner questing for the pull of the rod.

"Oh, rummage it," Dido muttered. "This is a fine time for Aswell to feel like a chat."

Very unwillingly she followed Cris, who was now proceeding at a steady pace back along the alleyway. At the top she went left, passing the jail again, and entered a grass-grown yard at the side of a windmill. Someone was inside the mill: there was a faint rim of light around the door. Dido looked inquiringly at Cris, who shook her head.

"Hush! I can almost hear it now!" she breathed. "Why are you so faint, Aswell?"

Their eyes were used to the dark; they could see the round stone in the middle of the yard, and the wellhead. Cris moved slowly toward this, listening all the time. Dido took two or three steps after her, glancing warily around.

"*Cris!* Yan said we oughta get under cover!" she whispered urgently.

"Hush!" Cris, heedless of Dido's warning, seemed to be listening through every pore of her skin. She murmured, "I can't make it out—Aswell seems to be in trouble—"

There followed a pause which seemed nerve-rackingly long to Dido, then Cris added with the beginnings of doubt in her voice,

"*Is* it Aswell?"

At that moment something struck Dido on her wrist. She rubbed the place and whispered, "*Do* come on, gal, we dassn't stay scambling about here so near the lock-up—"

"Could Aswell be down *there?*"

Like a bird dog, Cris was pointing to the well—not with her hand, but with her whole attention.

"In the *well?* Look, Cris, it just ain't sensible to stay here—"

Two more pellets struck Dido's hand; purely by chance she caught one of them and rolled it unthinkingly between her fingers. Something about the feel and shape of it attracted her notice; she sniffed it, peered at it, tested it with the tip of her tongue. It was a Joobie nut.

"Hey! Where did that come from?"

She knelt down to look at the millstone covering the well; as she did so, a fourth nut hit her on the cheek. It had come, there was no doubt at all, through the round hole in the well lid.

"What the dickens is going on round here?" she whispered to Cris. "Surely to goodness Aswell ain't shooting Joobie nuts at us from down the well?"

Even while she said the words her mind had leapt ahead and found the explanation.

"Tobit!"

She squatted down by the stone and leaned so that her face was over the hole. A nut struck her cheek. "Hey, Tobit!" she called softly. "Are you down there, boy?"

She could feel the well's hollowness carry her voice downward.

"Yes!" An urgent whisper came echoing back. "I'm halfway down here, hanging on a bucket. Can you pull me up? Some men threw me down here. Is that Dido? Are you on your own?"

"Rabbit me, *now* what are we going to do?" Dido muttered. "We don't dare waste time hunting for Yan—how does this pesky well open up?"

She felt all over the millstone; tugged upward; it was immovable.

"They musta shifted the stone somehow to get him *in*—"

All this time Cris had been standing silent, apparently dumbstruck; now she murmured in bewilderment,

"It's *not* Aswell!"

"O' course it's not Aswell, you noddy!" whispered Dido, hauling unavailingly at the millstone. "It's your brother. It's Tobit. Give us a hand, do!"

"No, but Aswell *is* saying something now—listen! Aswell says—wait, I'm getting it—Aswell says sideways. Push the stone sideways."

"What, like this?" More than doubtful, Dido gave the stone a shove, and nearly tumbled headlong in herself as it swung around, evidently on a pivot, to reveal a black crescent-shaped hole. The loud grinding rumble it made terrified the girls; Cris ran on tiptoe around to the far side of the stone; she and Dido eased it farther around, inch by inch; even so it seemed to make a hideous row in the quiet night. It would not go all the way; feeling around, Dido discovered that the rope had somehow jammed underneath it, which was why, evidently, the bucket had stuck halfway down and broken Tobit's fall.

"Anyways, I reckon there's room for him to clamber through," she whispered to Cris. "We can't wind up the bucket, though—we'll just have to haul him up. Brace yourself, Cris! It's lucky Tobit's skinny like you."

Heaving and straining, trying to stifle their gasps, they dragged Tobit on the bucket nearer and nearer to the top. When he was only a few feet down, Dido, changing places with Cris to get a closer purchase on the rope, fell or stumbled against the millstone and contrived to loosen it so that with a loud rasping thud it shot back the final foot; the freed rope would have run back down the well but Dido flung herself on it and reached down a hand to grab Tobit. She caught his hair and he let out a yell.

"*Quiet!* Grip on my hand, boy! Cris, you hold my feet."

Somehow, all struggling together on the brink, they managed to haul him out, losing a good deal of skin in the process.

There was a noise from inside the mill. Rapid steps came toward the door and they heard the sound of bolts being drawn.

"Quick!" gasped Tobit. *"He's* in there!"

No one asked who. Without a word they flew around to the back of the mill and dropped behind a stack of old farm implements grown over with brambles.

They heard the door open and a voice shout, "Pelmett? Where the devil are you?"

Somebody ran out. There was another shout, then silence.

"They've seen the well's open," Dido guessed. "Now what'll they do? Go off into the town, most like—they'd not expect anyone to be hiding around here."

Cris, Dido, and Tobit huddled in a heap, among the nettles and the rusty harrow blades.

"Keep your breathing down, you two—try *not* to breathe, can't you!" Dido whispered.

There was no more sound from the other side of the mill.

After five minutes had gone by, Dido said,

"Guess it'd be all right to mizzle off? We'd best climb over this wall behind us and circle round. Agreeable? Tobit, give Cris a hoist over the wall, can you?"

With the utmost caution they climbed, by means of the junk heap, on to the wall, which was not very high. There was much more of a drop down on the far side, into a field; Dido realized that this was in fact the town wall.

Without speaking, Dido grabbed Cris's hand, gestured her to take that of Tobit, and led off at a silent trot, under the wall, until they came to a small copse. Striking a footpath, they turned along it, through a gate, across another field, all the time skirting around the edge of Petworth which they could see as a few twinkling lights in the distance. At last their path met another which led back toward the town; they followed this warily, ready to duck into the hedge if they heard anybody approaching. But they met no one, and the path presently brought them out beside a big house at the bottom of the High Street.

"Right," muttered Dido. "You two bide here—duck down behind them bushes if you hear anybody coming—and I'll scout on ahead and make sure all's clear. Don't either of you dare to say a word!"

8

Luckily there was no cockfight that evening, and the
yard at the rear of The Fighting Cocks Inn was empty
and dark. Before going in, Dido glanced through the
kitchen window and saw Miss Sarah Gusset knitting
socks by the fire; nobody else was in the room. Dido
slipped softly in the back door.

"There you are, then, dearie," Miss Sarah remarked
placidly, finishing off her sock and adding it to a large
heap of others. "Where's t'other little lass? And did you
find the one you went to look for?" She spoke as if
rescuing people from jail were a perfectly normal occupation.

"Yes, ma'am, we did," Dido said quietly. "They're
a-waiting outside—I was wondering where we'd best put
'em—it wouldn't do for anyone to lay eyes on 'em."

"No indeed, dearie. They'd best go in our Gentlemen's cellar, the one the Wineberry lads uses in wintertime; they'll be cozy as two mice in a nest there. Just you fetch them in, poor little scrumplings—I daresay you can all do with a bowl of my soup."

Reassured by this calm welcome, Dido went off to fetch her companions. Halfway down the High Street an alley led in from the left. Just as Dido reached its entrance, a man came hurrying out of it; unable to check herself in time, she ran straight into him.

"Croopus, I'm sorry, mister—" she began, and then, getting a sudden glimpse of his face by the glimmer of a street lantern, "Why, it's *Pa!*"

The man's mouth fell open in utter dismay. "Great fish swallow us, it can't be Dido?" he muttered, gave her a hunted look, and made off at top speed up the hill.

Dido stared after him for a moment, biting her knuckle. But the first need was to get Tobit and Cris under cover; she went on down the hill. When she reached the point at which she had left them they were not to be seen. She gave a soft whistle.

"All clear, it's me—Dido!"

After a pause, long enough for her to grow anxious, Tobit and Cris crept out from behind two bay trees in tubs that ornamented the closed front of a greengrocer's shop.

"That man came by," Tobit whispered nervously. "I think he was hunting for me."

"Humph," Dido muttered to herself. "Here's a fine start. How's my pa got muxed up in this?" But aloud she was encouraging: "There was a chap, but he's gone —went off up the hill. Come on now—look sharp!"

Silently as three fish in a river they ran up the High Street and around to the back of The Fighting Cocks. Miss Sarah was waiting at the back door to let them in.

"That's the dandy," she said comfortably. "Come you down into the cellar now, while there's no folk about."

An iron spike with a side of bacon hanging from it stuck out of the bricks on one side of the big kitchen fireplace. Miss Sarah gave this a sharp tug; a large section of bricks opened outward like a door, revealing a narrow flight of stone steps.

"Take this rush dip, sweetheart, and go you down," Miss Sarah told Dido. "I put the soup on the hob and I've a pair of beds a-warming—I daresay the liddle 'uns'll be middling weary." She spoke as if Tobit and Cris were about six years old and gave them a kindly smile. "Then, when you've settled 'em, dearie, you come up and tap twice to be let out—I know you'll be wanting to have a look at your Cap'n. He's no different, but seems comfortable. Oh, just take the socks as you're a-going down, lovey, will you—I try to keep those Wineberry chaps socked up regular, their poor feet do get so wet."

The brick door closed behind them.

After descending about twenty winding steps they found themselves in a dry, brick-paved, brick-vaulted cellar which was so large that Dido guessed it must extend under the house next door as well as the inn kitchen. At the far end were about forty massive casks, labeled Sack, Rhenish, Canaries, Oporto, etc.; there were also bales of tobacco, crates of corkscrews and clay pipes, and half a dozen fourteen-quart kegs of brandy. Ten hammocks were slung from the ceiling, neatly made up with patchwork quilts; from two of them the handles of copper warming pans protruded. Ten seats, made from sawn-off sections of tree trunk, were ranged in front of a small but hot fire which burned in a kind of hollow pillar, open at one side, in the middle of the room; evidently its chimney ran up into that of the kitchen fireplace in the room above. A pot of soup stood on the hob.

"Jeeminy, this is snug," Dido said with approval. "It's a sight better than jail, *or* Mother Lubbage's parlor, hey, Cris?" Cris gazed around wonderingly; so did Tobit. Then Dido recollected something.

"Oh, Cris, this here's your brother Tobit; Tobit, meet your sis; reckon you ain't hardly had a chance to look at each other yet."

There followed a silence while they did so and Dido added with friendly impatience, "Well—go on! Don't you want to *say* summat to one another?"

It seemed they did not. They stared and stared. Tobit twisted a lock of his hair around his finger; Cris sucked a finger and rubbed it against the collar of her sheepskin jacket. At last Dido said, "Well, if you don't feel like talking, best eat," and ladled soup into earthenware bowls. Tobit gulped his down ravenously; Cris almost forgot to eat, watching every movement he made. Still neither of them spoke.

"Rumple me," Dido thought. "If I'd only just met my brother for the first time I'd have a sight more to say, I reckon. What a rum pair they are!" She stacked the soup bowls, put a couple of logs on the fire, and added aloud,

"Sweet dreams, then, mates. Us'll talk about plans in the morning. Now, don't you go a-making any ruckus, or chattering all night. Those is your hammocks a-warming. I'd best go and look after my Cap'n now."

She left, feeling that the silence behind her was closing and thickening, and becoming colored, like water into which a brilliant dye is slowly being poured; she had the fancy that if she turned and tried to go down the stairs again she would find it almost impossible to push her way.

When she had tapped twice and been let out by Miss Sarah, she went up to the attic and hung anxiously over Captain Hughes. His condition was unchanged, but he certainly seemed peaceful enough, and appeared to have been tidied up a good deal.

"I took off all those nasty old cobwebs," Miss Sarah explained, "and wrapped him up from head to toe in brandy leaves; that's why he smells so medical."

"What's brandy leaves, missus?"

"Lily leaves soaked in brandy; my old mother always used to say they'd cure any trouble but a broken heart. Now don't you fret about him, dearie, we'll get him better one way or another. My stars! He's a fine-looking fellow, isn't he—handsome as a herring. Yan sent a message to say he'd be round in the banquet hall at screech o' dawn for a confabulation. He went to the Angel but could get no news, he said to tell you. So you'd best get a bit o' sleep yourself. I had to put you in the loft, as all our guest rooms are full, but you'll sleep as soft as a silkworm there, for that's where the owlers keep their packs."

"What's owlers, ma'am?" Dido asked, as Miss Sarah opened a small trap door over the attic stairs, which led to the roof.

"Wool smugglers, dearie."

And indeed Dido discovered that all the space between the joists was packed with wool to a depth of several feet, so that it was like sleeping on a marvelously thick, springy mattress the size of a whole room. She burrowed herself a nest and lay in luxury. She could hear genuine owls calling, among the chimney pots outside; the owl hoots changed imperceptibly into the chattering of starlings, and she found that splinters of light were making their way between the tiles and that Miss Sarah had stuck her head through the trap door and was calling softly,

"Morning time, love! There's a bowl o' porridge keeping hot for you in the kitchen!"

While Dido gulped down her porridge, Miss Sarah, busy frying twenty eggs for the inn guests, said,

"I'll see to the Cap'n presently, don't you fret your head about him. And I reckon the liddle 'uns down below can sleep a bit longer yet; I've not heard chirp nor cheep from them. You can take down their break-fastses when you come back from seeing my nevvy Yan."

So Dido slipped out to the banquet hall and found Yan Wineberry already there, carving a whistle from an elder twig. His brown face looked less cheerful than usual and he greeted Dido soberly.

"I've not been able to find out anything about the boy, my duck. That Tegleaze be missing too—" he was beginning, when Dido, first glancing cautiously about the big empty room, whispered,

"Hush! It's all rug, we got him!"

"Nay! You never!"

As Dido described the mysterious way in which Cris had discovered, without being told, that Tobit was down the well, he looked more and more astonished.

"Well! That beats cockfighting!" he said at length. "I'd allus heard as twins was a bit uncanny and could understand each other wi'out talking but I never heard naught to equal that! And fancy you two liddle things being able to shove that gurt stone back and wrastle him out—he'd a bin drowned for sure by now, if you hadn't. That well be a hundred foot deep, easy. Who put him down there?"

"He just said some men. He and Cris was both a bit dumbstruck when I got 'em back here last night. But I reckon as how it was old Mystery."

Yan nodded. "Cousin Will said he'd not been back to the Angel all night, nor that mate of his, the fellow who plays the hoboy. They must still be out, searching for the boy—guessed he'd climbed outa the well when they saw the top shoved back, I daresay."

"What can we do with Tobit and Cris?" Dido said. "They can't stop in your aunt Sary's cellar forever."

"I've been thinking about that, duck. I reckon it'd be best if they came up to London with us, on our run."

"Croopus," said Dido, somewhat taken aback. But then she began to see that this was a sensible suggestion. "It'd keep them out o' trouble here for sure; and no one'd be looking for them in London. But what about on the way—how can you keep them hid?"

"We're all hid together, duckie—'tis a secret way we go, see?"

"And what happens when you get there?"

"Well," Yan said, "they could stop with my auntie Grissie in Wardrobe Court, where we always puts up; she'd keep an eye on 'em. And I was thinking—we always takes a load o' corkscrews and two-three tubs of Hollands to Sir Percy Tipstaff—he's the Lord Chief Justice, you know—I could tell him as how there'd been a frame-up on young Tobit. Sir Percy knows I'm a trustable chap—I reckon he'd pay heed to me."

"Oh, Yan!" Dido hugged him warmly. "That's a prime plan. It's no use talking to old Lady Tegleaze or any of the nobs down here—the ones as hasn't a screw loose is all in it together, thick as gutter mud."

"And I'll take your letter to Lord Forecastle too."

"I wish I could come along," Dido said wistfully.

"You're kindly welcome, my duck."

"No, I'd best stay with poor old Cap'n Hughes. And

if I'm seen about the town, Mr. Mystery and Sannie and the rest of 'em'll likely think that Tobit and Cris are still stowed here too, and that'll put 'em off the scent."

Yan agreed with this.

"But you take care of *your*self, lovey," he cautioned her. "Don't you go getting chucked down a well."

"I'm fly!" said Dido. "No one's liable to sneak up on me 'thout my hearing 'em. Now, where should Tobit and Cris come—where do you start your run?"

"We meets at the Cuckoo Tree. The ten-shilling men pick up the stuff at Appledram Camber and fetch it so far—then five of us takes it on to London."

"Cris and Tobit better not go back to the Cuckoo Tree now old goody Lubbage knows that's where Cris used to go."

"No," Yan agreed. "I reckon they'd best get the carrier's cart to Pulborough—my uncle Ned's the driver, he'll take 'em hid inside a pair o' cider barrels or summat—get off at the White Hart pub by Stopham Bridge, and one of us Wineberry chaps'll meet 'em there. And you give them Cap'n Hughes's letter and I'll see it's delivered."

This sounded like a watertight plan, but still Dido hesitated.

"Which day d'you reckon to get to London?"

"Tuesday—if we don't have too many deliveries along the way."

"Suppose there was trouble here—spose summat went

wrong and I wanted to get in touch with you afore you got to London?"

"There's three pubs along the way where I'll ask for a message: the Rose at Run Common, the Ring o' Bells at Ripley, and the Rising Sun in Wandsworth."

"The Rose, the Ring, and the Rising Sun—that's easy to remember. And you'll take mortal good care o' the Cap'n's Dispatch, won't you—I've a notion it's someway connected wi' the coronation, and that's why the Cap was so desperate anxious to get it there the day before."

"Don't you worrit—I'll keep it locked up, along o' the Lord Mayor's dallop of tea and the Lady Mayoress's pipkin of pink lemon perfume," he promised.

"And if so be as you're chatting with old Lord Forecastle," Dido said, "could you ask him to send a decent doctor down here? That Subito's too scared of Mother Lubbage to be any more use than a pastry pickaxe."

Yan said he would see to it.

That seemed to take care of everything. "I'll be getting back then," Dido said, and slipped into the alley, looking vigilantly all around her. After a cautious interval, Yan followed her.

Dido carried bowls of porridge down to Cris and Tobit. They were awake, and seemed quite content with each other's company, but still could not, or need not, talk together. They had gone back to their old occupation of staring at one another's faces.

Dido, finding their silence rather fidgeting, asked Tobit how he had come to be in the well, and he told her the whole tale.

"So it *was* old Mystery—and he's your cousin from furrin parts. No wonder he likes to come a-sneaking around Tegleaze after cockshut, measuring the flower-beds and sizing up the pigsties," Dido said thoughtfully. "But what a murksy set-out to push you down the well. Anyway I bet he's in a proper taking now—a-looking for you right, left, and rat's ramble. And you say the luck-piece fell down the well too?"

"I should think it must have. And so far as I care, it can stay there—Grandmother was only waiting for me to come of age so she could get hold of it and sell it for gambling money, my cousin wants it to sell to the Margrave of Bad Somewhere to pay for a Hanoverian plot—and it's never done *me* any good."

Dido was inclined to agree.

"Anyhow it can bide there for the time—nobody but us knows it's there, reckon it's safe enough." She chuckled. "I'll lay old Mystery's tearing out his hair in handfuls wondering where it's got to—he probably reckoned *you* made off with it."

"Well, so I did," said Tobit proudly.

Dido had observed a change in him since his adventure. It was hard to put into words, but he seemed more sensible, less given to play-acting and senseless dares.

She explained the plan in regard to Uncle Ned and the carrier's cart and the trip to London. Tobit's eyes certainly brightened at the thought of perhaps being able to see the coronation after all, but he was not so

wildly excited as Dido had thought he would be; while Cris seemed very little interested in the prospect.

"The cart don't pass here till dusk, so you'll have to stay down here for the day. You'd better play cat's cradle or summat—you can't just sit *staring* all day."

Neither Tobit nor Cris knew how to play cat's cradle; Dido pulled a length of string out of her pocket and instructed them, looping it over Tobit's hands, crossing it, and showing Cris how to take hold of the crisscrosses, pull them under and out, and so make a new framework. In no time they had got the hang of it and were completely absorbed.

Dido dumped a log on the fire and went upstairs, feeling rather lonely.

I wish I *was* a-going up to London with them and the Wineberry Men, and not staying here in this spooky little town, she thought enviously. And don't I just hope the Fust Lord of the Admiralty sends back some decent doctor as can put the poor old Cap'n to rights.

It was another driply foggy day; twilight came early, long before the arrival of Uncle Ned. During the afternoon Dido helped Uncle Jarge and his son Ted pack Tobit and Cris into sacks, with handfuls of wool and all the smugglers' socks Miss Sarah had knitted to stuff out the crannies so that they looked like a load of grain or seed. Then Uncle Ted arrived in his ancient covered wagon drawn by a spavined gray mare who went along so slowly that her driver never bothered to stop her, but simply loaded and unloaded as she wandered along. The canvas cover was pulled aside, the two sacks were placed on the cart. Dido did not dare call good-bye, as two or three other people were hoisting goods on at the same time, so she gave each sack a friendly pat under pretext of settling them in place, and jumped down on to the cobbles again.

"Eh, dear," she thought. "I do hope Cap'n Hughes's Dispatch will really be all right."

She had given it to Tobit, with strict instructions to hand it over to Yan Wineberry as soon as they were alone together.

"Jub on, mare," said Uncle Ned, the mare plodded slowly on up the hill, and Dido went off to Wm. Pelmett, Chymist, to get some more treacle, since Captain Hughes had finished the first gallon. The apothecary's shop was open for an hour on Sunday evenings, for the sale of treacle and cough jujubes, because so many people made themselves hoarse singing hymns in church.

"I can see you've a sweet tooth, missie," said Mr. Pelmett, handing her the treacle with a gluey smile.

Dido gave him a scowl in return.

As she was carrying the heavy jar up the High Street she caught a glimpse, in the distance, of a lanky, familiar figure, just turning left in the direction of the church.

"I'll not lose him twice!" Dido vowed. Thrusting the jar of treacle into the arms of a startled small boy she told him to carry it to The Fighting Cocks Inn and ask Miss Sarah for a spoonful.

"Say I said you was to have one!" And she made off at top speed in pursuit of the retreating figure. As he had not seen her and did not realize she was after him, she was able to dodge swiftly around the block and so meet him face to face in front of the church.

"Hello, Pa dear!" she greeted him affably. "Ain't you a-going to speak to me? Your own little Dido? How's Ma? And Penny-lope?"

Mr. Twite—for it was undoubtedly Dido's father—would have turned and run once again, but his daughter had him firmly by the jacket buttons.

"Now, Pa! Don't you try and scarper! Jigger it, some dads would be *pleased* to see their child as had been twice round the world and given up for drownded. Come and sit down on a tombstone and tell us the family news."

"Why, there's none that I know of, my chickadee. Indeed, for the last year or so I have been a happy man, free from family afflictions." But seeing there was no help for it, he allowed her to lead him to a dry tombstone behind a hollybush in the churchyard, where they could talk unobserved. "Your dear lamented mother was lost to us when Battersea Castle blew up—so was your aunt Tinty and your cousins—your sister eloped with a very ineligible young fellow who traveled in buttonhooks—and *I* am under the painful necessity of supplying hoboy music for a strolling puppet troupe, since the Bow Street runners conceived a wholly unjustified suspicion that I was in some way connected with the Battersea Castle explosion."

"Swelp me," said Dido. "The whole family's gone, then?" She was not particularly cast down, since her mother had never been at all fond of her. "But what about Simon? And our house in Rose Alley?"

"Sold, sold, alas—or so I understand, not having been able to inquire personally—to pay some few trifling debts. So I have not even a home to offer you. As to Simon— the young boy who used to lodge with us?—I really cannot say." Mr. Twite sighed. He pulled a hoboy from the front of his waistcoat and played a few melancholy notes on it, then, becoming enthusiastic, launched out into a spirited jig.

"Ah," said Dido, "I suspicioned it was you playing, soon as I heard the hoboy tuning up for old Mystery's Mannikin show. So you're Mystery's mate, are you? How long've you been with him, Pa?"

"Why, but a few weeks, child. I was introduced to him by a most respectable gentleman, a Colonel Fitz-Pickwick. I understand Mr. Mystery has only recently come from one of our delightful colonies."

"And is already up to his whiskers in a plot to pinch Tegleaze Manor and put Bonnie Prince Georgie on the throne, helped by those old witches and that dicey pair o' footmen; Pa, Pa," said Dido sorrowfully, "why *will* you let yourself get imbrangled with such a jammy-fingered set o' coves? It's sure to lead to trouble."

"Not if we succeed, my dove; it'll be all garnets and gravy then, and Sir Desmond Twite, conductor at Sadlers Wells, and a house in Cheyne Walk."

"But you won't succeed, Pa."

"Oh? And why not, my sprite?" Mr. Twite gave her a sharp look.

Dido was tempted to tell him that the Tegleaze luck-piece, which was to have paid for the conspiracy, had been dropped in a well, but she resisted the urge. She said,

"Stealing may be respectable in your circles, Pa, but attempted murder ain't going to be so easy to laugh off."

"Humph," muttered Mr. Twite. "I wondered, when I came back and found the well stone had been pushed aside, if your little meddling hands had been at work. I had the devil of a job to get it back. So the boy *did* escape, did he?"

"Some trustable chaps as I know of are on their way to London this minute to lay an information about the whole affair before the Lord Chief Justice," Dido went on, impressively. "So if I was you, Pa, I'd mizzle while the mizzling's good."

"Oh, ho!" said Mr. Twite gaily, not a bit impressed. "But suppose I told *you*, my dear little chickadee, that some trustworthy chaps *I* know are perfectly informed about *your* trustworthy chaps and plan to get their information off them and destroy it before they reach London. Hey, dee, marathon me, what a set of simple souls those Jacobites be!" he hummed.

Dido gaped at him, utterly taken aback by this news.

"Yes, yes," Mr. Twite went on agreeably, "our friend Mystery—ah, there's a clever spark for you—got an equally clever old lady called Mrs. Lubbage to find out through some timid-hearted relative of one of those gallant Wineberry Men all about their so-called secret route to London. Unknown to the Preventive Men, maybe, but not to us; a concealed canal, I understand, all the way from the Arun River to the Thames, along which the barge of contraband plies its worthy way. With *one* extra crew member on board, ho ho, snug between the lavender water and the Lapsang Souchong and the spirits of licorice! So this famous Dispatch will vanish before it ever reaches London; and by Thursday, you know, it won't matter if *twenty* Lord Chief Justices know about the affair, it will be too late; too late, too late, too late, to retaliate," he sang joyously.

> "Sir Christopher Wren
> Let fall his goosefeather pen
> But, he said, whatever else falls
> It won't be St. Paul's.

Ah me, ah me, even the best of us are sometimes faulty in our judgments, are we not?"

"Sir Christopher Wren?" said Dido slowly. "The Wren's Nest?"

Mr. Twite suddenly stopped short in his caroling.

"You didn't know that, then, my duckling? Well, as it's too late now to prevent it, I'll strike a bargain with you. I will unfold to you the whole Wren's Nest project —ah, and what a startlingly sublime and sweepingly satisfactory scheme it is—in return for one small piece of information which doubtless you have at your clever little fingertips. What has become of that volatile pair, the youthful Tegleaze heir and his bewitching twin, like as one pin to another pin? Oh where and oh where can they be, with their noses turned up and their toes turned out, afloat on the bonnie blue sea? Or words to that effect," he added, suddenly darting another sharp look at his daughter.

But Dido was hardly heeding him.

"I couldn't say where they are, Pa, I'm sure," she truthfully replied.

"Oh, well, in that case, no cash, no crumpet."

"That's right," Dido said inattentively. "I must go, Pa, my Cap'll be wanting a dose of treacle."

"Indeed, indeed, the gallant Dispatch bearer. Poor fellow, what a misfortune that his coach should overturn, and he on his way to town with tidings of such urgent import."

"So long, Pa." As impatient to leave him as she had been to question him, Dido gave her father a hasty nod and almost ran in the direction of The Fighting Cocks. Had she looked back she would have seen him staring thoughtfully after her. But she did not look back.

9

Dido was panting and breathless when she arrived back at The Fighting Cocks Inn.

"Gracious, dearie, what's amiss?" inquired Miss Sarah, placidly stirring a caldron of soup with a spoon in one hand while she rotated five sizzling chickens on a spit with the other.

"Miss Sarah, I've got to get arter those Wineberry chaps at once! There's a spy among 'em that's going to pinch the Cap's Dispatch!"

"Eh, dear, there's a fanteague. Who could that be, I wonder?" Miss Sarah, still unruffled, basted her chickens, took a china mug down off the mantelshelf, and counted out five gold guineas from it. "Well, that Dapple horse is still there eating his head off in our stable, they've never sent for him from the Dolphin, so you'd best take him. Here's a bit o' cash—it never comes amiss."

"The Cap'n—" Dido began.

"Bless your heart, don't you worrit about him, dearie, I'll see to him as careful as if he was my Hannibal that was struck by lightning in a rowboat full of corkscrews, fifteen year last Michaelmas. Terrible fierce thunderstorms we had in those parts when I was a girl. Ah, it's a hard profession being a Gentleman."

Dido ran up to have a last look at the Captain, who seemed to be having pleasant dreams, lapped in his brandied lily leaves.

"Wrap up warm against the sea fret now," warned Miss Sarah when she came down. "Do you know where to go?"

"To the White Hart Inn?"

"That's it, but don't you cross the river. There's an old narrow bridge they call Stopham Bridge; *you* stop on this side, and follow the river upstream. Then you'll come to where the secret canal begins—"

"How be as it's so secret, ma'am?"

"Well, you see, dearie, it's a long way from any highroad, running through the farmers' fields. O' course the farmers knows about it, but they don't reckon to mention it, not when they finds a keg of Bergamo Water or two-three corkscrews in the hay barn now and again. And the canal's all grown over with maybushes, right the whole way up, so you'd hardly notice it was there. Ah, dear, in May month it surely is a pretty way to go to London, a-gliding along under the maybushes and a-listening to the nightingales sing—many's the time I've done it with my Hannibal in bygone days. Well, when you find the canal, 'tis easy enough; all you've to do is follow along till you come up with the barge, the *Gentlemen's Relish* she's called; she doesn't go faster than mule pace, it shouldn't take you that long to catch up with her. If you meet anybody, just you say Yan, Tan, Tethera, Methera, and they'll know you're on Gentlemen's business and not hinder you."

"I'm obliged to you, ma'am. And I'll pay back the dibs as soon as I can—or work it off helping you in the kitchen."

"Ah, pshaw, child, run along with you."

Dapple was not pleased to be harnessed and ridden off along the Pulborough road on a foggy November night, but he had been well fed and rested in the stable of The Fighting Cocks; he went briskly and biddably enough, through the little village of Fittleworth, up a long hill, and then down a winding road through evergreen woods. Now Dido began to smell water; they were coming into a valley. Ahead of her the road curled around and she could just make out a narrow stone bridge spanning the misty river; on the far side glowed the lighted windows of the White Hart pub.

"Keep on this side, Miss Sarah said. Us wants a gate, Dapple." Dido reined him in, and walked him along, searching for a way into the water meadows; with her head turned to the left she never heard quick soft footsteps; never heard a rope whistle through the air; the first thing she knew was that a noose dropped over her,

tightening sharply and jerking her from Dapple's back.
That was the last thing she knew, too; she fell, helplessly, her head thudded against the road's stony surface,
and the dark fog seemed to rush in through her eyes,
nose, and ears.

The party on board the *Gentlemen's Relish* were carefree enough. She was a forty-foot barge, with a galley
bigger than the bar parlor of The Fighting Cocks, and
below that, a series of roomy holds, packed now with
corkscrews, orris root, eau de cologne, eau de vie, eau
de nil, and spirits of licorice; in fact she smelt like a
mixture between a scent factory and a distillery as she
glided along, drawn by Moke and Choke, a pair of mules
who picked their careful way up the towpath, heads
lowered to avoid the overhanging red-berried, rusty-
leaved branches of the hawthorn trees.

"Well, yes, 'tis a bit okkerd, the hogo," Yan agreed
when Tobit remarked on the smell. "That's why we
likes to come canal-way because it's fine and far from
the turnpike. In springtime, o' course, no one'd be like
to notice, because o' the scent o' the may-blow, but at
this time o' year it *is* a bit remarkable."

There were five Wineberry Men on the boat, looking
after cargo and navigation: Yan, Tan, Tethera, and
Methera (who were brothers) and Pip, recently rescued
from jail. The other five, Yan explained, did the ten-
shilling run from the sea to the Cuckoo Tree.

"But o' course we all shares the profits; 'tis a grand
steady line o' trade."

"Don't you have adventures?" said Tobit, disappointed.

"Not if we can help it, my duck," said Yan, grinning. "That's why we keeps the paddlequacks, see?" Tobit and Cris had wondered why there were so many ducks on board: half a dozen different families, all with broods of lanky pin-feathered ducklings. "There be naught to equal a paddlequack for a night watchman; rouse up if a stranger comes within a hundred yards, they will."

"What do you do then?" Tobit asked, all agog.

"Why, we rummage off, right smart; up the bank and away."

"And just leave the boat and cargo?" Tobit thought this very poor-spirited. "I'd stay and fight!"

"Nay, that'd be right ardle-headed," remonstrated Tethera, a bony redhead, who spoke little but seemed extremely devoted to, and popular with the ducks; whenever he sat down, as many as could find room came and perched on him. "What's the *ship*, what's the *cargo*? Uncle Samson, in Appledram Camber, he'd allus fettle us up another barge; and we can allus get us another cargo; but it ain't so easy to get another *us*."

A slow smile broke over the face of Cris. She, like Tethera, played little part in the long, lazy conversations, but she enjoyed listening, and the ducks had taken to her at once, too; she had a brood of parti-colored ducklings now, scrabbling for the warm place under her chin. Bunches of red-leaved thorn twigs and swags of golden bracken were fastened thickly all over the decks and cabin of the *Gentlemen's Relish*, to help her merge into the background as she floated along; Cris and the ducks had burrowed themselves a kind of nest in the bracken, and there they were all snuggled together in the mild November sun.

Pip and Tethera jumped ashore and mounted Moke and Choke (whose real names were Mercy and Charity) to encourage them to amble along a little faster; Tan and Methera went below to re-stow some of the corkscrew cargo, which had worked loose and was clanking. Yan sat in the stern steering, when it was needful, playing on his devil's box, or harmonium, in between times, and softly singing old songs—"The Milkmaid of Wisborough Green," "Sweet Sally of Smock Alley," and a very aged ditty that seemed to consist principally of the words,

> "Eh! how they do bound about
> At Roundabout."

"How about a game of cat's cradle?" Tobit said to Cris.

She nodded, and pulled a length of string from her pocket. They had hardly spoken since leaving Dido; after coming aboard the previous evening, they, with the rest of the crew, had been busy for a couple of hours, fastening down the cargo, then Yan had shown them a pair of sweet-scented little cabins between the orris root and the eau de cologne, where they had slept in bracken-lined bunks, until called on deck for a breakfast of brown bread, scrambled duck eggs, and licorice tea.

After they had been playing for a while, Tobit said, "D'you know what? It's our birthday!"

"So it is!"

"We're of age!"

They both thought this very funny. Cris, leaning back and looking up at the gleams of sunshine coming through as they moved along under red hawthorn leaves, said,

"I didn't even know what coming of age meant, this time last week."

Presently Tobit said,

"Do you remember me at all?"

She shook her head.

"Or the place where we were born?"

"No."

"I didn't think *I* did, but since I've seen you I'm beginning to. I can remember a pair of big iron gates, and two rows of trees with moss on them. There was a fountain."

"Why," said Cris slowly, "*so* there was. And a big white house with balconies—wasn't there a sandy track under the trees? They used to put us there in our wicker cradles—"

"That's right!" said Tobit excitedly. "And once—there was a snake in the sand—"

"And our father came and killed it!"

"He was a big man with a black beard."

"He used to sing—he used to sing a song about the

moon and a mockingbird," said Cris, frowning with effort as she dragged the memory from some nearly closed cupboard in her mind. Then she added rather slowly, "Can you remember our mother?"

Tobit thought for a minute.

"A yellow dress?"

"Yes! And a necklace of big orange beads. I used to bite them when my gums were sore."

"Father used to hold us both at the same time, one in each arm."

"Oh," said Cris—she was crying a bit, "what happened to them? Why aren't they here?"

"There was a storm—a very bad storm."

"So there was. First it was hot—and a lot of crabs came—"

"And the wind blew like a scream that went on and on."

"All the trees fell down."

"The house fell down too."

"I don't want to remember any more." Cris rubbed her eyes. "It's too miserable."

"They got killed in the storm," Tobit said soberly. "I can remember someone saying. They were out in the carriage. We were in the cellar with Tante Sannie so we were all right."

"Horrible old Tante Sannie. Why didn't I remember that?"

"She wasn't horrible then. It was only in England that she turned horrible."

"We used to have a parrot that sat on a perch."

"That's right—so we did! Mother used to give it bits of orange peel."

"Father named it when someone gave it to us—he called it—he called it—"

"Polygot!" said Tobit triumphantly. They beamed at one another. Then, remembering something Tethera had said half an hour before, he added, "I tell you what, Cris, it's miserable that Father and Mother were killed in the storm, but aren't we lucky to have found *us!*"

Dido was unconscious a long time. When she began to take notice again, she found that she was lying on a damp stone floor listening to voices which apparently were discussing her future.

"Polish off the little canker, *I* say. Drop her in the river," suggested one voice, which Dido recognized, with little enthusiasm, as that of Mrs. Lubbage.

"Is much best," agreed Tante Sannie's voice. "Isn't no more trouble from her then."

"Here, hold hard!" protested a man—Dido's father. "The individual you allude to in this utilitarian way is my own chick—the youngest living sprig on the tree of Twite. Consider a father's feelings, I beg!"

"Does she know about the Wren's Nest?" That was Colonel FitzPickwick.

"She says not. She appears ignorant of the matter."

"So, once that meddlesome Captain's Dispatch is destroyed, she can't give a warning?"

"No."

"Oh well, in that case, all we need do is leave her trussed up here for two days—that will serve our turn. Wind an extra length of cord about her wrists and secure her to the pillar."

Dido was dragged a few feet across gritty ground; her wrists were jerked out in front of her and made fast to a post. Nevertheless she went on resolutely keeping her eyes shut.

At this moment she heard footsteps.

"Who's that?" said Colonel FitzPickwick sharply. "Oh, it's you, Godwit. What kept you, man? Have you the levers—the machinery? Are you ready to start?"

"No I haven't, and I'm not, and I'm not coming," replied a thin, dry voice—Dido instantly recalled the wrinkled little ironmonger and conspirator in his rimless glasses.

"*What*'s that? Not *coming*? What the deuce has got into you? Explain yourself, man!"

"I supplied rollers as per specification. I installed them by night, encountering difficulties which would make—which would make a *camel* weep," said Godwit. "Have I been paid? I have not—bar a mere pittance. Now you ask me to do this other job which is a difficult job and a highly risky job. Very well, I say. Where's the money for the rollers? Where's the money for the next job? Any more work I undertake on behalf of you and your colleagues is strictly cash in advance."

Colonel FitzPickwick let out an oath.

"I tell you, Godwit, the money's as good as in the bank. Tegleaze has gone to sell the miniature to the

Margrave of Bad Fallingoff. He will be back anytime this next seven days."

"That wasn't what *I* heard," said Godwit. "*I* heard as how he'd scarpered from the Angel leaving his luggage and without paying his score, and it was thought he'd pocketed the Tegleaze luck-piece and gone back to the Americas. That's the talk in the town."

"Rubbish, man!" Colonel FitzPickwick spoke with forced confidence. "Twite here will say that's a pack of moonshine, won't you, Twite. You'll pay the score at the Angel, won't you, Twite?"

"Not pesky likely!" replied Mr. Twite. "What, when that unfeeling Mystery required me to sleep in the stable along with those heathen mannikins—*me*, an artist on the hoboy as has played before all the margraves and pagraves of Europe in my palmier days? No, if Mystery has really snudged off, I'm clearing off too; unless you're wishful to pay the month's wages he owed me, Colonel?"

"Don't be ridiculous, man; of course you will be paid in full when our cause triumphs."

"If I had an ounce of flour for every time I'd heard *that*," muttered Twite, "I'd be able to make a birthday cake the size of the Houses of Parliament. No, friends and colleagues, this is where Twite says good night. I like plots as is carried on businesslike and money down; none o' this havey-cavey cabbing around on credit. You a-going back to Petworth, Mr. Godwit? I'll ask the favor of a lift in your conveyance."

There was a long silence after the two men had left.

The Colonel began cursing in an undertone. "Flay, spike, and hamstring that Mystery. I wonder if he *has* made off with the luck-piece. If so, what'll we do? By the great Coolin, it's enough to make a man become a —a fishmonger; to have the whole project so near coming off, and then to be at a stand for want of a bit of motive power!"

"Me and Sannie could do your little job for you, Colonel," said Mrs. Lubbage softly. "Us doesn't need all that gurt old machinery and levers. All us needs is *folk*, hey, Sannie?"

Sannie didn't answer in words, but she gave a little chuckle that made Dido's hair prickle.

"*Could* you now?" said the Colonel thoughtfully. "Could you really?"

"Ah, we could! We could make a right avick as'd finish off King Dick for ye once and for all. And the only pay we'd want'd be a passage to Tiburon—"

"On a great white ship a-sailing, sailing—"

"Over the white waves and the black waves—"

"With us a-wrapped in silk satin—"

"Well, well, I daresay that could be arranged without undue trouble," the Colonel said hastily.

"It better had," Mrs. Lubbage muttered. "Or who's to say our fine Colonel won't end up in the same mizmaze as old piecrust-promises Mystery?"

"What's that, you old hag?" the Colonel said sharply. "What do you know about Mystery?"

"Why, nothing, Colonel, nothing! He be in Bad Fallingoff, you said so your own self!"

"Humph!" the Colonel grunted, sounding only half satisfied. "Well, wherever he is, *we* had best start for London without delay. There is no time to be lost. I left my carriage at the White Hart yonder. I'll tell them to set-to new horses, and will expect you in ten minutes."

"Us'll have to go back to Petworth, Colonel-mister," said Sannie. "For to get Mystery's mannikin box."

"What d'you want that for? How do you know he has not taken it with him?"

"He not take it, no, no," Sannie said chuckling. "He not need mannikins where he be now, in Bad Fallingoff. Those mannikins a-waiting in Angel stable, a-lying so still. Those mannikins like to play new game, old Sannie teach to play new game."

Lying on the wet stone floor Dido was cold already, but Sannie's tone made her feel even colder.

"Right; back to Petworth and pick up the puppets. What about the girl; should she not be gagged?"

"No need; old Sannie put her to sleep directly."

Oh no you don't, missus, Dido thought.

"Ten minutes, then." The Colonel left.

"Open eyes, dearie! Old Sannie knows you not be asleep."

Despite her intention not to, Dido opened her eyes. She was in a curious little octagon room, quite bare and empty. It had small windows in each of its eight walls, and an iron pillar in the middle, to which she was tied. Beyond the open door she could see weeping willows, and the river flowing. But in front of her stood

Mrs. Lubbage and Tante Sannie with their four eyes fixed on her like four glittering metal skewers.

"Now, miss!" The face of Mrs. Lubbage was red and shiny and gleeful. She looked as if she had been given a splendid birthday present. "Where's Cris and Tobit? You'd best tell us or you'll be turble sorry, I can promise ee."

"*That* I won't!" said Dido stoutly. But her heart sank at the expression on their faces.

"You like spiders?" Sannie asked softly. "You like spiders come and climb on you?"

Spiders happened to be things that Dido particularly disliked. But she shrugged, in what she hoped was an indifferent manner.

Crouched in front of Dido, wrapped in her black-and-white blanket, old Sannie looked like the Queen of the Spiders herself. She reached out a tiny, bony, furry arm, flicking her fingers sideways in front of Dido's face, and Dido felt something tickle her cheek; a thread of spiderweb had caught and attached itself crossways. With her hands tied, she could not rub it away; she moved her head, trying to dislodge it.

"Now another!" whispered Sannie, and moved her hand upward; a thread crossed Dido's eye and stuck to her eyelash.

"Now one for the other eye," chuckled Mrs. Lubbage, and drew her hand across Dido's face so that five tendrils of sticky thread, one from each finger it seemed, clutched and clung simultaneously.

"Stop it, you old witches!" Dido shouted angrily.

"Weren't it for you," crooned Mrs. Lubbage, drawing another handful of spiderwebs along Dido's cheek and around the back of her neck, "weren't it for you, Miss Fine-Airs, we'd be sailing to Tiburon on a white ship this minute. You don't like spiders, eh?"

"I don't mind 'em, I tell you."

"Oh, so you don't mind 'em, dearie? Well—before your eyes is all matted over with black webs—jest you have a look by the wall there, eh?"

By the wall there seemed to be a heaving mass of things about the size of bantams' eggs, each with a pair of tiny red eyes, all looking at Dido.

"Take your nasty little cold claw off'n the back of my neck, will you, missus Sannie?" Dido said politely, quelling a horrible heave of her heart. "Yan, Tan, Tethera," she said to herself, "Methera, Pip, Sethera, Wineberry, Wagtail, Tarrydiddle, and Den! It's all a load of hocus-pocus. There's nothing by the wall but a pile o' dead leaves."

She looked at the wall again. Were they dead leaves —or were they hairy, wicked-looking spiders, beginning to scurry silently in her direction?

She stared and stared—so hard that she did not notice the shadow in the doorway, nor hear the patter of paws on the stone floor, until Mrs. Lubbage suddenly let out a wild screech of terror, which was echoed an instant later by Sannie. The two old women sprang away from Dido and bolted for the door, jibbering and wailing— struggled in the entrance a moment, each trying to get

out first—then Sannie slipped ahead, Mrs. Lubbage
followed her, and they were gone.

"Well!" Dido muttered, trying to get her breath—
and the spiders *were* only dead leaves—"That was sudden,
but I won't say it warn't a welcome riddance. Whatever
put the old besoms in sich a fright, though?"

Whatever it was had gone around to the back of her;
she could hear a sniffing and snuffling close behind, and
feel warmth on her hands, tied to the metal post. With
some difficulty she worked her head sideways against the

pillar, so as to peer out of the corner of her eye, and saw quite a large tiger, all black and yellow stripes, with a head the size of a cider barrel, and eyes that blazed like marigolds.

"Oops!" said Dido.

"Yan," Tobit asked, as the crew of the *Gentlemen's Relish* sat in the galley eating supper (brown bread and fried ducks' eggs) "why ever did the ducks kick up such a row last night? They were quacking away for over an hour? What was the trouble?"

"Well, I don't rightly know," said Yan. "I was in a rare puzzle myself about it. When I heard them kick up all the ruckus I thought there must be Bush officers a-tracking us, but Pip and I had a good sharp look-around, up the cut and down the cut, and there wasn't a soul for miles. Then it seemed as if the paddlequacks was a-fussing about summat *on* the boat, so we had a look-see all around the cargo, in case anyone had got down there that shouldn't."

"Yes," Cris said softly. "*I* thought it was something down in the hold that was upsetting them. I had Lady Webb and her children with me in my bunk, and they all acted the way chickens do when there's a rat in the nesting box, stealing the eggs."

"Oh well," Yan said, "maybe it was a rat. Rats never yet took to eating orris root and eau de cologne and corkscrews, not as *I* heard of. A rat aboard won't do us much harm."

10

Dido was still gazing over her shoulder at the tiger, and the tiger was still sniffing thoughtfully at the back of her neck, when a huge gray shadow obscured the door and four windows of the octagon room, as if a battleship had berthed outside.

Dido heard a kind of scuffling slither, a gentle voice said, "Stand, if you please, Rachel," and a gentleman entered the room.

"Dear me," he said. "Sunflower, come here."

The tiger—Sunflower was its name, apparently—padded around, rubbed its head against the gentleman very lovingly, and sat down beside him. Dido studied him with interest. He really *was* a gentleman, she decided—as opposed to a Gentleman. He wore black small-clothes, white silk stockings, black shoes with silver buckles, a black velvet jacket, and a snowy white stock, beautifully tied. His hair, what little there was of it, was also snowy, like very clean thistledown. His face looked as if he sat indoors a good deal, reading, but the eyes behind gold-rimmed pince-nez were a very clear bright blue. On one hand he wore a silver ring with a large pink stone in it.

"Dear me," he said again. "That waygoing fellow gave me to understand that there were picnickers, and he was quite right, evidently. When *will* the public learn that this is private property? Not that I mind in principle, you understand—they do little real damage beyond leaving orange peel and bits of marrowbone pie on the ground—but it is frightening for the animals to have strangers about. But people will do it—they come up the river in boats—"

Shaking his head he crossed to Dido, absently surveyed the rope that tied her to the pillar, drew from his pocket first an inkhorn, then a snuffbox, finally a small silver penknife with which he cut the cord—

"Eat their lunch in my gazebo, play ring-o'-roses in my park, and then go on without saying so much as good afternoon or thank you," he continued sadly.

"I'm sorry, sir," said Dido. "I didn't come here a-purpose. I was fetched."

She rubbed her wrists to get the stiffness out of them; then her face. There were no cobwebs on it. "My name's Dido Twite," she added.

"Lord Sope," said the gentleman.

"Soop?"

"You spell it s-o-p-e and pronounce it soup—confusing, I agree. What can I do for you, Miss Twite?"

"I suppose there ain't a dapple-gray horse outside?" she said hopefully.

He looked out, and drew his head in again to say, "Not a *horse*, not at present. You have lost a horse?"

"I was supposed to be taking an urgent message, you see, to some chaps a-going up to London. But I was stopped and tied up in here, and I spose that mardy lot have gone off with my Dapple. D'you reckon I could hire a nag at the White Hart, sir? Mister? Lord?"

"You need a horse? I could accommodate you with one I imagine—I am almost certain I have a horse."

Dido stood up, and nearly fell down again from weakness. It suddenly seemed a terribly long time since her last bowl of soup at The Fighting Cocks. Yesterday? The day before?

"You are a little enfeebled," said Lord Sope. "Allow me." He took her arm and piloted her from the gazebo, the tiger padding behind them. Just outside stood an elephant, with a kind of opera box on its back, from which dangled a rope ladder made of red silk cord.

"After you, Miss Twite."

Rather shakily, Dido climbed the rope ladder and sat on one of the red velvet chairs. Lord Sope followed and took his place beside her.

"Home, if you please, Rachel," he said. The elephant started, at a deceptively smooth stroll which carried them rapidly across an open grassy park to a handsome gray stone mansion. On the way Dido observed a couple

of giraffes, a small group of zebra, and a lynx rolling about on its back and playing with some dead leaves, watched in a vaguely puzzled manner by a flock of sheep.

"Doesn't some of 'em chase the others?" asked Dido.

"I teach them not to, of course," Lord Sope replied.

The elephant reached the house by climbing on to a terrace.

"Just wait outside here a short time if you please, Rachel," Lord Sope instructed it, and politely assisted Dido down the ladder.

Passing through a pair of french windows into a library, he took down a speaking tube from a hook on the wall, said into it, "Lunch, if you please, Diggens," and replaced it.

"Pray sit down," he said to Dido, "and excuse me one moment."

Left alone in the library, Dido gazed rather blankly at the leather and gilt volumes, and the numerous paintings of wild animals that covered the walls. She felt tired, and hungry, and sad. Too much had been happening; she was suddenly shaken by a small, dry sob.

"I wisht Pa hadn't gone off like that and left me," she thought.

Lord Sope returned, followed almost immediately by a footman in a beautifully powdered wig, who arranged dishes on two small tables beside Dido and his master, and then withdrew.

"Frumenty," said Lord Sope. "And I think this note

must be for you: the waygoing character who told me about the picnickers left it."

The note, simply addressed to DIDO, said, "Dear Daughter, maybe you were right. Things is somewhat Sticky, so I am going to Cut and Run. If I was you, I would do Similar. But I reckon you will be Alright; you always was a Clever Chick. See you some Turpentine Sunday. Your loving Pa."

Frumenty seemed to be a kind of porridge made with wine and spice; after two spoonfuls Dido felt wonderfully better. It was followed by apple pie, with cheese, and a jam-lined omelet, which was very good but difficult to eat politely.

"Now—you say you require to go to London quite fast?" said Lord Sope, removing his jammy stock, throwing it into the fire, and receiving a clean one from the footman who had come back to clear away the dishes.

"Yes. It's to do with the coronation. An urgent message may have gone astray," Dido explained, licking a blob of jam off her elbow.

"In that case, without a doubt, the best thing I can do is to put Rachel at your disposal. She is quicker than any horse, and very reliable. Also, she is well acquainted with the route, for I nearly always take her when I go up to my club."

"Croopus; I mean—that's ever so kind of you, mister —lord. Will she go for me, d'you reckon?"

"She is particularly partial to being ridden by a young female."

"I need to call at three pubs on the way—the Rose, the Ring o' Bells and the Rising Sun."

"There will be no difficulty about that. Rachel is quite accustomed to wait for me outside places of refreshment. In fact she will stop automatically at such places."

"Well, I *am* obliged to you, sir—lord," said Dido. "If you really means it, I'd best be on my way directly. Oh—please can you tell me what day it is?"

"It is Monday, Miss Twite. You do not wish to wait for the two old ladies whom I observed making off at some speed as I approached the gazebo?"

"No, thank you, lord. They wasn't really friends." She put Mr. Twite's note in her pocket and went out on to the terrace, where the wigged footman was just descending the red cord ladder after placing a hamper in the box seat on top.

"I thought you might be glad of a few provisions on the way," Lord Sope explained. "I usually reckon that it takes nine or ten hours to reach London—with the usual pauses for refreshment, of course. Now, Rachel, you are to stop at the Rose, the Ring of Bells, and the Rising Sun—and anywhere else the young lady requires, naturally. Is that perfectly clear? Capital. Allow me, Miss Twite."

He helped her up the ladder.

"I'm *ever* so obliged," Dido said again. "I'll bring her back directly after the coronation."

"Such a lot of extravagant fuss and display," sighed

Lord Sope. "Still, kings have to be crowned, I understand. On your way, Rachel."

He raised his hand in farewell, Dido settled herself in the red velvet seat, and Rachel rolled off smoothly across the park.

It was plain that when Lord Sope and Rachel went to London, they followed a direct, cross-country route; Rachel ambled through fields and woods, over streams and rivers, by copses and commons, but seldom went near a road. Presently it began to rain; Dido discovered that various capes and covers were provided against this contingency, waterproof on the outside, lined with camel fur. She wrapped herself up snugly and, lulled by Rachel's smooth-flowing motion, went to sleep.

An hour or so later she woke because Rachel had stopped. Night, she found, had fallen; they were halted outside a small, cheerful-looking public house situated by a canal lock; its sign, illuminated by a lantern, showed a red rose.

"Crumble me—thanks, Rachel," muttered Dido, yawning and scrambling to her feet. "I'd never awoken if you hadn't stopped. Just hang on a minute, will you, while I pop in and inquire."

The landlady of the Rose was black-eyed, pink-cheeked, and smiling.

"Well I never!" she exclaimed, looking past Dido. "If that isn't Lord Sope's elephant. Aren't you a lucky young lady! Going up for the coronation, then, are you? Is Lord Sope going too? I *am* surprised!"

"No, ma'am. He says he can't abide fuss," said Dido, drinking the glass of milk she had ordered.

"I daresay his elephant'll be glad of her usual bite," said the landlady and went to fetch this, which turned out to be a bagful of buttered buns.

"Ma'am," said Dido as Rachel munched, "could you tell me, please, if a barge called the *Gentlemen's Relish* has been past yet?"

"Why yes, dearie, they went by early this morning, afore sunup. They'll be a long way up the cut by now."

Dido thanked her, and tried to pay for the buns, but the landlady refused, saying that Lord Sope was an old friend. The refreshment appeared to have been very welcome to Rachel; the minute her passenger was aboard again she started off as if competing in the Calcutta Derby.

Since there was nothing to be seen in the dark wet night, Dido went back to sleep.

Next morning, at gray of dawn, they came to the Ring of Bells, and again Rachel stopped of her own accord. Dido had hoped that, swinging along at Rachel's more rapid pace, they might have caught up with the barge by now but the landlord, whom she found dousing his head under a pump in the yard at the back, reported that the *Gentlemen's Relish* had passed by early the previous evening.

By now Rachel was beginning to grumble and mutter as she rolled along, and to look back at her rider in a reproachful and significant way, which Dido took to be an intimation that it was time for rest and breakfast; so they halted in a hazel copse near Esher. Rachel, after more buns, provided by the Ring of Bells, had a standing nap, with her huge ears folded tidily over her eyes, while Dido sampled Lord Sope's hamper. It proved to contain egg salad in a silver bucket, currant wine, cheese straws, and a marmalade pie. There was also a pot of frumenty, and instructions for heating it up in a chafing dish to be found under the red velvet seat, but Dido was impatient to press on, ate it cold, and gave the marmalade pie to Rachel as compensation for having to start again after an hour's nap.

By now they were no great distance from London and houses were more frequent: large, handsome mansions, most of them; many were gaily decorated with flags and wreaths and colored bunting in honor of the next day's event.

Dido had expected to cause some surprise by riding through the suburbs on an elephant, the more so as Rachel, cheered by her nap and breakfast, was now trumpeting cheerfully to herself as she proceeded; but in fact no one seemed to find their appearance at all remarkable, either because this was Lord Sope's regular route, or because people took it for granted that Rachel was to form part of the coronation procession.

"Gee up, Jumbo, you'll be late for the crowning!" shouted a cheerful group of boys coming out from morning school in Merton village; they showered Rachel and her passenger with peppermint drops and Michaelmas daisies, which Rachel rapidly sorted, swallowing the former and tossing back the latter with a dexterity that filled the boys with admiration.

"How far to the Rising Sun in Wandsworth?" Dido called, leaning over the side of her box.

"Matter o' five mile, duck; she'll do it before you can make these into a daisy chain," they called back, bombarding her with the rejected daisies.

Wandsworth was a small, ancient village, not unlike Dido's native Battersea, situated about a mile south of the river Thames, and perhaps eight or nine miles up that winding river from London Bridge. The Rising Sun was evidently not one of the inns where Lord Sope was accustomed to stop for refreshment. There had been a good many of these along the way and Rachel was beginning to grumble again at being expected to pass them by without her usual fifteen-minute pause outside each. So both companions were pleased to arrive at their third point of inquiry, which proved to be a tiny, gabled public house in Allfarthing Lane, on the banks of the river Wandle.

"Has the *Gentlemen's Relish* been by yet?" Dido asked the landlord.

He was a thin, sandy-haired, sharp-faced character; he gave her a very searching scrutiny before replying:

"No, missie. She ain't. And what's more she's powerful late—I've been expecting her these three-four hours."

Dido's heart sank. What could have happened to delay the barge? Had she better start back along the banks of the Wandle? She was not quite sure where this river was joined by the Gentlemen's secret canal, but if she followed the towpath she must be sure to find the junction somewhere. But then she would be farther away from London when they met, and would have to bring the Dispatch all the way back again—it was difficult to know what to do for the best. In the end she decided to remain by the Ring of Bells for two hours and then, if the *Gentlemen's Relish* had not yet arrived, start back.

On the west bank of the Wandle just at this point there was a pleasant little park, so they crossed the river —Rachel preferred to swim, ignoring a perfectly good bridge—Dido, dismounting, sat under a tree and Rachel sank down alongside like a neat and silent avalanche.

They waited. There was no difficulty in telling the hour hereabouts. Three churches, just across the Wandle, struck all the quarters, and if they did not agree absolutely to the minute, at least there was a general certainty that time was passing. One o'clock, half past, quarter to two, quarter past. And still the *Gentlemen's Relish* did not appear.

"Rachel," said Dido at three o'clock, "I reckon we'd better go back along the towpath."

Rachel, who had been asleep, lifted her ears away from her eyes with a movement like a shrug, and began gloomily clambering to her feet.

But just at that moment, far away along the winding Wandle, something came into view that might have been a traveling hedge, or a sliding grove, or a piece of moving moorland.

"Hang on a minute, Rachel. What's that?"

The landlord of the Rising Sun had come out of his bar parlor and was standing on the opposite river bank gazing upstream. He nodded to Dido.

"That's the old *Relish,*" he called. "Dear knows why she's so late."

Dido ran across the bridge and Rachel waded through the river.

"Don't they worry about Preventives?" Dido asked. "Coming along in daylight, so bold?"

"Not in these parts, bless you—we're all good King's men round here. Nary a Bush officer'd dare show his face."

At last the garlanded barge slid alongside. Yan and Tan, who had been riding the tow mules, tied them to a lamppost.

"Well, Yan?" called the landlord, "Brought my drop of licorice water, have ye? What makes ee so late?"

"Hollo there, Bob. We had a bit o' trouble in the night wi' our paddlequacks." Then Yan saw Dido and the elephant. "Hey!" he said. "What's amiss? I didn't think to see you here, dearie."

"Oh, Yan! Am I pleased to see *you!*" Dido was about to jump on board, but she thought better of it, and beckoned him to come around the corner into Allfarthing Street.

"Listen!" she whispered urgently, "You've got a spy on board! Where's the Dispatch?"

"A *spy?* Nay, dearie, that just can't be! All us chaps has worked together since we was lads at school."

"Just the same, there is one." Dido repeated what Mr. Twite had said. "Is the Dispatch safe?"

"Surelye! I've got it packed in among the orris root."

"What was that about trouble in the night?"

"Our paddlequacks all swam away. We had the devil's own job a-pacifying and a-fetching them back—running up and down the banks, they was, roosting in trees, quacking and clacking and carrying-on—took us hours to catch 'em all, and when we'd caught 'em there was nothing for it but to shut the lot of 'em in young Cris's cabin—they takes kindly to *her*."

"What upset them?"

"'Twas a black mystery—we never did find out. There was no stranger around. And the cargo was trig enough —not a corkscrew out o' place. In the end we reckoned as it might a bin an outsize rat as scared the ducklings."

"A *rat?*" Dido stared at Yan, her eyes big as saucers. "Here—come back on board, *quick!* Show us where you've got the Dispatch."

She grabbed his hand and fairly raced him back to the barge. They picked their way hastily across the bushy deck while Tethera, Methera, and Pip, who were unloading kegs of licorice spirit for the Rising Sun, gazed at them in astonishment.

"Where's Cris and Tobit?" Dido panted, as they dropped down the hatch into the galley.

"Playing cat's cradle, I reckon. They spends most o' the day doing that, and hashing over old times," Yan said tolerantly. He led Dido through the spacious galley with its central stove, kitchen table, and benches. Here, before continuing, he took a lantern from a hook, lit it, and gave it to Dido to carry. They crossed a series of communicating cabins filled with bales and crates which smelt strongly of lavender and licorice, then came to a passageway leading between closed doors. Yan tapped on one of these and threw it open.

Inside, an extremely cozy scene was revealed. Cris and Tobit were sitting on the floor playing cat's cradle. Dido noticed at once that they had made great strides in this game since she had given them their basic instruction—when? Two days ago? Tobit held between his outspread fingers an immensely complicated network of string like the mesh of colored ribbons around a maypole. Cris was carefully studying it from all angles.

Perched all around the cabin, and on Cris's head and shoulders, were thirty or forty ducks and ducklings, also, it seemed, attentively watching the game.

However, when the door opened everybody looked around.

"Why, it's Dido!" said Cris with mild surprise.

"All right, everyone in here, are you?" Yan asked.

"Yes, why?" Tobit said. "Look, Cris, take those two with your hands and *those* two with your teeth—" he pointed with his nose.

"Ducks all right? No more upsets? We're a-going down below to make sure the Dispatch is safe."

"We'll come too," said Tobit jumping up, but carefully so as not to disturb any ducks, or his network, which he carried along with him.

Yan led the way down two more ladders and into a dark, narrow region, even more strongly scented, where they had to scramble over and between large prickly sacks of corkscrews and tacky bales of licorice.

"Now—" Yan paused in front of a shut door and pulled out a bunch of keys—"I keeps the Dispatch in the lock-up—no one goes in here but me." He carefully inserted the largest key, turned it, and flung open the door.

Dido, just behind him, held the lantern high.

There was a sudden scuffle and scurry. Something jumped off the wide shelf which ran around three sides of this hold, and dashed across the shadowy floor. But Tobit, acting with most unexpected dispatch and address, bounded forward past Yan, his hands held low and wide with the net stretched tight between them, and caught the thing on the floor, instantly twisting and gripping his net to prevent its escape.

"*Dang* it, what's that?" exclaimed Yan. "Here, Dido, bring the light closer!"

The creature in Tobit's net screamed. It was a horrible sound—a scream of rage and defiance, not fear at all. It was like a human scream but higher and shriller. The creature struggled, causing the net to swing furiously.

"Halloo, what's amiss—what the devil's going on below there?" cried startled voices from the deck. Tan and Methera came clattering down.

"Mercy sakes, what *have* you got hold of?" Tan gasped. Dido held the lantern close and Tobit's prisoner was revealed as an immense brindled rat, its eyes flashing, its whiskers bristling, its long yellow fangs bare in fury.

"Don't you let it bite you, boy," Yan warned. "I'll lay every one o' those grinders is as full o' poison as a deadly adder's tooth."

As they stared at the beast Cris said rather shakily, "That's Auntie Daisy's rat."

"Are ye certain, gal?"

"Yes, I reckon she's right," Dido said. "It's brindled just the same."

Yan began to curse.

"What a gurt muttonheaded fool I am. Why didn't I think? Where the dickens did the brute get in?"

"Never mind that, where's the Dispatch?"

"'Twas on the coaming yonder," said Yan with a groan. "In an oilskin packet—"

"Here's a bit of it on the floor," Cris said, springing forward. "The rat must have knocked it off—"

She picked it up gingerly. The red string and seal fell to the floor with a shower of leaf-sized bits of paper. Half the document had been gnawed away.

"Let's go up where it's light and have a look at what's left," Dido said. "Maybe we can make out what it's about. Mind how you hold that monster, Tobit— don't let him get away."

"Wait till I fetch my qualiver, I'll blow him to forty bits," vowed Yan. The rat squealed angrily.

They went on deck. "All that cat's cradle come in handy, anyhows," muttered Tan to Tethera. "Which was more than I'd a prognotified yesterday."

[247]

Tobit was having great difficulty in keeping a grip on the struggling rat which darted its head this way and that, trying to squeeze through the meshes of the net. Nobody could take it from him because it snapped so savagely.

Just as Yan came back with his hand gun the rat finally succeeded in thrusting its body through a gap and bounded on to the deck, screeching with triumph. Yan fired but missed. The rat scurried over the side and could be seen swimming across the river, a dark V of water spreading away behind its pointed head.

"*Plague* on it—" Yan hurriedly reloaded. But as he did so, Tobit sprang over the side and went after the rat.

"Tobit! Come back, boy! You'll never catch it!"

"Oh, Tobit!" wailed Cris. "Do be careful."

But he did not answer. Hunter and quarry both disappeared into the dusk on the far side of the Wandle.

"Well, here's a right hugger-mugger!" said Yan furiously.

Dido had spread the rest of the chewed Dispatch on the cabin roof and was poring over it, by the light of the lantern and the last rays of the setting sun.

> "To my Lord Forecastle Master of the
> lace horse and Westminster Foxhou
> First Lord of the Admiralty.
> Sir: Whilst interrogating prisoner
> captured French frigate *Madame de Ma*
> I was lucky enough to discover detail
> laid and diabolical plot to assassina
> well-beloved Prince of Wales on the oc

his Coronation. The details are as
Cathedral of St. Paul's has already be
mined & its foundations rest merely
at a given signal or impetus these rol
set in motion and the whole Sacred Edif
slide with uncontrollable speed in
River Thames. Proof of this can
visiting the Crypt. I there
it right to communicate the fright
tidings without delay. I remain
     Your lordship's
     Charles Tran
      Rear-Admi

Dido read through this very carefully three times.

"Holy Peggotty!" she said then. "What time's the coronation tomorrow?"

"Ten in the morning."

"Us has got to hustle," Dido said.

"Why, what's it about?" Yan peered over her shoulder at the damaged Dispatch. But he said, "You've got more book-learning than I have, reckon, ducky; blest if I can make trotter nor tail of it. What's it say?"

"Why," said Dido, "near as I can reckon, some admiral is writing to this here Lord Forecastle about a plot to push St. Paul's Cathedral into the Thames, with the whole coronation a-going on inside it. That's what they means when they keeps talking about the Wren's Nest! Oh, the villains! Here, I'm off—where does Lord Forecastle live, Yan?"

"House in the Strand. How'll you get there?"

"Lord Sope lent me his elephant."

"I was wondering where that came from," Tethera said.

"Shall I come with ee, duck?" said Yan. "Old Lord Forecastle is a tiddy bit slow and given to argufication. But he knows me, reckon I could help get the notion into his noodle as there's need to hurry."

"That'd be prime, Yan. How about the ship?"

"The others can bring her on the reg'lar way, and we'll all meet at Aunt Grissie's in Wardrobe Court."

"But Tobit!" said Cris, half crying.

"Look, gal, us simply can't wait to hunt for him now," Dido said. "But he's got sense. He can ask his way to Wardrobe Court—you told him where that is?" Yan nodded. "He'll be all right, I reckon. Besides, wouldn't Aswell give you a warning if he was in any kind o' trouble?"

"Aswell?" Cris looked vaguely puzzled.

Dido stared at her, equally astonished. Had she already forgotten about Aswell? But there was really not an instant to waste. Yan slipped what was left of the Dispatch into another oilskin case, he and Dido jumped ashore, and ran to where the elephant was patiently waiting.

11

Steering Rachel through the streets of London to Lord Forecastle's residence proved considerably more difficult than letting her find her own way from Stopham Park to Wandsworth. In fact it proved impossible. Rachel had her own theories about the right route into London and whether they threatened, pleaded, thumped, or tried to lead her, she pursued her own course, quite regardless of their wishes.

"Oh well, let her take her own way," said Dido at length. "She seems to have a powerful strong notion o' where she wants to go."

She took them across Wandsworth Bridge and along the King's Road, Chelsea.

"Why," exclaimed Dido, "that's Doc Furneaux's Academy of Art! Hang on just a moment, Rachel, my ducky, I used to have a pal as learnt painting there. I'll just nip in and ax if anyone knows where he is. I've been trying to get in touch with him—he'd be a right useful cove in a fussation like this—chap called Simon."

And she slid down the rope ladder like a powder monkey, muttering to herself.

"Oh I *does* hope he's still alive."

But Dr. Furneaux's Academy of Arts presented a very blank and silent aspect: in the wide forecourt, usually choc-a-block with students eating impromptu meals and doing their laundry in the fountain, no one was to be seen but an aged Chelsea pensioner, who was slowly and thoughtfully trying to remove a Dutch cheese from the hole in the middle of a statue where someone had rammed it.

"Where's all the folk?" Dido asked. The old man turned bleary eyes on her.

"What folk?"

"The students!" Dido said impatiently. "And the teachers! And Doc Furneaux! Where are they?"

"Gone for to put up the decorations in the cathedral. And in Threadneedle Street and Paternoster Row and Cheapside. Fancy wasting a good bit o' cheese like that," said the old man in disgust, giving it another vain poke.

Dido scurried back to the elephant.

"No good . . . You can roll on, Rachel." So Rachel continued, looking neither to right nor left, along the King's Road, across Sloane Square, through Belgravia, across Green Park, and presently drew up outside what was presumably Lord Sope's club in St. James's. It was called Toffy's and, judging by the white steps, polished brass, window boxes, and the uniformed porter, was very grand indeed.

"What'll us do now?" Dido said. "Leave Rachel here and call a cab?"

But Yan, all excited, exclaimed, "There! There he is!"

"Who?"

"Lord Forecastle. He just got out of that phaeton and went into the club."

"Oh, well, that's prime," Dido said. "We'll go in too."

But this was easier said than done.

The uniformed porter, who was about seven feet tall, said coldly,

"Lord Sope's elephant always gets taken around to the back."

"Well, you do that, will you?" Dido said. "Us has an urgent errand with Lord Forecastle. Just ax him to step back and speak to us for a minute, can you?"

"I *beg* your pardon," the porter said in frozen tones. "I fear that will be quite out of the question."

"Why?" demanded Dido.

"Gentlemen when availing themselves of the facilities of this establishment may not be disturbed for *any* reason whatso*ever* by *any*body. It is the first club rule. Why, when the Battle of Trafalgar was won, they had to wait for two days till Mr. Pitt came out before they could tell him."

"What did he say? I'll bet he was right vlothered that everyone else had known for two days before him."

"History does not relate," the porter said snubbingly.

Then his tone changed to one of outrage and he exclaimed,

"*Where* do you think you are going?"

"In, to look for Lord Forecastle, if you won't."

"Persons of the female sex are not on *any* account *ever* allowed into these premises."

"Yan, *you* better go," Dido said crossly.

Yan looked daunted.

"When d'you reckon his lordship's liable to come out?" he asked the porter.

"I cannot possibly undertake to say."

"Oh, drabbit!" said Dido. She retired to the street, filled her lungs to their maximum capacity with air, and bawled,

"LORD FORECASTLE!"

Yan, approving of this tactic, joined her, filled *his* lungs, and shouted even louder,

"LORD FORECASTLE!"

Rachel, entering into the spirit of the enterprise, joyfully trumpeted. Windows were opened in clubs all up and down St. James's. About a hundred white-wigged heads and scandalized old faces poked out. "Like cheese mites," Dido said.

The elderly gentleman who all this time had been slowly climbing the red-velvet-carpeted stairs of Toffy's club, slowly retraced his steps.

"What is all the commotion about, Prothero?" he demanded. "Pray cause it to cease."

"Begging your humble pardon, your lordship, but

Lord Forecastle

there is a—a person, and a—a *young* person that are desirous to have words with your lordship."

"Indeed? Where are they?" inquired Lord Forecastle icily.

"In the street, your lordship."

"I can hardly converse with them in the street, can I?"

"The young person is of the female sex, your lordship."

This might have been insoluble, but luckily Lord Forecastle, peering through the entrance, observed,

"Dear me, there is old Plantagenet Sope's elephant. I'd no notion he was coming up for the crowning. Planty! Planty! D'you care to come and take a dish of tay with me?"

"Lord Forecastle!" said Yan, springing on him like an active thrush on a very ancient snail, before he could discover his mistake and retreat inside the club again. "You knows me—Yan Wineberry, as delivers your corkscrews and organ-grinder's oil."

"Good gracious, my good fellow—" Lord Forecastle was scandalized, "St. James's Street is *not* the place to allude to such commodities."

"Well, I ain't a-going to," Yan said reasonably. "We bring you half a Dispatch from Rear-Admiral Charles Tran."

"Charles Tran? I have no acquaintance of that designation. And in any case, this is not a suitable place to bring me a dispatch, or half a dispatch. I am off duty, I am in mufti! Take it to the office—take it to the

Admiralty. I will look at it on Friday. Or, no, on Friday I shoot partridge at Ravenscourt Park—Monday. Monday will be better. Charles Tran? Some imposter, I daresay; never heard of the fellow."

"Look, Lord Fo'c'stle, this is *urgent*," said Dido. "We borrowed Lord Sope's elephant special to come and find you. Are you a-going to the coronation tomorrow?"

"Of course I am, child. What has that to say to anything?"

"Well then you won't be in the Admiralty on Monday, I can tell you that. You'll be squished in sixteen feet o' Thames mud under twenty thousand ton dead-weight o' fancy stonework."

"My dear young person, are you raving? Shall I be obliged to call the Watch?"

"See here," said Dido, and spread out the gnawed Dispatch under his eyes.

"Tut! What is this rigmarole?" he said peevishly. "French frigate Madame de Ma? There is no such vessel. Cathedral has been mined? Unthinkable rubbish. Why, the fellow who wrote this must have been drunk —half the sentences are incomplete. Either drunk or mad! Tush—take it away—I dare swear the whole thing is an arrant fraud."

"It ain't!" said Dido indignantly. "Captain Hughes o' the *Thrush* asked us to bring it to you."

"Ha!" said Lord Forecastle triumphantly. "*I* know Hughes—sensible, reliable, gentlemanly sort of officer —excellent disciplinarian—know *he*'d never act in such an irregular manner. Why not bring it himself, pray?"

"He's ill—he was wounded at sea, and in a carriage accident, and overlooked by a witch."

"Fiddledeedee! Be off with you, miss—pray don't try such Billingsgate stories on me. A witch—Owen Hughes—there's a likely fairy tale. Why, my great friend Rear-Admiral Charles Transome, under whom he serves, thinks the world of Hughes."

"Transome!" exclaimed Dido. "Don't you see this letter *is* from Transome, you clutter-headed old—"

"Steady, steady, ducks!" cautioned Yan. "No use setting his whiskers on fire!"

Lord Forecastle was indeed in a dangerously empurpled condition.

"Wineberry!" he sputtered. "I've always found you a businesslike fellow in our dealings. What you are doing with this disgracefully impudent young person who appears to be mentally deranged as well, I cannot imagine, but I wish you will take her away!"

"But, sir, what she says is quite true. 'Tis they bothering Hanoverians, at it again—digging away under St. Paul's like mouldywarps, they be."

Lord Forecastle cooled down a little. He read the Dispatch again.

"Well," he said at length, "if this really is from Charlie Transome—though why he cannot sign himself properly I quite fail to comprehend—"

"The Dispatch was gnawed by a rat—"

"A rat? Oh, good gad, man, how can you expect me to believe such a farrago of preposterous balderdash?"

"Because it's the truth!" exclaimed Dido, with such

indignant and passionate conviction that a number of people in the street turned to look at her.

A spare, shrewd-looking gray-headed gentleman who happened to be driving past in a curricle reined in his horses.

"Evening, Fo'c'stle!" he called. "Is Planty Sope in town, then? I see his beast there."

"No, he is not," said Lord Forecastle peevishly. "So far as I can make out this precious pair appear to have purloined his elephant in order to come and tell me a ramshackle tale of rats and witches and a plot to dig up St. Paul's—I wish you will call up your constables, Sir Percy, and have them consigned to the Tower—"

"Sir Percy!" exclaimed Yan joyfully, while the gray-headed gentleman, seeing Yan at the same moment, remarked,

"Nay, that's young Wineberry, who brings me my Hollands every month, regular as the Bank of England. I can't believe he'd be mixed up in anything havey-cavey."

"Sir Percy, do but take a look at yon message!" Yan begged. "It bean't a ramshackle tale, indeed it bean't. It got chawed by a rat aboard the *Gentleman's Relish*, but you can see it's from Rear-Admiral Transome and it's mortal important—"

With obvious relief, Lord Forecastle passed over the Dispatch to the gentleman in the curricle, who read it attentively.

"That's Sir Percy Tipstaff," Yan muttered in Dido's ear. "He'll pay a bit more heed, I'll lay—"

"Humph," grunted Sir Percy. "This certainly bears *some* appearance of a genuine warning. I feel it had best be looked into. I'll put matters in train, shall I, Fo'c'stle, and spare you the trouble?"

"Do, Tipstaff—do—if you really think it is not a hoax. And now, if you'll pardon me, I am sadly late for an appointment to play backgammon with the Bishop of Bayswater—" Plainly much relieved at being able to wash his hands of the business, Lord Forecastle gave a final disapproving glare at Dido and Yan, turned, and stumped up the steps of Toffy's club.

"You two had best come in my carriage," said the Lord Chief Justice. "Then you can tell me the details as we ride."

"What about the elephant?"

"Prothero!" called Sir Percy.

"Yes, sir? What can I do for you, Sir Percy?"

"Put away this elephant; see she is fed and rubbed down."

"Begging your pardon, sir, can't undertake to stable her without Lord Sope himself personally consigns her to our stable."

"Oh, tush—" Sir Percy was beginning, when Yan interposed.

"Excuse me, sir, but best not waste time in arguing; I daresay my auntie Grissie will oblige if they ain't willing here."

So Rachel was allowed to follow behind Sir Percy's curricle, and this was perhaps just as well, for it was plain that she had every intention of doing so anyway.

Yan and Dido sprang into the vehicle, Sir Percy touched up his horses, and the procession whirled away toward Piccadilly.

"Now," said the Lord Chief Justice, skillfully guiding his team through the crowds, which became denser and denser as they approached the City of London, "you know more about this murky business than is mentioned in the Dispatch, hey? How do the miscreants propose to topple over St. Paul's?"

"Well, sir," Dido told him. "One night I heard two coves, as I know to be mixed up in this, a-talking together and one of 'em said, 'The rollers is mounted already. All we want now is motive power.'"

"Rollers? Good gracious. Do you mean to suggest that the whole cathedral is already mounted on castors like —like a sofa?"

"Yes, sir. We reckons so."

"How very shocking. Well, proceed! What about the motive power—have you ascertained how they propose to give it the final push?"

"They ran into a bit o' trouble when it came to that, sir," said Dido, and explained about the defection of Mr. Godwit. "Someone run off with a valuable bit o' property that they was going to sell to pay for the levers and stuff, you see."

"So our worries are at an end? They cannot start the cathedral rolling?"

"I ain't so sure about that, sir," said Dido. "There's these two old witches—"

"*Witches?* Come, come, child. Do not try my credulity

too far. Rollers are one thing, witches are quite another. Let us leave magic and spookery out of the business, pray!"

"But they *can* do queer things, sir! They put poor Cap'n Hughes in a sleep and no one can't rouse him—"

"A drug or a blow on the head would do as much—"

"They can make folk see things as isn't there—"

"Bah!"

"Well, anyways, Colonel FitzPickwick believes they can fix it."

"FitzPickwick, eh? I always suspected he had Hanoverian leanings," Sir Percy said thoughtfully. "But this talk of sorcery and such jiggery-pokery, you know, is the outside of enough."

By now the curricle, with Rachel in anxious pursuit, had rolled briskly along the Strand, along Fleet Street, up Ludgate Hill, and had turned left below the towering bulk of St. Paul's Cathedral. They drew up outside the Old Bailey.

"The Yeoman of the Guard and just about the whole of the London constabulary are quartered here in readiness for tomorrow," Sir Percy explained. "And Lord Raven, the Home Secretary, is certain to be here, so we can put the whole matter before him and decide on a proper course of action."

This sounded promising. But when Lord Raven presently appeared, in a small gloomy office to which Sir Percy had led them, Dido's heart sank.

The Home Secretary was a tall, gaunt, draggled-looking character with rusty black hair and a rusty black beard and such very thick drooping black eyebrows that it seemed unlikely that he could see much unless he looked sidelong.

He listened to Sir Percy's outline of the plot to dispose of King Richard the Fourth, along with the Archbishop of Canterbury, all the nobility and gentry of the land, as well as members of parliament, clergy, choir, St. Paul's Cathedral itself, and a congregation of several thousand, in a discouraging silence.

"So you see," concluded Sir Percy, "whether or not these dastardly plotters have, since our young friends left them, actually discovered a means of shifting the edifice or not, it is urgently necessary to survey the foundations before tomorrow's ceremony, so as to remove any risk of such an attempt."

The Home Secretary ran one hand through his beard, looked at it, ran the other hand through, looked at it, and after a thoughtful pause replied,

"Can't be done."

"What is that you say, man?" exclaimed Sir Percy. "How do you mean, can't be done?"

"Cathedral's not my province. Can't set foot in it without permission of the Dean. Certainly can't arrest anyone in it."

"But, good heavens, man, there's a double cordon of your constabulary officers all around the place this minute. I noticed them as we came up Ludgate Hill."

"That's to keep people out," replied Lord Raven. "Cathedral's already filling up fast—tomorrow's congregation will all be there by invitation. About the only ones left to come now are members of parliament and peers."

"The congregation's there already?"

"A cathedral's not like a teapot—you can't fill it and empty it in five minutes," Lord Raven said sourly. "Every person who'll be there tomorrow has to have a pass—every pass has to be countersigned by ten different constabulary officers—takes hours to get 'em all in and out again."

"Well, we must obtain passes so that we can go and look at the crypt—I presume that is where the malefactors will have placed their rollers," said Sir Percy impatiently. "And surely conspirators could be arrested in the crypt?"

Lord Raven ran one hand through his beard, ran the other hand through, and replied, "Can't get passes."

"Why not, in the name of St. Pancras?" demanded the Lord Chief Justice, in a high state of exasperation.

"Passes have to be issued by the Dean."

"Very well, then let us go to the Dean, for goodness' sake."

"Can't. The Dean is passing the night with His Majesty, in meditation and serious talk."

"Oh." Sir Percy considered, and then said, "Just the same, in a case of such danger and urgency—Where are they having this talk?"

"In St. Paul's library."

"In the *cathedral?* You mean His Majesty is there *already?*"

[264]

"That is so. He arrived just after lunch, and will not leave until after tomorrow's ceremony."

"But, in that case—good gracious, don't you see that the danger is critical *now?* Why, if everybody is inside it already—except the peers and M.P.s and who cares about them—if the plotters have by now found some means of moving the building, there's not a thing to stop them doing so *at any time*—supposing they knew His Majesty is in there. Good heavens, man, the whole thing is perched at the top of Ludgate Hill like a boot on a roller-skate, just waiting for someone to give it a shove. We *must* get inside, I tell you!"

"Can't, without a pass," replied the Home Secretary immovably.

Dido plucked Yan's hand and drew him from the room.

"Come on," she whispered outside. "That pair will be at it for hours, to and fro. I wouldn't give a buttered biscuit for Sir Percy's chances of getting into St. Paul's. Dismal old croaker, that Lord Raven, ain't he?"

Yan could only agree.

"What'll us do? Got any notion, duck?"

"Let's go up to your aunt Grissie's," Dido suggested. "If she lives in Wardrobe Court, that's right handy for St. Paul's, and maybe the others'll have got there by now; they might have some good ideas."

They walked up the short but steep hill—Rachel following—and admired the great west front of the cathedral, which had been garlanded all over, presumably by the students of Dr. Furneaux's Academy, with purple daisies and bunches of red autumn berries. The roadway down toward the City of Westminster had been kept clear by Yeomen, but in all the houses, and everywhere that people were allowed to stand, the crowds were massing thicker and thicker. People were all in their holiday best. There was an atmosphere everywhere of jubilation and expectancy.

Yan turned right, off Ludgate Hill, into a tiny cobbled street, and right again, under an arch. Rachel, unable to squeeze through, trumpeted mournfully.

"Just you wait there a minute, Rachel my duck, and we'll bring you something nice," Dido reassured her.

Wardrobe Court was a tiny enclosure, in which two plane trees were dropping their pale yellow leaves on to soft green grass. Around the sides of the court were peaceful little old houses which looked as if they had grown there, like the trees. Up above, the sky, for once, was clear; its luminous green, with one or two stars prickling out, gave promise that the next day would be fine.

They knocked at Number Four. Aunt Grissie, a small cheerful old lady exactly like a nut, hugged Yan and said, "There! I made sure I'd see you directly. I've been a-watching the old *Relish* a-tying up at Mermaid Wharf from my kitchen window. But how is it you're ahead of her, Yan, boy?"

"We had a bit o' business to do, Auntie, so we left the ship at Wandsworth. This here's Dido Twite, and we've left an elephant outside, if so be as you've any buns."

Aunt Grissie made no difficulty about producing buns —"I always lays in plenty of provisions when the Wineberry lads are due," she explained to Dido, giving her a trayful. While Aunt Grissie and Yan were exchanging family news in the neat little kitchen Dido wandered back through the parlor—with its painted glass ornaments, pictures made from butterflies' wings, red chenille tablecloth, and wax fruit under glass domes. Outside the window a larger dome, that of St. Paul's, faced the house over the roofs of Wardrobe Court.

"If St. Paul's does go a-skating down into the river," Dido thought, carrying the buns to Rachel, "it'll take Aunt Grissie's house with it. *And* topple in right on top of the old *Gentlemen's Relish*."

Rachel, appeased by buns, was content to wait in the street. As Dido returned to the house the rest of the *Gentlemen's Relish* crew trooped into the court, hungry, highly scented, and cheerful.

"Well, did you fix things with his lordship?" asked Tethera.

Cris ran to Dido and caught her by the hand.

"Oh Dido—I'm so worried about Tobit!"

"He's not back yet? Oh well, I daresay he'll be along by and by," Dido soothed her.

"But *I keep getting messages from him!*"

Dido's skin prickled.

"Like when he was in the well?"

[267]

"Yes! No, not quite like that—it doesn't seem so much that he's in danger—but he's stuck somewhere and can't get out, and he wants to tell me something and I can't understand it."

"Like it was with Aswell sometimes?"

"Aswell?"

Blimey, thought Dido, has she clean forgotten? "You remember Aswell, that you used to talk to in the Cuckoo Tree?"

"Oh," said Cris slowly, "yes—I *think* I do—but I was just a child then. That was a long time ago. Was it someone I used to believe was up in the sky? I've almost forgotten."

"Oh well, no matter. D'you reckon if we went upstairs, or somewhere quiet, you might hear better?"

Cris thought this might help. As the tiny house was now crammed with Wineberry Men shaving, washing their socks, eating bacon and eggs, and discussing Lord Raven's behavior, Dido and Cris went out through Wardrobe Court, gave Rachel a passing pat, and strolled on into St. Paul's churchyard.

"This is better—but let's keep going." Cris tugged Dido along toward the cathedral. Since the double line of constables prevented the crowd from entering and kept urging people to move on, Dido and Cris continued going east—anti-clockwise—until they were around on the north side of St. Paul's. Here the crowd was thicker still. Every now and then somebody who had a pass showed it and was allowed to go in.

"Can't *we* go in?" Cris said impatiently. "I'm almost sure Tobit's voice is coming from inside there."

"That's funny," Dido thought. "Well, I suppose if Tobit had come straight, he *could* have got here while we was argufying with old Fo'c'stle, but why? And how did he fetch up inside? And how can we?"

Her last question was answered at once.

"Buy a pass, dearie?" muttered a voice in her ear. "Only two guineas to *you*, for I've took a fancy to you. You've a lucky face."

She turned to find a little man like a blackbeetle at her elbow. "Passes for the North Door and Lord Mayor's Vestry—you'll never be sorry you took the chance," he urged her. "Only two guineas—in an hour's time you won't be able to get 'em for twenty!"

"Does I look as if I had two guineas?" Dido began tartly, and then remembered that as a matter of fact she *had*; thanks to Miss Sarah Gusset she had five. She glanced about and realized that in fact a brisk trade in illegal passes was going on. Pity old Raven couldn't come up here and buy a few, she thought.

"Please, *please* let's go in," besought Cris, who had seen Dido's hand move toward her pocket.

"Oh, very well!" Dido brought out four of the five guinea pieces, and received in exchange two large pieces of pasteboard all covered with lions, unicorns, balls, crosses, and croziers, that said, "Admit bearer to North Transept. (Signed) Thos. Talisman, Dean." They looked very official.

The salesman, having taken their money, vanished into the crowd like a lemming. Cris and Dido showed their passes, were allowed through the double line of constables, and climbed the steps to the North Door. "Wonder if I oughta let Yan know?" Dido thought. "But we needn't stay long, and this does seem a chance. We mightn't get in so easy another time."

12

Although born and bred in London, Dido had never before set foot inside St. Paul's Cathedral. When they had passed through the entrance vestibule and came out into the north transept, she was amazed at the size of the place. It was like being in some clearing among giant trees. Underfoot were black and white marble squares, an enormous checkerboard stretching away in every direction. Massive pillars led the eye upward to a roof that was a series of lofty white domes, encircled by dark-brown rings. Although there were so many people already in the cathedral, they seemed tiny in its hugeness.

The students from Dr. Furneaux's Art Academy were still running to and fro, busily at work on the decorations. Up and down the pillars, on the choir stalls, statues, monuments—wherever stone, wood, marble, or ironwork provided a hold, they were fastening great festoons of autumn leaves, brown, gold, and rust colored. And among the leaves hung oranges and lemons in profusion, so that the principal color everywhere was gold—it seemed like a forest of gilded trees, seen in the half dark, with the infrequent rays of light picking out pale gold, bright gold, rich gold, dark gold. The tiny flickering tapers carried by the students to give light for their labors enhanced this effect—the dusk among the majestic pillars, under the soaring arches, seemed powdered with a dazzling shimmer.

"Why all the oranges and lemons?" Dido asked a boy who carried a basket of these fruits and was pinning them with skewers among bunches of oak and beech boughs over the tomb of an old gentleman who was lying uncomfortably balanced on a pile of cannons.

"The new king is very fond of marmalade."

"My stars!" murmured Dido. "He'll be able to make enough outa what's here to last him the rest of his days." Then she asked the boy,

"Hey, are you from Doc Furneaux's place?"

"That's right."

"D'you know a cove called Simon—Simon as used to live in Rose Alley?"

He shook his head. "Can't say as I do. The only Simon I know is the Duke of Battersea. He's the gaffer in charge of all this set-out—Master of the King's Garlandries, he is."

"Oh, no, it wouldn't be him," Dido said, greatly disappointed. Cris plucked her arm.

[272]

"Can we go up, do you suppose? The voice seems to be coming from up there."

She pointed toward the white vault overhead.

"*Can* we go up?" Dido asked the boy.

"Sure—if you can get through the crowd. Door to the stairs over there on the south side." He pointed across the nave.

They edged their way through, Cris tugging Dido's hand, and found the door; beyond it, the crowd thinned somewhat, and they were able to make their way up the stairs. These were wide, shallow wooden steps, winding upward in what seemed an endless spiral; Dido lost count after a hundred and fifty.

"What the blazes would Tobit be doing up here?" she panted. "If all the doings is down below?" But Cris kept on doggedly.

At last, however, she turned off through a little doorway into a stone passage so narrow that if two people had met in it, one would have had to go back. After following this, up steps and down, mostly feeling their way in the dark, though it was lit by an occasional lantern, they emerged in a great circular gallery that must have lain under the central dome, for it looked down directly into the middle of the cathedral; the students below, scurrying hither and thither with their festoons of leaves, looked like ants carrying tiny shreds of grass.

"Ah: now it's *loud*," murmured Cris. "Where can he be?" She started walking around the gallery. Echoes

came strangely to them in this place; Dido felt as if she, too, could hear Tobit, urging them to hurry.

On the opposite side of the gallery another little passage led off; Cris followed it, past some doors, and presently paused outside one that seemed made for dwarfs. She tried it: it appeared to be locked. But a voice from inside whispered,

"Cris? Is that you?"

"Yes!"

A key rattled and the door opened; Cris and Dido slipped through into a tiny stone room that looked out on to a leaded roof. Tobit was there. He and Cris looked at one another in that queer way they had; as if, Dido thought, nobody else existed.

"What a time you took to get here!" he said.

"I came as fast as I could."

"Listen, we must do something fast! Old Sannie and FitzPickwick and Mother Lubbage are down below—"

"How did *you* get here, Tobit?"

"I followed the rat," he said impatiently. "I kept peppering it with Joobie nuts from my peashooter, and it ate one or two and got slow and sleepy—*I'm* not ever going to touch those things again, I can tell you—it went wandering along a lot of dirty streets and across a bridge —I couldn't catch it but I could keep it in sight. Over the bridge—Blackfriars, it was called—the rat crawled into an empty house. There were cellar stairs, and the rat went down, and I went down, and there was a passage, and I went along it, and it came out under here."

"In the crypt?"

"No, under that. There's a huge open space, big as—big as Tegleaze park, with all these rollers."

"What are they made of?"

"I dunno—iron—some kind of metal—all wrapped around with sheepswool. They're big—higher than me—and there's hundreds of them. The whole place is sitting on top of them. The rat went staggering out into this place and then it fell over and went to sleep. I was having a look around when I heard Sannie and Fitz-Pickwick and old Lubbage, so I hid behind a roller to listen."

"Not Mr. Mystery?"

"No, he wasn't there."

"What are they fixing to do?"

"It's something to do with old Mystery's puppet show. They've got the theatre down there, and baskets full of puppets, and they're planning to bring it up by and by—they've got leaves tied all over, so it looks like the rest of the decorations. And they've got trays and trays of Joobie nuts and two boys to take them round—"

"Oh, rabbit it," said Dido. "I reckon I know what they're a-going to do. Did they see you?"

"No, while they were dressing the puppets I found a ladder up to the crypt behind one of the rollers, so I thought I'd try to get out and find you. But you can't get out of the cathedral once you're in—the line of constables won't let you past."

"Couldn't you get back along the passage?"

"I thought of that, but when I went back FitzPickwick and the others were just coming up into the crypt—I only just got away without being seen. And I could feel you weren't far off, Cris, so I hoped you'd come."

"And how d'you reckon *we're* going to get out if you couldn't?" inquired Dido acidly.

Tobit's face fell. "I don't know. Can't you think of something?"

"We'd best find the Dean," she said more kindly. "He's somewhere about, a-chatting to the king and helping him with his cogitations."

"And he'll get in some of the constables to deal with FitzPickwick?"

"I ain't so sure about that," Dido said. "I reckon we has to go as if we was a-walking on eggs. We *are* on eggs. Start a ruckus wi' the Hanoverians, and we may set the whole place a-rolling. I can feel it rock right now."

It was true, there was a strange uncertain vibration in the cathedral, more plainly to be felt in its upper rooms and galleries. The whole building swayed gently, like the branches of a tree, like an anchored ship in a slight swell.

"Hushaby, Kingy," muttered Dido. "Let's hope it don't blow a gale in the night, or we may all get a surprise, FitzPickwick as well."

She led the way from Tobit's hiding place back toward the great circular gallery. Looking down over the rail they could see that the cathedral had filled up considerably even in the short time they had been talking.

Some girl students from the Chelsea Art Academy had

threaded goodness knows how many oranges and lemons alternately on to a long rope and were busy hanging this enormous necklace in swags all around from the balustrade of the gallery.

"Can you tell me," Dido asked one of them, "where his Reverence and King Dick are having their chat?"

The girl put her finger on her lips. "Hush! Nobody's supposed to know the king's here yet."

"But he is here, ain't he?"

"Oh yes; Doctor Furneaux just took them in a basket of oranges and a bottle of marmalade wine because the Dean sent a message to say they were getting rather dry. They're in the north gallery. But of course they mustn't be disturbed."

"O' course not," said Dido, and led the way past a sign that said "To the North Gallery."

After more stairs, more passages, they came to a closed door with a sign: "No Entry Except by Special Permission of the Dean." Dido considered knocking, and decided against it. She walked boldly in. Tobit and Cris followed with less confidence, Cris holding on to Tobit's hand.

They found themselves in a long room furnished with a refectory table, chairs, and gorgeously colored Persian rugs; on the walls were maps of London and pictures of Old St. Paul's before the Great Fire; a small fire burned briskly in a marble fireplace; nearby stood an open clavichord with some music on it; in front of the fire, on a low table inlaid with silver, two men were building card houses. In the corner of the room opposite the door hung a set of coronation robes, glimmering in the firelight; for a moment, as Dido entered, she fancied this was a ghost.

Cris shut the door softly behind her. At the same moment the card house, which had reached seven stories, fell down.

"May the foul fiend fly away wi' the cartes!" exclaimed the younger of the two men. "What ails ma hand this e'en, that I canna build higher than seven?"

He started building again.

"It must be the wind, your Majesty; I notice the smoke from the fire keeps eddying out in a most unusual manner."

"But 'tis a braw, still nicht, man! Nae breeze at a'!"

"It ain't the breeze, your Royalship," said Dido, walking forward. "It's on account of a mess o' Hanoverians down in the cellar who've stuck the church up on rollers. That's why it keeps rocking back and forth."

The king's hand paused for a second in the act of delicately depositing a card; then he laid it carefully in place. Next moment there was another puff of smoke from the fire and the new card house fell down.

"You see," said Dido.

"There wad appear tae be a possibeelity that the lassie is speaking the truth," said the king. "What is your opeenion, Reverence?"

The Dean had jumped to his feet, very scandalized at such an unauthorized intrusion.

"Who in the world gave you leave—" he began.

"Whisht, man! Let's hear what they have tae say. Explain yersel', lass!"

Dido and Tobit told their tale, keeping it as short as possible. When Dido mentioned Captain Hughes, as being the original bearer of the Dispatch, the king exclaimed,

"That's no' Captain Owen Hughes, o' the sloop *Thrush*? Why, I ken his son weel, and a canny braw laddie he is, and ettling to carry my train the morn's morn."

"Captain Hughes's son? In London?" Dido was delighted. "Why, then he can come back with me to Sussex—I reckon that'll be more likely to rouse the old Cap than anything. We can't wake him, you see," and she went on to explain why, and what she suspected the Hanoverians were planning.

"Aweel, aweel," said the king, "ilka path has its puddle. My puir auld dad had trouble wi' the Hanoverians aft eneugh, it wisna tae be expectit that I'd gang free o' them. Whit had we best do, Reverence?"

The fire smoked again, and the room gave a perceptible lurch. It was plain that, as the cathedral filled up and more people were moving around downstairs, the whole structure was becoming more tippy and unstable.

"Your Majesty must leave the building at once—without losing a minute!" announced the Dean.

"Na, na, man, I'll not do sid a thing while a' the folk doon yonder are in danger."

"Well then we must get *them* out—" the Dean began.

Then he stopped short and exclaimed, "Botheration!" in tones of the deepest dismay.

"What fashes ye, sir?"

"Nobody is to be allowed out before tomorrow's ceremony unless they have a special pass signed by the Home Secretary."

"Weel, send someone for him, man!"

"They couldn't get out."

"Losh," said the king thoughtfully, after a pause. "Here's a powsowdie. Whit'll we do the noo?"

"*You* could leave, your Reverence, surely—and fix things with Lord Raven?" suggested Tobit with some diffidence.

"Leave his Majesty in such peril? Never!" declared the Dean.

"Seems to me," said Dido, "no disrespect to your Royalty and your Reverence, that there's a lot of obstinate, clung-headed thinking going on round here."

"*Really*—" the Dean began, but King Richard said, "Nay, I like a plain-spoken lass. Let her have her crack."

"Well then. Us doesn't want any scrimmage, right? Acos that would start the place a-rocking. So no sense sending for a lot o' big flat-footed constables. The *main* thing is to get the place pegged down someway, so we needs to send a message about that."

"But how—"

"Fust of all, though," pursued Dido, "is there any food in the place?"

"Food? Not a crumb," said the Dean. "Except for the choirboys' buttons, of course."

"What's those?"

The Dean explained that in the fourteenth century, when choirboys were likely to faint from hunger, an act had been passed requiring the regular supply of small macaroons to the cathedral by city bakers. Choirboys were better fed nowadays, but the act had never been repealed, and over the centuries a large supply of these cakes had accumulated; they were kept in a special lead-lined room, safe from fire and mice.

"They'll do," said Dido. "Have 'em taken round and handed out free to everyone downstairs. Folk who've had a bite already ain't so likely to nibble on Joobie nuts."

The Dean departed to arrange for this, murmuring that it was all sadly irregular and how he would account for the disbursement to the Church Commissioners, heaven only knew.

"Now," Dido went on. "Us needs a lot o' rope."

"Lord Forecastle wad be the proper pairson to apply to, I jalouse."

"He *is* such a picksome old cuss, though," objected Dido. "Could *you* write him a note, mister king? He'd pay heed to you, likely."

"Aye, lassie; I'll stress the oorgency o' the matter. Two thousand ells o' best cable," the king said, scribbling. "But who'll deleever the message?"

"We know five active, sensible chaps not a stone's throw from here. All we need *is* a stone," said Dido, and glanced about. On a glass-fronted shelf were some carved pieces of masonry—relics of Old St. Paul's before the fire. "That's the dandy." She selected one. "Now for a bit o' leather."

At this juncture the Dean returned, having arranged for free distribution of choirboys' buttons. When applied to for leather he seemed puzzled, but thought the librarian would undoubtedly have a supply, for bookbinding; at a nod from Dido, Tobit went with him to choose a suitable strip.

"Odds fishikins," said the king, laughing, "ye should ha' been a general, lassie—whit name do ye go by?"

"I'm Dido Twite, your Royalship."

"Dido Twite? Nay, I've heard *yon* name before—and on the lips of an auld friend. Dido Twite. Well, weel! He'll be blythe and canty to hear ye are weel."

"A friend of your *Majesty*—who in the world—?" Dido began, but now Tobit and the Dean reappeared with a leather strip and some thongs, from which Tobit constructed a sling with considerable dispatch and skill. While he did so the Dean, on the king's instruction, signed five cathedral passes for Yan, Tan, Tethera, Methera, and Pip. ("I know yon names too," said His Majesty, "they used tae supply claret wine to my dad") and Dido wrote a letter:

"Dere Yan, Were stuk in Sint Palls. Things is disey. Can yoo tell Home Seck to see Sint Palls is tide down tite as quik as poss. Then slope allong here fast for Them Hanno Veerins is agwine to Brake loose enny minnit. luv Dido.

"P.S. His Majesty sez this is troo."

"You sign it too, sir, then he can show it to Lord Raven and Sir Percy."

So the king signed Dido's letter, which was then, with the note about rope to Lord Forecastle, and the five passes, and a note from the Dean to Lord Raven asking that no more people be allowed into the cathedral, all placed together in an outer covering addressed to Mrs. Grissie Gusset, 4 Wardrobe Court, One ginny reward to him as Delivers this, and Dido's last guinea was enclosed, since neither the king nor the Dean had any money on them. The whole package was securely tied to the lump of stone.

"The foot of Saint Erconwald! The only piece of his tomb left!" lamented the Dean.

"Wheesht, man! Ye'll get it back."

"Now, where's the best place to send it from?" Dido asked Tobit.

"Higher up."

So the whole party left the north gallery.

"Your Majesty had best remain out of sight," remonstrated the Dean; but the king said, havers, this was the daftest ploy he'd been engaged in since he was a sackless callant, and naething would gar him miss any o' the whim-whams.

They had to pass around the circular gallery in order to reach the southwest tower, which Tobit reckoned would be the best spot for his purpose.

Looking down over the balustrade into the nave, Dido let out a groan.

[284]

"Confizzle it! They're a-setting up that blessed theatre. Us'd best make haste."

"In my north aisle!" said the Dean, outraged. "Wait till I go and—"

"No, your Reverence! We *dassn't* start a row! Feel how the place sways."

The motion was even more noticeable now, and sometimes, when there was a sudden shift in the crowd below, the cathedral bells could be heard faintly jangling in the north tower.

"The rollers are uneven sizes," Tobit said. "I heard FitzPickwick complaining that Godwit had cast them in small batches and they were all different."

"The skrimping skellums," muttered King Richard.

They hastened on to the south tower, climbed up a steep, narrow spiral stair, past the works of the cathedral clock with its three massive bells, Great Tom, Great Paul, and Great Fred, on, up, to a high outer gallery from which half London could be seen, smoky and twinkling in the clear frosty twilight.

"By my certie," said the king, "yon's a braw parochine! Where do you aim, laddie?"

"Down yonder." Tobit showed him the tiny oblong of Wardrobe Court, easily to be recognized by its two plane trees. He inserted the stone foot of Saint Erconwald, with message attached, into his sling, took careful aim, and let fly. The projectile whirled away, soaring over the churchyard, over the rooftops, dropped, and was lost to view.

"Send it lands on the planestanes, and disna smash some citizen's losen-glass!" said the king anxiously.

They waited, peering, straining their eyes. One minute went by—two—five—seven.

"If there's no one about in Wardrobe Court," Dido muttered.

"If it lodged in a tree—fell in a window box—" Cris worried.

But then suddenly a figure appeared on the roof of a house that must, surely, be on the south side of Wardrobe Court. The light was too dim and he was too far off to be recognized, but he carried a long pole attached to the end of which was, without any shadow of doubt, Aunt Grissie's red chenille tablecloth. He waved the pole once, twice, three times, and the watchers on the tower let out a unanimous gasp of joy and relief.

"Though dear knows we're nae oot o' the wanchancie business yet," remarked the king, as they retraced their steps down the spiral stair. "Let's see what yon skytes are abune the noo."

When they returned to the gallery and looked down they could see that a change had taken place in the random shifting and drifting motion of the great crowd assembled below. The crowd's attention was now focused on the puppet theatre which a figure in black fur, wearing a mask, had almost finished erecting in the north transept. Dido stared fixedly at this character. From his height she guessed him to be Colonel Fitz-Pickwick—or was it Mystery come back? She could not be certain.

There was an upheaval going on in the crowd. People were pressing and massing in front of the theatre. With another fourteen long hours before the coronation ceremonies would begin, any promise of distraction was welcome as water in the desert.

Evidently this commotion did not suit the puppeteer's purpose, for he could be seen to send out a sharp message; presumably that no performance was to be expected for a long time yet; a disappointed ripple passed through the crowd, which eddied back.

"Forbye, they're growing fretful and capernoited," muttered the king, knitting his brows. "Where be your laddies wi' the cakes, Dean?"

"There they go." The Dean pointed downward to where a dozen choirboys in white surplices could be seen threading their way among the crowd, each carrying a big silver tray heaped high with macaroons. These were handed out liberally, and eagerly received; for the moment the puppet theatre was forgotten. Plainly this development did not meet with the puppet master's approval; he consulted with two shorter assistants, also masked—were they Sannie and Mrs. Lubbage?

"What'll they do?" Dido wondered. "They're as stuck as we are; they dassn't start a performance too soon."

At this moment, however, King Richard solved the puppeteers' problem, while adding greatly to that of his own supporters. Observing the giant necklace of citrus fruit that hung in swags around the balustrade, he reached down with his penknife to remove an orange and, by mischance, cut right through the cord; the entire necklace of fruit went cascading down on to the crowd in the nave, who naturally looked up to see what had caused this rain of oranges and lemons.

A great gasping murmur went up!

"The King! Granny, look, 'tis His Highness! Ma! look up there, it's His Majesty's own self!"

"Sir!" exclaimed Dido. "Duck! Don't let the Hanoverians see you!"

Too late! Plainly the puppet master and his two assistants had discovered the king's presence. Full of excitement and purpose, they were bustling about their theatre. And some smaller assistants were now making their way up and down the nave carrying trays full of what were presumably Joobie nuts.

"Oh, croopus," Dido said. "Sir, you'll have to talk to the people. Now the Hanoverians know you're here I reckon it don't make much odds."

"I am e'en o' the same mind," agreed the king and, leaning over the balustrade, he called, in a voice that, though not particularly loud, was remarkably clear and carrying:

"Friends! Will ye leesten tae me a meenit? This is yer ain appointit king, Davie Jamie Charlie Neddie Geordie Harry Dick Tudor-Stuart, wishfu' tae hae a crack wi' ye. I came tae spend the nicht here, in seerious meditation afore being crownit tomorrow, and blythe I am tae see sae mony o' ye keeping me company. But, friends, I maun warn ye. There's *un*friends amang us too."

"For *mussy*'s sake, sir, don't mention the rollers!"

[288]

Dido whispered urgently in his ear. "It'd start a panic—they'd all helter-skelter for the doors. It'd be murder!"

King Richard nodded reassuringly, while continuing to address the crowd.

"These unfriends, wha I willna scruple tae ca' by their richtfu' name, which is Hanoverians, are aboot tae gang aroond, offering ye nuts. *Dinna eat yon nuts!* They are a kind of poison, they will mak' ye sick, and in your sickness ye will see ghosties and hobgoblins and deil kens what! Drop the nuts on the floor, wamp them under foot!"

"No, no! Not on my tiles!" the Dean was heard to protest in agony.

"But, friends, if ye are hungry—and it's a lang watch till the morn—my gude friend, his Reverence the Dean here has kindly sent oot some almond cakies—those ye can eat a' ye've a mind to."

The crowd down below could be seen responding to this advice by dropping handfuls of Joobie nuts on the black-and-white tiles and scrunching them underfoot as instructed; the puppeteers were plainly angered and taken aback by this development; King Richard nodded with satisfaction.

"Now: anither thing, friends. Bear wi' me patiently and I'll not trouble ye much farther. These ill-deedy Hanoverians have also set up yon puppet theatre in the cathedral. They plan to distract yer minds with gal-dragonries and marvels! Weel, 'tis a free country—thank the Lord—I'll not forbeed ye tae look. But dinna tak it unco seeriously. (But dinna mistreat the Hanoverians either—we want nae rampauging in the cathedral.) Those that love me best, and loved my old dad, Jamie Three, will maybe not look at a'. For my part, I like plays and puppetries fine, but I jalouse they arena whit I'd wish tae watch the nicht afore I'm crownit. This nicht I aim tae spend in seerious thocht and hymn singing. And I'm aboot tae commence noo. Any friends wha care tae join in are kindly welcome!"

Without more ado, King Richard lifted his voice—a resonant baritone—in a tuneful rendering of Metrical Psalm 23.

There was a moment's pause, then a gale of sound followed him. The entire congregation had joined in.

"Saints save us!" breathed Dido. "Don't I just hope the noise ain't enough to upset the rollers."

The Dean, terribly agitated, glanced around him at his beloved building, waiting for the landslide to start. But the sound of the singing, though tremendous, was steady and ordered. The cathedral vibrated like a chimney in a storm, but it kept its position.

"Good boy, good boy!" murmured the Dean. "Ah, he'll make a decent king, if we're all spared. Only, does he know enough hymns to keep them going all night?"

The Dean bustled off to find a hymnbook. Dido, seeing that for the moment King Richard had the situation under control, turned back and climbed the spiral stair to the outer stone gallery below the dome, and looked down to see what was happening in the streets.

What she saw filled her with amazement and thankfulness.

On the north side of the cathedral the crowd had scattered to a considerable extent and the reason for this was that Yan, mounted on an elephant, presumably Rachel, was riding in and out, unrolling as he went what seemed an endless reel of rope. Each time he came close to the cathedral he tossed a loop of this rope to another of the Wineberry Men—Dido could not see which—who stood waiting to receive and make it fast; then the elephant dashed away to the outer perimeter of the open space around the cathedral, where another Wineberry Man stood ready to receive another loop of rope and tether it to whatever was at hand.

"Pegging it down just like a tent, bless 'em," muttered Dido, and rubbed the back of her hand across her eyes. "I might a known they'd do the job decent and seamanly. They surely never got the stuff from old Lord Fo'c'stle, though; I can't believe he'd come through with it so quick."

Yan, having secured St. Paul's at about forty different points on the north side, took a turn of rope completely around the cathedral and disappeared lickety-spit northward in the direction of Newgate, presumably to pass the rope round the block formed by Paternoster Row and Ivy Lane.

"Just so long as the rope holds," said Tobit anxiously. He had followed Dido on to the stone gallery. "I bet the cathedral's pretty heavy, once it starts to slide."

Cris ran out and caught Tobit's hand.

"Come quick! Things aren't so good inside."

They dashed at top speed down the shallow spiral stairs and back to the inner gallery.

When they looked down they saw that the puppet master had started his play. It was not, from where they stood, possible to see the puppets themselves, but, judging from the behavior of the audience, what they were doing was very sinister; remembering the Miller's Daughter, Dido knew how wild and strange they could be, even when acting something comical. The people standing near were gaspingly attentive; every now and then, at some bit of action, a portion of the crowd would jump nervously back.

"Blame it," Dido said. "It won't do to have much o' *that*."

As if to underline her words, there was an uneasy surge of the crowd at some startling occurrence, and the cathedral rocked on its unstable foundations.

Meanwhile the king, steadily singing, beating time as he sang, was still carrying a good half of the congregation with him, at the same time keeping a wary eye on the activities of the Hanoverians.

"Some o' the daft fules ate the nuts in spite o' the warning," he told Dido between two verses. "That's why they're sae nairvous and rintheroutacious."

It seemed that events on the puppet stage were approaching a climax. The light from the theatre shone blue and evil.

"I wonder what Sannie and co. plan to do if they start the church a-sliding?" said Dido.

"Oh, I heard that," Tobit told her. "They reckon it'll

slide south, that's why they put the theatre near the north door—as soon as it starts to move, they slip out the back way."

"Not so easily now, they can't." Dido grinned, thinking of Yan's network of rope. "I'm a-going down," she went on, "I want to see these here mannikins."

Cris and Tobit followed her. The stairs were beginning to fill up, as early-comers were crowded out of the nave and transepts; it was hard to squeeze their way down, but people were kind about letting them through; everybody was singing, even on the stairs, and there was a general atmosphere of cheerfulness and good will.

Out in the nave it was different.

About three quarters of the huge crowd now assembled in the body of the cathedral were singing. Those who could see the king were taking their time and tune from him, and the rest were following *them* (with some exceptions: Dido distinctly heard one old lady singing "O where and O where is my little dog gone," looking around her with a melancholy expression, which was certainly justified if she had brought her little dog into the cathedral). But the crowd, several hundred strong, directly in front of the puppet theatre were not singing; they were following the action on the stage with strained attention.

Wriggling, gliding, edging their way, Dido, Tobit, and Cris moved in the direction of the theatre. People in the crowd here were by no means so friendly and helpful as those on the stairs; they met with glares and mutters of "Keep back there! Give over shoving!" One man gave Cris a clout as she slid under his elbow; three more linked arms and tried to stop them getting through.

As, in spite of this opposition, they neared the stage, they began to hear the music: a sad, hypnotic wailing drone. It was the same tune that Mr. Twite had played on his hoboy, but it was now being rendered, Dido saw, by Tante Sannie and Mrs. Lubbage, wearing black fur clothes and black masks, playing on black combs wrapped in black tissue paper.

At last, by standing on tiptoe and craning sideways, they were able to get a view of the puppets.

The play was evidently about a war between goblins and humans. The humans were losing the war. And the goblins—little dark creatures, their faces wizened with malice, their eyes blazing with green light—were winning. They had poisoned blades to their swords and daggers; they sang a magic song which killed its hearers. Louder and louder wailed the sad, spooky music.

"Oh, Alfred, I feel rotten queer," said the woman beside Dido, absently swallowing a couple of Joobie nuts she held. "I believe I'm going to faint." She swayed, but there was hardly room to fall over. "You *can't* faint here, Lil, hold up, do!" said the man with her anxiously. However at this moment another woman did faint, crumpling on to the black-and-white tiles.

"We have won!" screamed the goblin king on the stage, triumphantly waving his poisoned sword. "Not one of our enemies is left alive!"

He turned toward the audience, his eyes blazing green,

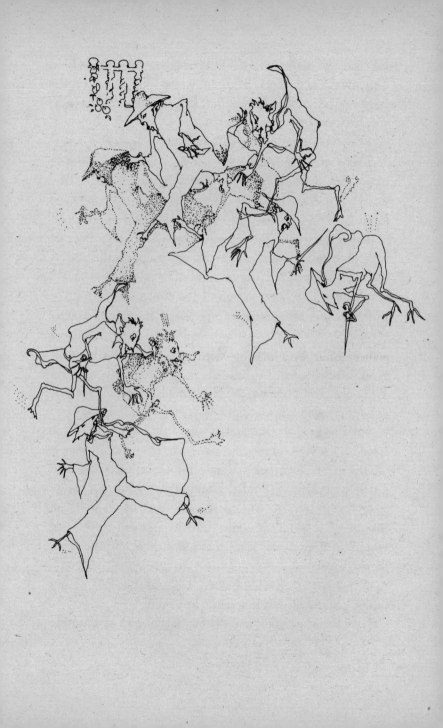

his army of dark, wicked little soldiers massing behind him—more and more of them came piling on to the stage. "And *now*," hissed the king, "now, my friends, we are coming to get *you!*"

The whole army of goblins poured off the stage.

There were screams, shouts of fright and disgust, gasps, moans. Both Dido's feet were stamped on heavily, as the crowd surged backward. Three more women fainted.

The situation in the nave was now as if one piece of a jigsaw were trying to shove its way through the rest of the completed puzzle; there was no room to move at all, and yet a whole huge section of the crowd was frantically pushing and struggling to get away from the puppet theatre.

Cris pounced forward and grabbed one of the puppets from the floor.

"Look!" she cried to the woman called Lil. "It's only a doll! It won't hurt you!"

But the woman, screaming and hysterical, was in no state to listen to sense.

"It's alive, it wriggled! I saw it!" she wailed. "It's got a poisoned dagger!" And she fought like a crazy creature to get away from it. Kicked and knocked by frantic feet, the puppets skidded about on the smooth tiles, and wherever they were seen they spread terror and pandemonium.

"They aren't alive!" shouted Dido at the top of her lungs. "Stand still! They can't hurt you!"

But at that moment she distinctly saw one of the little

creatures move toward her foot, jerking itself along the ground. Quelling a horrible swoop of her heart, she picked it up, and realized that it was propelled by a simple mechanism of a twig, a notched cotton reel, and a stretched, twisted piece of catgut. "*Look!* It's only a toy!"

She might as well have said so to Niagara.

"STAND STILL!" shouted the king. "Keep your heads! Stand still!"

But the crowd, five hundred strong, heaved sideways, once, twice, three times.

"Hold them!" shouted the king to the people farther away from the puppet theatre, who, unaffected by the panic, were still keeping their position and singing away. "Link your hands round and hold them!"

The cathedral began to rock.

"Guess this is what an earthquake's like," Dido said to Cris. They had been washed up against a pillar, as if by a flood; Dido grabbed an arm of Tobit, an arm of Cris, and braced herself against the stone. "Hark at the bells! Don't they half ring!"

The chandeliers with their tapers were swinging wildly; shadows leapt about; oranges and lemons rained down from the high vaulted roof. The puppet theatre toppled and fell, crushing a good many puppets underneath it. Dido peered through the mass of people, trying to discover where the puppet master and his two assistants had got to. She could not see them in the general muddle. It was like a battle; it *was* a battle.

The cathedral rocked a fourth time.

"Do you think it's starting to slide?" Cris said. She was rather pale. She let go of Dido's hand and clung to Tobit.

"Dunno. With all the ruckus, it's hard to say *what*'s happening."

But at that moment the cathedral did something definite. With a tremendous noise, louder than any sound hitherto produced by the crowd, with a kind of thunderous, rumbling scrunch, St. Paul's lurched sideways—shuddered in every stone—and sank about six feet into the ground, canted over at an angle of fifteen degrees.

And stood still.

"Some of the rollers must have buckled and given way," said Tobit.

"That's so—on account of Yan's anchoring it so tight," agreed Dido. "With all that rocking about, and the ropes holding fast, the rollers jist couldn't take the strain. Oh well—guess the old place is safe enough now—though it's going to be a right puzzle for his Reverence to jack it up level again. Why, look—there *is* Yan!"

At the moment of the cathedral's final subsidence, the north doors had swung open. There was a movement of the crowd to try and get out, but due to the angle at which St. Paul's was tilted, down at the southwest corner, the north entrance was now above ground level. Moreover Rachel the elephant was standing outside, blocking the way. The five Wineberry Men leapt in, off her back.

"The puppets!" called Dido. "Pick 'em up! Put 'em away!"

She, Cris, and Tobit, began tossing all the puppets they could see into a wicker hamper, evidently the container in which they had been brought. The Wineberry Men helped. Seeing this, the crowd began to settle down.

"Friends!" shouted the king from above. "It wad mateerially asseest matters if ye'd a' sit doon on the ground. The cathedral is quite safe—just a wee bit canted o'er. Ye hae nae groonds for appreheension!"

People were only too pleased to comply—with three exceptions. As the whole congregation sank limply to the floor, three desperate figures were seen trying to make their way to the south entrance: Sannie, Mrs. Lubbage, and the puppet master, who had been foiled in their attempt to get out at the north door.

"Get them, lads!" shouted Yan.

The three separated, Sannie and Mrs. Lubbage fleeing toward the crypt, while the puppet master darted through the door to the spiral stair.

Dido, Tobit, and Yan followed him.

"I'm afeered he means mischief to the king," Dido panted. "We mustn't let him get to the gallery!"

Yan nodded, pounding ahead. But there was really no risk, as they saw when they reached the narrow gallery entrance; it was jammed with people and the fugitive had evidently abandoned his plan and, in desperation, continued onward and upward with Yan close at his heels.

"Stop, you fool!" Yan shouted after him. "You can't escape that way!"

The puppet master evidently thought otherwise. Pausing an instant to discard his black fur cloak and hood, which were hampering him, he rushed along a narrow passage that led off the stairs. Now they could recognize the fair hair and mustache of Colonel FitzPickwick.

"He can't escape that way," said a voice behind Dido. She looked around and saw the Dean. "It leads only to the roof."

But FitzPickwick had unbolted the door and sprang out into darkness, followed, an instant later, by Yan. Light from inside showed a lead-lined valley between two roof ridges.

"Yan! Take care!" called Dido anxiously.

She started after him, but the Dean grabbed her arm.

"Don't go, child! It's too dangerous in the dark: That's the nave roof—it ends in a sheer drop over the west front."

Nonetheless, Dido would have gone—but at that moment they heard a wild shout of rage, or defiance, or despair. A moment later Yan came back to them, looking pale and appalled.

"He jumped . . . clean off the end of the roof."

"Heaven forgive him," said the Dean.

Downstairs, they found that a general calming-down and tidying-up process had taken place. Another issue of choirboys' buttons had been dealt round and most people, exhausted by all the excitement, had gone to sleep, lying as comfortably as they could on the sloping cathedral floor. The king, having delivered a calming speech, had retired to the north gallery. Here the Wineberry Men were summoned to be thanked for the speed and skill with which they had secured the cathedral.

"You saved it from destruction," the Dean kept repeating, with tears in his eyes. "I'll never forget it, never!"

"Losh, lads, ye did wonders," agreed the king.

"How did you get the rope so quick?" Dido wanted to know.

"Got it from the Old Bailey. They've allus got plenty there—for tying up prisoners. Sir Percy fixed for us to have it—he and Lord Raven were still arguing when we took along his Reverence's note. We could see the cathedral a-swaying about from there, so I reckoned there wasn't time to go along and argue the toss wi' Lord Fo'c'stle."

"I'll no' say but that ye were richt," agreed the king. "Weel, lads, if ye wish for pensionable, kenspeckit poseetions in the government, Davie Jamie Charlie Neddie Geordie Harry Dick Tudor-Stuart's the man tae see ye'll get them."

Yan and the rest thanked him politely, but said on the whole they would prefer to continue plying their trade as Gentlemen.

" 'Tis what we're used to, you see, sir."

"Aweel, I'll no' quarrel with ye; 'tis a gey frack profession, fit for gallant lads like yersel's. Whene'er ye veesit Westminster I'll be blythe tae buy claret from ye as my dad did afore me. And I hereby gie ye leave to write Appointit tae His Majesty on the brattach o' your boat."

Much impressed by this royal favor, the Wineberry Men withdrew, pulling their forelocks.

"Would Your Grace wish to see the two prisoners?" the Dean inquired.

"I canna say I do, but I doubt I had better," said the king reluctantly.

Tante Sannie and Mrs. Lubbage were led in; they had been taken in the crypt without difficulty, for the subterranean passage was blocked when the southwest corner of the cathedral sank into the ground.

The two witches were a sorry spectacle. Sannie seemed to have shrunk; she had always been small, now she was tiny, hardly bigger than a five-year-old. She whimpered out miserably, on seeing the king,

"Oh, dear King-sir! Is will be kind to poor old Sannie? Old Sannie never meant harm! Only to go back where the sea she do sing, and isn't no cold nor rudeness, but love apples and sweet grass, and old people is loved and given quilt stuffed with happiness feathers—"

"What does she mean?" asked the king.

"She wants to go back to Tiburon," Dido said.

"And the other one?"

But no one, ever again, would be able to tell what Mrs. Lubbage wanted—if she wanted anything. She had half a dozen Joobie nuts, with which she played, smiling like a baby, trickling them from one hand to the other without speaking; she never said another word.

"Take them away," said the king. For the first time he sounded tired. "Take them away and let them be looked after somewhere. . . ."

"Shall you let them go back to Tiburon, sir?" Dido asked when they had gone.

"Och, weel, they'd be out of mischief there."

But old Sannie died in the night; whether from age, or lost hope, no one could say.

"Whit aboot ye three?" the king said to Dido, Cris, and Tobit. "Gin ye hadna brought yon message in the faurst place, we'd nane of us be here noo. I'd be blythe for ye tae carry my train the morn, alang wi' young Owen Hughes—would ye like to?"

Dido glanced at the others; they nodded.

"Thanks, Mister King; we'd be right pleased. If I can get back to Sussex directly arter, that is; I shan't feel easy till I see how my old Cap's a-getting on. And I promised Lord Sope I'd return his elephant."

So that was how Dido Twite, along with Tobit and Cristin Tegleaze, came to carry the train of King Richard IV at his coronation. And the Master of the King's Garlandries, arriving at the last minute for the ceremony, because he and his helpers had been working all night replacing the scattered decorations on the cathedral, looked down from the Whispering Gallery and exclaimed,

"Good heavens! That's Dido!"

13

Dido, Tobit, and Cris started for Sussex the very instant the ceremony, which was held at six in the morning, had finished. They had been invited to stay for the junketings, but declined. Dido was anxious to get back to her Captain; Tobit and Cris, armed with an injunction, signed by the Lord Chief Justice, against anybody trying to stop them taking possession of Tegleaze Manor, in particular one Miles Tuggles, alias Tegleaze, alias Mystery, were anxious to see what was happening at home; and Rachel, too, was dreadfully homesick; right through the crowning she had stood just outside, in St. Paul's churchyard, trumpeting mournfully.

Just before they left, Dido received a message to say that the Duke of Battersea would like to see her, as soon as he had fixed up some toppling garlands.

"Duke o' Battersea? Who's he?" she said, puzzled.

"Well, look, tell him I'm right sorry but I can't wait now. Ax him to write to me."

Rachel swung through the outskirts of London at a rattling pace. Along with Dido, Tobit, and Cris, traveled Captain Hughes's son Owen; he seemed a pleasant enough boy, though rather silent and anxious at the moment. This was hardly surprising, since the Captain's family had not heard from him for several years, had thought him dead in the Chinese wars, and now the news of his mysterious illness was hardly encouraging.

"Don't you fret, though, I reckon the king's doctor will be able to set him to rights," Dido kept saying consolingly. "He seemed a right sensible cove."

The king's doctor, who had an allergy to elephants, was to follow them in his own curricle with a supply of medicines, directly the coronation banquet was over.

Rachel took them over heath and common, through woods, fields and copses, straight as a bird to Stopham House, where she trumpeted outside the library window until Lord Sope came out and patted her cheek.

"Well, well, well, Rachel; that will do! I am delighted to see you back, but do not deafen me, pray! How do you do, Miss Twite," he said to Dido. "Were you able to deliver your message? That's good, that's good. . . . I see you have friends with you. Would you all care for a little refreshment?"

"That's ever so kind of your lordship, but I reckon we'd best get on. Oh, here's a note from Lord Forecastle, inviting you to take a dish of tay with him next time you're in town. He sent a messenger posting after us with it on a Derby 'chaser.'"

Dido had been planning to hire a carriage at the White Hart for the last bit of the journey, but Lord Sope hospitably put his phaeton at their disposal, so they drove in it on to Petworth, where they received a great welcome from the Gusset family at The Fighting Cocks.

"There, I *am* pleased to see you, dearies!" exclaimed Aunt Sarah, embracing them all impartially. "You'll never guess what's happened, *never!*"

"What?" Dido asked anxiously. "Is the Cap'n all right?"

"At twelve o'clock midnight last night," said Miss Sarah impressively, "just as I was a-taking a last look at the Cap'n, poor dear soul, sleeping up in the attic, so innocent and quiet as a babby, what does he do?"

"What *does* he do?"

"Sits up! Looks about him calm as a Christian and, if you'll believe me, says, 'Ma'am, who are *you*? Where the deuce am I? What's become of my Dispatch? And where's Dido Twite?' He's sitting in an armchair in the little parlor—a bit weak, but a-mending fast—drinking a mugful of huckle-my-buff—at this very minute. He *will* be pleased to know you're back, dearie."

"He'll be even more pleased than that," said Dido. "This here's his son Owen, that he hasn't seen for dunnamany years."

"Oh, dearie! He'll be right dumbfounded with joy."

"Owen," Dido suggested, "why don't *you* go in and

[306]

see your pa fust—he won't want too many of us a-crash-
ing in on him if he's weak yet."

Owen nodded, and went through the door indicated
by Mrs. Gusset. They heard him say,

"Father?" and Captain Hughes exclaim,

"That's never *Owen*?"

Then there was a long silence.

"Eh, bless him! That'll do him more good than doctor's medicine," said Aunt Sarah, wiping her eyes.
"Now, how about the rest of you? Would you like a
bowl of my soup, eh?"

They were glad of soup, having had nothing since a
scanty breakfast before the ceremony, and while they
ate they told Aunt Sarah, Uncle Jarge, and his boy Ted
the whole tale of the events leading up to the coronation,
and discussed the astonishing fact that, at the exact
time when Mrs. Lubbage and Tante Sannie realized
their plan had failed, Captain Hughes had recovered
the use of his senses.

"There's something mighty odd about it all," Miss
Sarah said over and over. "But I'm right glad he's on
the mend, for I've not laid eyes on a better-looking man
since my Hannibal was struck by lightning in the rowboat full of corkscrews. And that's a nice-looking boy,
too; do you reckon *he'd* fancy a bowl of my soup?"

"Guess he would," Dido said. "While you're giving
it to him, ma'am, I'll take Tobit and Cris on to Tegleaze,
before it gets dark, and then come back to have a talk
with the Cap. Oh, there's a letter for him from Lord

Fo'c'stle giving him six months' leave so's he can go home to Wales."

"I've always fancied a holiday in Wales," Miss Sarah said thoughtfully, tucking Lord Forecastle's letter in her apron pocket.

Dido, Tobit, and Cris returned to the phaeton and continued on their way. Some three quarters of an hour after their departure, the doctor's curricle arrived. The doctor had brought with him a passenger who inquired for Miss Dido Twite and, on hearing that she had gone to Tegleaze Manor, decided to follow her, after a brief pause for refreshments.

Dido, Cris, and Tobit drove through the village of Duncton, and up steep Duncton hill, where they dismounted and walked beside the horse. Dido was rather silent, but Tobit and Cris kept up a nonstop flow of talk.

"We'll keep a lot of sheep—Mr. Firkin will be the chief shepherd—and we'll breed horses again—Granny will like that, she knows a lot about horses when she's off the Joobie nuts—we'll mend all the things that are falling to bits—have Dogkennel Cottages repaired and find new tenants—set Tegleaze Manor to rights—"

"What'll you use for cash?" Dido asked.

"Well, there's bound to be *some,* now old FitzPickwick isn't taking it all for his Hanoverian plots—"

"What about the luck-piece?"

"Oh, well, it won't run away. We'll give it to that museum in London. Neither of us wants it. But there's other things to do first—that can wait."

(It waited for a year, and when they finally sent down a diver to rescue the Breughel miniature, which was dangling from a nail in the brickwork of the well, they also found the bones of Miles Tegleaze, alias Miles Mystery, lying at the bottom, where he had fallen when he rushed from the mill that dark November night.)

"And we'll do something about those magistrates in Petworth, so people can't be transported on false evidence," Tobit said.

"And we'll look after poor old women, so they don't get a grudge against everybody and take to witchcraft," said Cris.

They passed Dogkennel Cottages. Mr. Firkin was up on the side of the down with his sheep and dog Toby.

"I'll go and see him tomorrow," Cris said.

They reached Tegleaze Manor. While Dido was tethering Lord Sope's horse to the marble pillar, Tobit and Cris walked through the great door hand in hand. The big white dog Lion flew down the stairs like a bolt from a catapult, barking and whining with joy. When he saw that there were *two* of them, he was quite astounded, and did not know which face to lick first. Old Gusset, wandering about the hall with a feather duster, also nearly fainted from astonishment.

"Mas'r Tobit, sir! Miss Crissie! Bean't you transported to van Dieman's Land? Nor murdered? Nor taken up by the Bow Street runners? Nor magicked by Mother Lubbage?"

"None of those things," Tobit said. "And Tante

Sannie's never coming back, nor Colonel FitzPickwick, and we're never going to allow another Joobie nut on the place, and things'll all be different from now on. Where's Granny?"

"Why, she's been a bit brighter than usual, Mas'r Tobit. She be in Mr. Wilfred's bedroom, a-playing tid-dlywinks with him."

"We'll go up and surprise her. Want to come, Dido?"

But Dido said she thought she would be getting back.

"Thanks for the ride, then. Maybe we'll come over to Petworth tomorrow to see you."

Hand in hand, without looking back, they ran up the stairs.

Old Gusset, gazing after them, shook his head.

"Well, I declare! Who'd a beleft it? So all's right, is it, Missie Twido Dite?"

"Yes," said Dido slowly. "All's right, Mister Gusset. The king's been crowned, and Cap'n Hughes is better, and if that Mystery turns up again, he'll get his come-uppance. And your boy Yan got a special thanks from the king, and permission to put By Royal Thingummy on the *Gentlemen's Relish*. And they're coming back by the cut, and he said to tell you he'd see you at the Cuckoo Tree the day arter tomorrow."

"Ah, that be champion," the old man said happily. "I knew nothing'd harm my boy Yan, acos I bought him that liddle wooden charm piece from owd Mother Lubbage—but thanked by His Majesty! Think o' that!"

He looked up the stairs again, thoughtfully rubbing his whiskers with the feather duster.

"All the same," he muttered, "those two young 'uns ought to offered you a glass o' cowslip wine. Uncivil, that was. Or would ee like a biscuit, now, missie?"

"That's ever so kind of you, Mister Gusset, but I really does want to be getting back."

Just the same, before doing so, Dido went into Cousin Wilfred's little study to have a look at the Tegleaze family tree. Triplets, back in Charles the First's time: Tobias, Christopher, and Miles Aswell Tegleaze.

"Mister Gusset?"

"Yes, Missie Dwite?"

"Do you know the name of the other triplet? Tobit and Cris's brother who died at birth?"

"No, missie. I never did hear. Likely he was never christened."

"Maybe not."

Dido unhitched the phaeton, and drove off. All of a sudden she felt lonely—almost choked with loneliness. Tobit's got Cris, she thought, and Cap'n Hughes has his boy Owen, but who've *I* got?

Such thoughts were not sensible, she knew. A warm welcome awaited her back at The Fighting Cocks. She could probably go to Wales with Captain Hughes and Owen, if she wanted, the king had invited her to stay at Westminster, and Mr. Firkin would certainly be pleased if she went back to Dogkennel Cottages. But all the hospitality in the world is not the same as having someone of your own.

As she neared Dogkennel Cottages she saw that the sheep were down in the pasture, which meant that Mr.

Firkin was home. So she stopped in to tell him about Captain Hughes's recovery and the collapse of Mrs. Lubbage. While she was telling her tale, a curricle dashed by, going toward Tegleaze.

"Eh, fancy old Mis' Lubbage being brung so low!" Mr. Firkin exclaimed wonderingly. "The poor owd mawther! Like a babby, is she? Tell 'em to send her back here, darter, and I'll keep an eye on her, surelye; she 'on't come to no harm herealong when folks knows she'm afflicted."

Dido promised she would do this.

"Mr. Firkin," she said suddenly. "I've a fancy to walk along to the Cuckoo Tree. Can I leave the carriage here for twenty minutes?"

"O' course, darter! And time ee comes back, I'll have a cup o' tea a-mashed for ee."

Dido walked across the pasture, up the chalk track, through the beech grove, across the saddle of rough down grass, along the path under the hanging yew trees. And she finally came to the little crooked, aged Cuckoo Tree, leaning out sideways from the slope of the hill, as it had leaned for many, many hundreds of years, and would lean for many hundreds of years more.

"I wonder if a cuckoo ever really did build a nest in it?" she thought. "No, Cris said cuckoos don't build nests. Cuckoos don't *have* nests. All they have is other birds' nests."

She climbed up into the tree and looked down at the wide, spreading stretch of country below, beginning now to be hazy with the blue of evening. She remem-

bered how she had first come to the tree and heard Cris, apparently talking to nobody.

"It was right queer about Aswell, Cris just forgot him, once she met Tobit. I wonder if *he*'s lonely too."

Half seriously, half not, she put out both hands and shut her eyes. She remembered Cris saying, "When we first start talking I can feel him put his hands in mine."

"Aswell?" said Dido. "Is you there, poor old Aswell? Can you hear me?"

She waited.

And waited. But nothing happened, and presently she opened her eyes again.

And, meanwhile, through the beech grove, across the saddle of down, along the yew-hung path, her friend Simon, Sixth Duke of Battersea, came searching for her, following the directions Mr. Firkin had given him.

JOAN AIKEN, daughter of American writer Conrad Aiken, was born in Rye, Sussex, England. She has engaged in a variety of professions, including features editor for a magazine and copywriter for a large London advertising agency. Now she devotes her time to writing.

In 1969, Miss Aiken received the *Manchester Guardian* award for children's fiction.

Her hobbies are painting and gardening at her home, an ex-pub in Petworth, Sussex, England, where she lives with her two children.

Hair-raising, rib-tickling
tales of long ago by

JOAN AIKEN

master of mystery and suspense!

___THE WOLVES OF WILLOUGHBY CHASE

Life at Willoughby Chase takes a dangerous turn for the worse when Bonnie and her cousin Sylvia are left in the care of a truly evil governess!

49603-9 $3.25

___BLACK HEARTS IN BATTERSEA

Can a cellar full of guns, a wild balloon ride and a pack of hungry wolves keep Dido Twite and her friend Simon from saving the King of England?

40904-7 $3.25

___NIGHTBIRDS ON NANTUCKET

Dido Twite and Dutiful Penitence survive a creepy sea voyage only to wind up in the clutches of cruel imposter pretending to be Dutiful's aunt!

46370-X $3.25

Masterful mysteries by

(**Winner of the Edgar Allan Poe Award**)

☐ **NIGHT CRY**   40017-1 $2.95

Scaredy-cat Ellen Stump <u>really</u> has something to worry about when a suspicious stranger starts hanging around her house just after a local boy is kidnapped.

☐ **THE WITCH'S SISTER**   40028-7 $2.95

Lynn is convinced her sister, Judith, is a witch—especially after she sees her conjure up a real live boy from the middle of a lake!

☐ **WITCH WATER**   40038-4 $2.95

Lynn and her best friend, Mouse, are off on another witch hunt—only this time it's a spooky old neighbor that they're after...

For a complete listing of these titles, plus many more, write to us at the address below and we will send you the Dell Readers Service Listing.

 DELL READERS SERVICE LISTING
P.O. Box 1045
South Holland, Illinois 60473